STORE

Resurr

Anne Perry was born in London and lived abroad for some time before moving to her present home in the Scottish highlands. She has established a reputation for bestselling murder mysteries of the highest quality. You can find more information about Anne and her books on her of cial website, www.anneperry.net.

BY THE SAME AUTHOR

ANNE PERRY

RESURRECTION ROW

HarperCollins*Publishers*

This novel is a work of ction. The names, characters and incidents portrayed in it are the work of the author s imagination. Any resemblance to actual persons, living or dead, is entirely coincidental.

HarperCollins*Publishers*
77—85 Fulham Palace Road,
Hammersmith, London W6 8JB

The HarperCollins website address is:
www.**fire**and**water**.com

This paperback edition 2001

1 3 5 7 9 8 6 4 2

First published in USA by
St Martin s Press 1981

Copyright ' Anne Perry 1981

The Author asserts the moral right to
be identi ed as the author of this work

ISBN 0 00 651123 6

Set in Times

Printed and bound in Great Britain by
Clays Ltd, St Ives plc

To MEG
for all her help

1

THE FOG SWIRLED thick and sour down the street, obscuring the distances and blurring the gas lamps above. The air was bitter and damp, catching in the throat, yet it did not chill the enthusiasm of the audience pouring out of the theatre, a few bursting into impromptu snatches of song from Gilbert and Sullivan's new opera, *The Mikado*. One girl even lilted from side to side in imitation of the little Japanese heroine, before her mother told her sharply to remember herself and behave with the decorum her family had a right to expect.

Two hundred yards away Sir Desmond and Lady Cantlay were walking slowly in the general direction of Leicester Square, intending to hail a cab; they had not brought their own carriage because of the difficulty of finding a suitable place to meet afterwards. On such a January night one did not wish to keep the horses standing or roaming the area to pick one up. It was too hard to come by a really excellently matched pair to risk their health in such an unnecessary fashion. Cabs were plentiful enough and naturally gathered at the coming out of any theatre.

"I did enjoy that," Lady Gwendoline said with a sigh of pleasure that turned into a shiver as a swirl of fog wreathed her and the damp touched her face. "I must purchase some

1

of the music to play for myself; it really is delightful. Especially that song the hero sings." She took a breath, coughed, and then sang in a very sweet voice, "A wandering minstrel I, a thing of rags and patches—er—what was next, Desmond? I recall the tune, but the words escape me."

He took her arm to draw her away from the curb as a cab swished by, splashing manure where the street sweeper had gone home too early to clear it.

"I don't know, my dear. I'm sure it will be in the music. It really is a miserable night, it is no pleasure at all to walk. We must find a cab immediately. I can see one coming now. Wait here and I'll call him." He stepped out into the street as a hansom loomed out of the mist, its slow hooves muffled in the blanketing damp, the horse dragging head down, almost directionless.

"Come on!" Sir Desmond said irritably. "What's the matter with you, man? Don't you want a fare?"

The horse drew level with him and raised its head, ears coming forward at the sound of his voice.

"Cabby!" Desmond said sharply.

There was no reply. The driver sat motionless on the box, his greatcoat collar turned up, hiding most of his face, the reins slack over the rail.

"Cabby!" Desmond was growing increasingly annoyed. "I presume you are not engaged? My wife and I wish to go to Gadstone Park!"

Still the man did not stir or steady the horse, which was moving gently, shifting from foot to foot, making it unsafe for Gwendoline to attempt to climb into the cab.

"For heaven's sake, man! What's the matter with you?" Desmond reached up and grabbed at the skirts of the driver's coat and pulled sharply. "Control your animal!"

To his horror the man tilted toward him, overbalanced, and toppled down, falling untidily off the box over the wheel and onto the pavement at his feet.

Desmond's immediate thought was that the man was drunken insensible. He would not be by any stretch the only cabby to fortify himself against endless hours in the bitter

2

fog by taking more alcohol than he could handle. It was an infernal nuisance, but he was not without a flicker of understanding for it. Were he not in Gwendoline's hearing he would have sworn fluently, but now he was obliged to hold his tongue.

"Drunk," he said with exasperation.

Gwendoline came forward and looked at him.

"Can't we do something about it?" She had no idea what such a thing might be.

Desmond bent down and rolled him over till the man was lying on his back, and at the same moment the wind blew a clear patch in the fog so the gaslight fell on his face.

It was appallingly obvious that he was dead—indeed, that he had been dead for some time. Even more dreadful than the livid, puffy flesh was the sweet smell of putrefaction, and a crumble of earth in the hair.

There was an instant's silence, long enough for the indrawing of breath, the wave of revulsion; then Gwendoline screamed, a high, thin sound smothered immediately by the night.

Desmond stood up slowly, his own stomach turning over, trying to put his body between her and the sight on the pavement. He expected her to faint; and yet he did not know quite what to do. She was heavy as she sank against him, and he could not maintain her weight.

"Help!" he called out desperately. "Help me!"

The horse was used to the indescribable racket of the London streets, and it was barely stirred by Gwendoline's scream. Desmond's shout did not move it at all.

He cried out again, his voice rising as he struggled to prevent her sliding out of his grip onto the filthy pavement and to imagine some way of dealing with the horror behind him before she regained her senses and became completely hysterical.

It seemed like minutes standing in the wreaths of coldness, the cab looming over him, silent except for the breathing of the horse. Then at last there were footsteps, a voice, and a shape.

"What is it? What's wrong?" An enormous man mate-

3

rialized out of the fog, muffled in a woollen scarf, coattails flapping. "What happened? Have you been attacked?"

Desmond was still holding Gwendoline, who was at last beginning to stir. He looked at the man and saw an intelligent, humorous face of undoubted plainness. In the halo of the gaslight he was not so enormous, merely tall, and dressed in too many layers of clothes, none of which appeared to be done up correctly.

"Were you attacked?" the man repeated a little more sharply.

Desmond jerked himself into some presence of mind.

"No." He grasped Gwendoline more tightly, pinching her without meaning to. "No. The—the cabby is dead." He cleared his throat and coughed as the fog caught him. "I fear he has been dead some time. My wife fainted. If you would be kind enough to assist me, sir, I shall endeavor to revive her; and then I imagine we should summon the police. I suppose they take care of such things. The poor man is an appalling sight. He cannot be left there."

"I am the police," the man replied, looking past him to the form on the ground. "Inspector Pitt." He fished absently for a card and turned up a penknife and a ball of string. He abandoned the effort and bent down by the body, touching the face with his fingers for a moment, then the earth on the hair.

"He's dead—" Desmond began. "In fact—in fact, he looks almost as if he had been buried—and dug up again!"

Pitt stood up, running his hands down his sides as though he could rub off the feel of it.

"Yes, I think you're right. Nasty. Very nasty."

Gwendoline was now coming fully to consciousness and straightened up, at last taking the weight off Desmond's arm, although she still leaned against him.

"It's all right, my dear," he said quickly, trying to keep her turned away from Pitt and the body. "The police are going to take care of it!" He looked grimly at Pitt as he said this, trying to make something of an order of it. It was time the man did something more useful than merely agree with him as to the obvious.

Before Pitt could reply, a woman came out of the dark-

4

ness, handsome, and with a warmth in the curves of her face
that survived even the dankness of this January street.

"What is it?" She looked straight at Pitt.

"Charlotte," he hesitated, debating for an instant how
much to tell her, "the cabby is dead. Looks as if he's been
dead a little while. I shall have to see that arrangements are
made." He turned to Desmond. "My wife," he explained,
leaving the words hanging.

"Desmond Cantlay." Desmond resented being expected
to introduce himself socially to a policeman's wife, but he
had been left no civil alternative. "Lady Cantlay." He
moved his head fractionally toward Gwendoline.

"How do you do, Sir Desmond?" Charlotte replied with
remarkable composure. "Lady Cantlay."

"How do you do?" Gwendoline said weakly.

"If you would be good enough to give me your address?"
Pitt asked. "In case there should be any inquiry? Then I'm
sure you would prefer to find another cab and go home."

"Yes," Desmond agreed hastily. "Yes—we live in Gadstone Park, number twenty-three." He wanted to point out
that he could not possibly help in any enquiry, since he had
never known the man or had the least idea who he was or
what had happened to him, but he realized at the last moment that it was a subject better not pursued. He was glad
enough simply to leave. It did not occur to him until after he
was in another cab and halfway home that the policeman's
wife was going to have to find her own way, or else wait
with her husband for the mortuary coach and accompany
him and the body. Perhaps he should have offered her some
assistance? Still—it was too late now. Better to forget the
whole business as soon as possible.

Charlotte and Pitt stood on the pavement beside the body.
Pitt could not leave her alone in the street in the fog, nor
could he leave the body unattended. He searched in his
pockets again and after some moments found his whistle.
He blew it as hard as he could, waited, and then blew it
again.

"How could a cabby have been dead for more than an

hour or two?'' Charlotte asked quietly. "Wouldn't the horse take him home?''

Pitt screwed up his face, his long, curved nose wrinkled. "I would have thought so.''

"How did he die?'' she asked. "Cold?'' There was pity in her voice.

He put out a hand to touch her gently, a gesture that said more than he might have spoken in an hour.

"I don't know,'' he answered her very quietly. "But he's been dead a long time, maybe a week or more. And there's earth in his hair.''

Charlotte stared at him, her face paling. "Earth?'' she repeated. "In London?'' She did not look at the body. "How did he die?''

"I don't know. The police surgeon—''

But before he had time to finish his thought, a constable burst out of the darkness and a moment later another behind him. Briefly Pitt told them what had happened and handed over responsibility for the entire affair. It took him ten minutes to find another cab, but by quarter-past eleven he and Charlotte were back in their own home. The house was silent, but warm after the bitter streets. Jemima, their two-year-old daughter, was spending the night with Mrs. Smith opposite. Charlotte had preferred to leave her there rather than disturb her at this hour.

Pitt closed the door and shut out the world, the Cantlays, dead cabbies, the fog, everything but a lingering of music from the gaiety and color of the opera. When he had first married Charlotte, she had given up the comfort and status of her father's house without a word. This was only the second time he had been able to take her to the theatre in the city, and it was an occasion to be celebrated. All evening he had looked at the stage, and then at her face, and the joy he saw there was worth every careful economy, every penny saved for it. He leaned back against the door, smiling, and pulled her towards him gently.

The fog turned to rain, and then sleet. Two days later Pitt was sitting at his desk in the police station when a sergeant

6

came in, his face puckered with unhappiness. Pitt looked up.

"What is it, Gilthorpe?"

"You remember that dead cabby you found night before last, sir?"

"What about him?" It was something Pitt would have preferred to forget, a simple tragedy but a common enough one, except for the amount of time he had been dead.

"Well," Gilthorpe shifted from one foot to the other. "Well, it looks like 'e wasn't no cabby. We found an open grave——"

Pitt froze; somewhere, pressed to the back of his mind, had been a fear of something like this when he had seen the puffy face and the touch of wet earth, something ugly and obscene, but he had ignored it.

"Whose?" he said quietly.

Gilthorpe's face tightened. "A Lord Augustus Fitzroy-Hammond, sir."

Pitt shut his eyes, as if not seeing Gilthorpe might take it away.

" 'E died just short o' three weeks ago, sir," Gilthorpe's voice went on inexorably. "Buried a fortnight. Very big funeral, they say."

"Where?" Pitt asked mechanically, carrying on while his brain still sought to escape.

"St. Margaret's, sir. We put a guard on it, naturally."

"Whatever for?" Pitt opened his eyes. "What harm is anyone going to do an empty grave?"

"Sightseers, sir," Gilthorpe said without a flicker. "Someone might fall in. Very 'ard to get out of a grave, it is. Sides is steep and wet, this time o' year. And o' course the coffin is still there." He stood a little more upright, indicating that he had finished and was waiting for orders from Pitt.

Pitt looked up at him.

"I suppose I had better go and see the widow and have her identify our corpse from the cab." He climbed to his feet with a sigh. "Tell the mortuary to make it look as decent as possible, will you? It's going to be pretty

7

wretched, whether it's him or not. Where does she live?''

"Gadstone Park, sir, number twelve. All very big 'ouses there; very rich, I shouldn't wonder.''

"They would be," Pitt agreed drily. Curious, the couple who had found the corpse had lived there also. Coincidence. "Right, Gilthorpe. Go and tell the mortuary to have his lordship ready for viewing." He picked up his hat and put it hard on his head, tied his muffler round his neck, and went outside into the rain.

Gadstone Park was, as Gilthorpe had said, a very wealthy area, with large houses set back from the street and a well-tended park in the center with laurel and rhododendron bushes and a very fine magnolia—at least that was what he guessed it to be in its winter skeleton. The rain had turned back to sleet again, and the day was dark with coming snow.

He shivered as the water seeped down his neck and trickled cold over his skin. No matter how many scarves he put on, it always seemed to do that.

Number twelve was a classic Georgian house with a curved carriageway sweeping in under a pillared entrance. Its proportions satisfied his eye. Even though he would never again, since his childhood as a gamekeeper's son, live in such a place, it pleased him to see it. These houses graced the city and provided the stuff of dreams for everyone.

He jammed his hat on harder as a gust of wind rattled a monumental laurel by the door and showered him with water. He rang the bell and waited.

A footman appeared, dressed in black. A thought flickered through Pitt's mind that he had missed his vocation in life—nature had intended him for an undertaker.

"Yes—sir?" There was the barest hesitation as the man recognized one of the lower classes and immediately categorized him as someone who should have known well enough to go to the back door.

Pitt was long familiar with the look and was prepared for it. He had no time to waste with layers of relayed messages, and it was less cruel to tell the news once and plainly than ooze it little by little through the hierarchy of the servant's hall.

"I am Inspector Pitt of the police. There has been an outrage with regard to the grave of the late Lord Augustus Fitzroy-Hammond," he said soberly. "I would like to speak to Lady Fitzroy-Hammond, so that the matter can be closed as soon and as discreetly as possible."

The footman was startled out of his funereal composure. "You—you had better come in!"

He stood back, and Pitt followed him, too oppressed by the interview ahead to be glad yet of the warmth. The footman led him to the morning room and left him there, possibly to report the shattering news to the butler and pass him the burden of the next decision.

Pitt had not long to wait. Lady Fitzroy-Hammond came in, white-faced, and stopped when she was barely through the door. Pitt had been expecting someone considerably older; the corpse from the cab had seemed at least sixty, perhaps more, but this woman could not possibly be past her twenties. Even the black of mourning could not hide the color or texture of her skin, or the suppleness of her movement.

"You say there has been an—outrage, Mr.—?" she said quietly.

"Inspector Pitt, ma'am. Yes. I'm very sorry. Someone has opened the grave." There was no pleasant way of saying it, no gentility to cover the ugliness. "But we have found a body, and we would like you to tell us if it is that of your late husband."

For a moment he thought she was going to faint. It was stupid of him; he should have waited until she was seated, perhaps even have sent for a maid to be with her. He stepped forward, thinking to catch her if she crumpled.

She looked at him with alarm, not understanding.

He stopped, aware of her physical fear.

"Can I call your maid for you?" he said quietly, putting his hands by his sides again.

"No." She shook her head, then, controlling herself with an effort, she walked past him slowly to the sofa. "Thank you, I shall be perfectly all right." She took a deep breath. "Is it really necessary that I should—?"

9

"Unless there is someone else of immediate family?" he replied, wishing he could have said otherwise. "Is there perhaps a brother or—" He nearly said "son," then realized how tactless it would be. He did not know if she was a second wife. In fact, he had neglected to ask Gilthorpe the age of his lordship: Presumably Gilthorpe would not have brought the matter to him at all if he could not have been the man on the cab.

"No." She shook her head. "There is only Verity—Lord Augustus's daughter, and of course his mother, but she is elderly and something of an invalid. I must come. May I bring my maid with me?"

"Yes, of course; in fact, it might be best if you did."

She stood up and pulled the bell cord. When the maid came, she sent the message for her personal maid to bring her cloak, and make herself ready for the street. The carriage was ordered. She turned back to Pitt.

"Where—where did you find him?"

There was no point in telling her the details. Whether she had loved him or it had been a marriage of arrangement, it was not necessary for her to know about the scene outside the theatre.

"In a hansom cab, ma'am."

Her face wrinkled up. "In a hansom cab? But—why?"

"I don't know." He opened the door for her as he heard voices in the hallway, led her out, and handed her into the carriage. She did not ask again, and they rode in silence to the mortuary, the maid twisting her gloves in her hands, her eyes studiously avoiding even an accidental glimpse of Pitt.

The carriage stopped, and the footman helped Lady Fitzroy-Hammond to alight. The maid and Pitt came unassisted. The mortuary building was up a short path overhung by bare trees that dripped water, startling and icily cold, in incessant, random splatters as the wind caught them.

Pitt pulled the bell, and a young man with a pink face opened the door immediately.

"Inspector Pitt, with Lady Fitzroy-Hammond." Pitt stood back for her to go in.

"Ah, good day, good day." The young man ushered

them in cheerfully and led them down the hallway into a room full of slabs, all discreetly covered with sheets. "You'll be after number fourteen." He glowed with cleanliness and professional pride. There was a basket-sided chair close to the slab, presumably in case the viewing relatives should be overcome, and a pitcher of water and three glasses stood on a table at the end of the room.

The maid took out her handkerchief in preparation.

Pitt stood ready to offer physical support should it be necessary.

"Right." The young man pushed his spectacles more firmly on his nose and pulled back the sheet to expose the face. The cabby's clothes were gone and they had combed the sparse hair neatly, but it was still a repellent sight. The skin was blotched and in places beginning to come away, and the smell was cloying sick.

Lady Fitzroy-Hammond barely looked at it before covering her face with her hands and stepping back, knocking the chair. Pitt righted it in a single movement, and the maid guided her into it. No one spoke.

The young man pulled the sheet up again and trotted down the room to fetch a glass of water. He did it as imperturbably as if it were his daily habit—as indeed it probably was. He returned and gave it to the maid, who held it for her mistress.

She took a gulp, then clutched onto it, her fingers white at the knuckles.

"Yes," she said under her breath. "That is my husband."

"Thank you, ma'am," Pitt replied soberly. It was not the end of the case, but it was very probably all he would ever know. Grave robbing was of course a crime, but he did not hold any real hope that he would discover who had made this obscene gesture or why.

"Do you feel well enough to leave now?" he asked. "I'm sure you would be more comfortable at home."

"Yes, thank you." She stood up, wavered for a moment, then, followed closely by the maid, walked rather unsteadily towards the outer door.

11

"That all?" the young man inquired, his voice a little lowered but still healthily cheerful. "Can I mark him as identified and release him for burial now?"

"Yes, you may. Lord Augustus Fitzroy-Hammond. No doubt the family will tell you what arrangements they wish," Pitt answered. "Nothing odd about the body, I suppose?"

"Nothing at all," the young man responded ebulliently, now that the women were beyond the door and out of earshot. "Except that he died at least three weeks ago and has already been buried once. But I suppose you knew that." He shook his head and was obliged to resettle his glasses. "Can't understand why anybody should do that—dig up a dead body, I mean. Not as if they'd dissected him or anything, like medical students used to—or black magicists. Quite untouched!"

"No mark on him?" Pitt did not know why he asked; he had not expected any. It was a pure case of desecration, nothing more. Some lunatic with a bizarre twist to his mind.

"None at all," the young man agreed. "Elderly gentleman, well cared for, well nourished, a little corpulent, but not unusual at his age. Soft hands, very clean. Never seen a dead lord before, so far as I know, but that's exactly what I would have expected one to look like."

"Thank you," Pitt said slowly. "In that case there is little more for me to do."

Pitt attended the reinterment as a matter of course. It was just possible that whoever had committed the outrage might be there to see the result of his act on the family. Perhaps that was the motive, some festering hatred still not worked through, even with death.

It was naturally a quiet affair; one does not make much of burying a person a second time. However, there was a considerable group of people who had come to pay their respects, perhaps more out of sympathy for the widow than further regard for the dead. They were all dressed in black and had black ribbons on their carriages. They processed in silence to the grave and stood, heads bowed in the rain.

Only one man had the temerity to turn up his collar in concession to comfort. Everyone else ignored the movement in pretense that it had not happened. What was the small displeasure of icy trickles down the neck when one was faced with the monumental solemnity of death?

The man with the collar was slender, an inch or two above average height, and his delicate mouth was edged with deep lines of humor. It was a wry face, with crooked brown eyebrows; certainly there was nothing jovial in it.

The local policeman was standing beside Pitt to remark any stranger for him.

"Who is that?" Pitt whispered.

"Mr. Somerset Carlisle, sir," the man answered. "Lives in the Park, number two."

"What does he do?"

"He's a gentleman, sir."

Pitt did not bother to pursue it. Even gentlemen occasionally had occupations beyond the social round, but it was of no importance.

"That's Lady Alicia Fitzroy-Hammond," the constable went on quite unnecessarily. "Very sad. Only married to him a few years, they say."

Pitt grunted; the man could take it to mean anything he chose. Alicia was pale but quite composed: probably relieved to have the whole thing nearly over. Beside her, also in utter black, was a younger girl, perhaps twenty, her honey-brown hair pulled away from her face and her eyes suitably downcast.

"The Honorable Miss Verity Fitzroy-Hammond," the constable anticipated him. "Very nice young lady."

Pitt felt no reply was required. His eye traveled to the man and woman beyond the girl. He was well built, probably had been athletic in youth, and still stood with ease. His brow was broad, his nose long and straight, only a certain flaw in the mouth prevented him from being completely pleasing. Even so, he was a handsome man. The woman beside him had fine, dark eyes and black hair with a marvelous silver streak from the right temple.

"Who are they?" Pitt asked.

"Lord and Lady St. Jermyn," the constable said, rather more loudly than Pitt would have wished. In the stillness of the graveyard even the steady dripping of the rain was audible.

The burial was over, and they turned one by one to leave. Pitt recognized Sir Desmond and Lady Cantlay from the street outside the theatre and hoped they had had the tact not to mention their part in the matter. Perhaps they would; Sir Desmond had seemed a not inconsiderate person.

The last to leave, accompanied by a rather solid man with a plain, amiable face, was a tall, thin old lady of magnificent bearing and an almost imperial dignity. Even the gravediggers hesitated and touched their hats, waiting until she had passed before beginning their work. Pitt saw her clearly for only a moment, but it was enough. He knew that long nose, the heavy-lidded, brilliant eyes. At eighty she still had more left of her beauty than most women ever possess.

"Aunt Vespasia!" He was caught in his surprise and spoke aloud.

"Beg pardon, sir?" the constable started.

"Lady Cumming-Gould, isn't it?" Pitt swung round to him. "That last lady leaving."

"Yes, sir! Lives in number eighteen. Just moved 'ere in the autumn. Old Mr. Staines died in the February of 1885; that'd be just short a year ago. Lady Cumming-Gould bought it back end o' the summer."

Pitt remembered last summer extremely well. That was when he had first met Charlotte's sister Emily's great-aunt Vespasia, during the Paragon Walk outrage. More precisely, she was the aunt of Emily's husband, Lord George Ashworth. He had not expected to see her again, but he recalled how much he had liked her asperity and alarming candor. In fact, had Charlotte married above herself socially instead of beneath, she might have grown in time to be just such a devastating old lady.

The constable was staring at him, eyes skeptical. "You know 'er, then, do you, sir?"

"Another case." Pitt did not want to explain. "Have you

14

seen anyone here who doesn't live in the Park, or know the widow or the family?"

"No, no one 'ere except what you'd expect. Maybe grave robbers don't come back to the scene o' the crime? Or maybe they come at night?"

Pitt was not in the mood for sarcasm, especially from a constable on the beat.

"Perhaps I should post you here?" he said acidly. "In case!"

The constable's face fell, then lightened again as suspicion hit him that Pitt was merely exercising his own wit.

"If you think it would be productive, sir?" he said stiffly.

"Only of a cold in the head," Pitt replied. "I'm going to pay my respects to Lady Cumming-Gould. You stay here and watch for the rest of the afternoon," he added with satisfaction. "Just in case someone comes to have a look!"

The constable snorted, then turned it into a rather inefficient sneeze.

Pitt walked away and, lengthening his stride, caught up with Aunt Vespasia. She ignored him. One does not speak to the help at funerals.

"Lady Cumming-Gould," he said distinctly.

She stopped and turned slowly, preparing to freeze him with a glance. Then something about his height, the way his coat hung, flapping at his sides, struck a note of familiarity. She fished for her lorgnette and held it up to her eyes.

"Good gracious! Thomas, what on earth are you doing here? Oh, of course! I suppose you are looking for whoever dug up poor Gussie. I can't imagine why anyone should do such a thing. Quite disgusting! Makes a lot of work for everyone, and all so unnecessary." She looked him up and down. "You don't appear to be any different, except that you have more clothes on. Can't you get anything to match? Wherever did you purchase that muffler? It's appalling. Emily had a son, you know? Yes, of course you know. Going to call him Edward, after her father. Better than calling him George. Always irritating to call a boy after his father; no one ever knows which one you are talking about. How is Charlotte? Tell her to call upon me; I'm bored to

15

tears with the people in the Park, except the American with a face like a mud pie. Homeliest man I ever saw, but quite charming. He hasn't the faintest idea how to behave, but rich as Croesus.'' Her eyes danced with amusement. "They cannot make up their minds what to do about him, whether to be civil because of his money or cut him dead because of his manners. I do hope he stays.''

Pitt found himself smiling, in spite of the rain down his neck and the wet trouser cuffs sticking to his ankles.

"I shall give Charlotte your message," he said, bowing slightly. "She will be delighted that I have seen you, and you are well.''

"Indeed," Vespasia snorted. "Tell her to come early, before two, then she won't run into the social callers with nothing to do but outdress each other.'' She put her lorgnette away and swept down the path, ignoring the skirts of her gown catching in the mud.

ON SUNDAY Alicia Fitzroy-Hammond rose as usual, a little after nine, and ate a light breakfast of toast and apricot preserve. Verity had already eaten and was now writing letters in the morning room. The dowager Lady Fitzroy-Hammond, Augustus's mother, would have her meal taken up to her as always. On some days she got up; far more often she did not. Then she lay in her bed with an embroidered Indian shawl around her shoulders and reread all her old letters, sixty-five years of them, going back to her nineteenth birthday, July 12, exactly five years after the battle of Waterloo. Her brother had been an ensign in Wellington's army. Her second son had died in the Crimea. And there were old love letters from men long since gone.

Every so often she would send her maid, Nisbett, down to see what was going on in the house. She required a list of all callers, when they came and how long they stayed, if they left cards, and most particularly how they were dressed. Alicia had learned to live with that; the thing she still found intolerable was Nisbett's constant inquiry into the running of the house, passing her finger over the surfaces to see if they were dusted every day, opening the linen cupboard when she thought no one was looking to count the sheets and tablecloths and see if all the corners were ironed and mended.

This Sunday was one of the old lady's days to get up. She enjoyed going to church. She sat in the family pew and watched everyone arrive and depart. She pretended to be deaf, although actually her hearing was excellent. It suited her not to speak, except when she wanted something, and occasional failure to know what was said could be not inconvenient.

She was dressed in black also, and she leaned heavily on her stick. She came into the dining room and banged sharply on the floor to attract Alicia's attention.

"Good morning, mama-in-law," Alicia said with an effort. "I'm glad you are well enough to be up."

The old lady walked towards the table, and the ever-present Nisbett pulled out her chair for her. She stared at the sideboard with displeasure.

"Is that all there is for breakfast?" she demanded.

"What would you like?" Alicia had been trained all her life to be polite.

"It's too late now," the old lady said stiffly. "I shall have to put up with what there is! Nisbett, fetch me some eggs and some of that ham and kidneys, and pass me the toast. I assume you are going to church this morning, Alicia?"

"Yes, Mama. Do you care to come?"

"I never shirk church, unless I am too ill to stand upon my feet."

Alicia did not bother to comment. She had never known precisely what ailed the old lady, or if indeed there was anything at all. The doctor came to call regularly and told her she had a weak heart, for which he prescribed digitalis; but Alicia privately thought it was little more than old age and a desire to command both attention and obedience. Augustus had always catered to her, possibly out of lifelong habit and because he hated unpleasantness.

"I presume you are also coming?" the old lady asked with raised eyebrows, then put an enormous forkful of eggs into her mouth.

"Yes, Mama."

The old lady nodded, her mouth too full to speak.

The carriage was called at half-past ten, and Alicia, Verity, and the old lady were helped into it one by one, and then out again at St. Margaret's Church, where for over a hundred years the family had had its own pew. No one who was not a Fitzroy-Hammond had ever been known to sit in it.

They were early. The old lady liked to sit at the back and watch everyone else arrive, then go forward to the pew at one minute before eleven. Today was no exception. She had survived the deaths of every member of her own blood, except Verity, with the supreme composure required of an aristocrat. The reburial of Augustus would not be different.

At two minutes before eleven she stood up and led the way forward to the family pew. At the end she stopped short. The unthinkable had happened. There was someone else already there! A man, with collar turned up, leaning forward in an attitude of prayer.

"Who are you?" the old lady hissed. "Remove yourself, sir! This is a family pew."

The man did not stir.

The old lady banged her stick sharply on the ground to attract his attention. "Do something, Alicia! Speak to him!"

Alicia squeezed past her and touched the man gently on the shoulder. "Excuse me—" She got no further. The man swayed and fell sideways onto the seat, face up.

Alicia screamed—at the very back of her mind she knew what the old lady would say, and the congregation—but it tore out of her throat beyond her helping. It was Augustus again, his dead face livid and bloodless, gaping up at her from the wooden seat. The gray stone pillars wavered round her, and she heard her own voice go on shrieking like a quite disembodied sound. She wished it would stop, but she seemed to have no control over it. Blackness descended; her arms were pinned to her sides, and something had struck her in the back.

The next thing she knew she was lying propped up in the

vestry. The vicar, pasty-faced and sweating, was crouching next to her, holding her hand. The door was open, and the wind rushed in, in an icy river. The old lady was opposite, her black skirts spread round her like a grounded balloon, her face scarlet.

"There, there," the vicar said helplessly. "You've had a most appalling shock, my dear lady. Quite appalling. I don't know what the world is coming to, when the insane are allowed loose amongst us like this. I shall write to the newspapers, and to my member of Parliament. Something really must be done. It is insupportable." He coughed and patted her hand again. "And of course we shall all pray." The position became too uncomfortable for him; he was beginning to get a cramp in his legs. He stood up. "I have sent for the doctor for your poor mama. Dr. McDuff, isn't it? He will be here any moment. A pity he was not in the congregation!" There was a note of affront in his voice. He knew that the doctor was a Scot and a Presbyterian, and he disapproved vehemently. A physician to such an area as this had no business to be a nonconformist.

Alicia struggled to sit up. Her first thoughts were not for the old lady, but for Verity. She had not seen death before, and Augustus had been her father, even though they had not been close.

"Verity," she said with a dry mouth. "What about Verity?"

"Don't distress yourself!" His voice became agitated at the thought of imminent hysteria. He had no idea how to cope with such a thing, especially in the vestry of the church. The morning service was already a complete disaster; the congregation had either gone home or was standing outside in the rain, impelled by curiosity to watch the last gruesome act of the affair. The police had been sent for, right here to the church, and the whole business was become a scandal beyond retrieval. He dearly wanted to go home and have luncheon, where there would be a fire and a sensible housekeeper who knew better than to have "emotions."

"My dear lady," he started again, "please be assured

20

Miss Verity has been taken care of with the utmost sensibility. Lady Cumming-Gould took her home in her carriage. She was most distressed, of course; who would not be—it is all quite dreadful! But we must bear these burdens with the grace of God to help us. Oh!'' His face lit up with something akin to delight as he saw the thick figure of Dr. McDuff come in and slam the vestry door. Professional responsibility could be shed at last—perhaps even shifted entirely. After all, the doctor must care for the living, and he himself was duty-bound to see to the dead, because no one else was properly qualified.

McDuff went straight to the old lady, ignoring the other two. He took her wrist and felt it for several seconds, then peered at her face.

"Shock," he said succinctly. "Severe shock. I advise you to go home and take as much rest as you feel you need. Have all your meals brought up, and don't receive any visitors except the immediate family, and not them, if you don't choose. Do nothing strenuous, and do not allow yourself to become upset about anything at all."

The old lady's face eased with satisfaction; the fierce color ebbed a little.

"Good," she said, climbing to her feet with his help. "Knew you would know what to do. Can't take any more of this—I don't know what the world is coming to—never had anything like this when I was young. People knew their places then and kept them. Too busy working to go around desecrating graves of their betters. Too much education of the wrong people nowadays; that's what's responsible, you know. Now they've got curiosities and appetites that are no good for them. It isn't natural! See what's happened here! Even the church isn't safe anymore. It's worse than if the French had invaded, after all!" With that parting shot she stumped out, banging her stick furiously against the door.

"Poor dear lady," the vicar muttered. "What a quite dreadful shock for her—and at her age, too. One would think she had earned a little respite from the sins of the world."

Alicia was still sitting on the vestry bench in the cold.

She suddenly realized how much she disliked the old lady. She could never recall a moment since the time she had become betrothed to Augustus when she had felt at ease with her. Until now she had hidden it from herself, for Augustus's sake. But there was no need any longer. Augustus was dead.

With a lurch she remembered his body in the pew, and on the slab in that bitter mortuary with the little man in the white coat who was so terrifyingly happy all the time in his room full of corpses. Thank goodness the policeman at least had been a little more sober; in fact, quite pleasant, in his way.

As if she had conjured him out of her thoughts the door swung open, and Pitt appeared in front of her, shaking himself like a great wet dog and spraying water from his coattails and off his sleeves. She had not thought of the police coming, and now all sorts of ugly fears crowded into her mind. Why? Why had Augustus risen out of his grave again like some persistent, obscene reminder of the past, preventing her from stepping out of it into the future? The future could hold so much promise; she had met new people, especially one new person, slim, elegant, with all the laughter and charm Augustus had lost. Perhaps he had been like that in his youth, but she had not known him then. She wanted to dance, to make jokes of trivial things, to sing something round the spinet other than hymns and solemn ballads. She wanted to be in love and say giddy and uproarious things, have a past worth remembering, like the old lady who sat rereading her youth from a hundred letters. No doubt there was sadness in them, but there was passion, too, if there was any truth in her retelling.

The policeman was staring at her with bright gray eyes. He was the untidiest creature she had ever seen, not fit to be in a church.

"I'm sorry," he said quietly. "I thought we'd seen the end of it."

She could think of no answer.

"Do you know of anyone who might be doing this, ma'am?" he went on.

She looked up at his face, and a whole abyss of new horror opened up in front of her. She had presumed it was an anonymous crime, the work of insane vandals of some sort. She had heard of grave robbing, body snatchers; but now she realized that this extraordinary man thought that it might be personal, deliberately directed at Augustus—or even at her!

"No!" She gulped, and the breath caught in her throat. She swallowed hard. "No, of course not." But she could feel the heat burning up her face. What would other people think? Twice Augustus had been uncovered out of his grave, almost as if someone were unwilling to let him rest—or, more pointedly, unwilling to let her forget him.

Who would do such a thing? The only one she knew was the old lady. She would certainly be annoyed if she thought Alicia could marry again, and so soon, this time for love!

"I have no idea," she said as calmly as she could. "If Augustus had any enemies, he never spoke of them; and I find it hard to imagine that anyone he was acquainted with, whatever their feelings, would do such a thing as this."

"Yes." Pitt nodded. "It is beyond ordinary vengeance, even to us. It's wretchedly cold in here; you'd better go home and warm yourself, take some food. There's nothing you can do now. We'll take care of it, see he's handled decently. I think your vicar's already ordered the proper observations." He walked toward the door, then turned. "I suppose you are quite sure it was your husband, ma'am? You did see his face quite clearly—it wasn't someone else, perhaps?"

Alicia shook her head. She could see the corpse with its gray-white skin in front of her sharply, more real than the cold walls of the vestry.

"It was Augustus, Mr. Pitt. There is no doubt of that at all."

"Thank you, ma'am. I'm extremely sorry." He went out and closed the door behind him.

Outside, Pitt stopped for a moment to glance at the remnants of the congregation, all affecting attitudes of sympathy, or else pretending to be there by chance and about to move; then he strode down the path and out into the street. The business had shaken him far more than the relative seriousness of the crime warranted. Far worse things were going on daily—beatings, extortions, and murders—and yet there was a relentless obscenity about this that disturbed some previously silent portion of his mind, an assumption that death at least was untouchable.

Why on earth should anyone keep on digging up the body of some elderly aristocrat whose death had been perfectly natural?

Or was this a bizarre but unignorable way of saying that it had not? Was it conceivable that Lord Augustus had been murdered, and someone knew it?

After a second disinterment it was a question he could not overlook. They could not simply replace him again—and wait!

There was nothing he could do today; it would be indiscreet. He needed to observe decorum or he would get no cooperation at all from those closest to him, and most likely to know or suspect. Not that he expected much help. No one wanted murder. No one wanted police in the house, investigations and questions.

Added to which, Sunday was his own day off. He wanted to be at home. He was making an engine for Jemima that pulled along on a string. It was proving harder than he had expected to make wheels round, but she was delighted with it anyway and talked to it incessantly in a mixture of sounds quite unintelligible to anyone else, but obviously of great significance to her. It gave him immeasurable happiness.

Late on Monday morning he set out through a fine, thick mist to ride to Gadstone Park and begin the questions. It was not as dismal as might be supposed, because he intended to call first upon Great-Aunt Vespasia. The memory of her in Paragon Walk brought a glow of pleasure to his mind, and he found himself smiling, alone in the hansom cab.

He had chosen his time with care, late enough for her to have finished breakfast but too early for her to have left the house for any morning business she might have.

Surprisingly, the footman informed him that she already had company, but he would acquaint her ladyship with Pitt's arrival, if he desired.

Pitt felt a surge of disappointment and replied a little tartly that yes, he did desire, and then allowed himself to be taken into the morning room to wait.

The footman came back for him unexpectedly soon and ushered him into the withdrawing room. Vespasia was sitting in the great chair, her hair piled meticulously on her head and a chin-high blouse of Guipure lace giving her a totally deceptive air of fragility. She was about as delicate as a steel sword, as Pitt knew.

The others in the room were Sir Desmond Cantlay, Lady St. Jermyn, and Somerset Carlisle. Closer to, Pitt observed their faces with interest. Hester St. Jermyn was a striking woman; the silver streak in her hair appeared quite natural and was startling against its black. Somerset Carlisle was not so thin or so angular as he had seemed in black by the graveside, yet there was still the same suggestion of humor about him, the slightly aquiline nose and the sharp brows.

"Good morning, Thomas," Vespasia said drily. "I was expecting you to call, but not quite so soon, I admit. I imagine you have already made yourself acquainted with the rest of the company, if not they with you?" She glanced round them. "I have met Inspector Pitt before." Her voice crackled with a world of unexplained meaning. Hester St. Jermyn and Sir Desmond both looked at him with amazement, but Carlisle kept his face impassive except for a small smile. He caught Pitt's eye.

Vespasia apparently did not intend to explain. "We are discussing politics," she offered to Pitt. "An extraordinary thing to do in the morning, is it not? Are you familiar with workhouses?"

Pitt's mind flew to the dour, airless halls he had seen crammed with men, women, and children picking apart and re-sewing new shirts from old for the price of their keep. Their eyes ached and their limbs stiffened. In the summer they fainted from heat, and in the winter bronchitis racked them. But it was the only shelter for those with families, or women alone who were too old, too ugly, or too honest to go on the streets. He looked at Vespasia's lace and Hester's minuscule pin tucks.

"Yes," he said harshly. "I am."

Vespasia's eyes gleamed in instant recognition of his thoughts. "And you do not approve," she said slowly. "Abominable places, especially where the children are concerned."

"Yes," Pitt agreed.

"Nevertheless, necessary, and all the poor law allows," she continued.

"Yes." The word came hard.

"Politics have their uses." She barely moved her head to indicate the others. "That is how things are changed."

He reversed his opinion of her, mentally apologizing. "You are moving to change them?"

"It is worth trying. But no doubt you have come about that disgusting business yesterday in the church. A piece of the most appalling distaste."

"If you please. I would appreciate speaking with you, if you will; certain investigations might be accomplished more—discreetly."

She snorted. She knew perfectly well he meant that they might be accomplished with a good deal less trouble, and probably more accurately, but the presence of the others prevented her from saying so. He saw it in her face and smiled.

She understood precisely, and her eyes lit up, but she refused to smile back.

Carlisle stood up slowly. He was more solid and probably stronger than he had appeared at the internment.

"Perhaps there is little more that we can do at the moment," he said to Vespasia. "I will have our notes written up, and we can consider them again. I fancy we have not yet all the information. We must supply St. Jermyn with everything there is; otherwise he will not be able to argue our case against those who have a few contradictions to it, however ill conceived."

Hester rose also, and Desmond followed her.

"Yes," he agreed. "I'm sure you are correct. Good morning, Lady Cumming-Gould—" He regarded Pitt indecisively, not able to address a policeman as a social equal, and yet confounded because he was apparently a fellow guest in the withdrawing room of his hostess.

Carlisle rescued him. "Good morning, Inspector. I wish you a rapid success in your business."

"Good morning, sir." Pitt bowed his head very slightly. "Good morning, ma'am."

When they had gone and the door was closed, Vespasia looked up at him. "For goodness' sake sit down," she ordered. "You make me uncomfortable standing there like a footman."

Pitt obeyed, finding the overstuffed sofa more accommodating than it appeared; it was soft and spacious enough for him to spread himself.

"What do you know about Lord Augustus Fitzroy-Hammond?" he asked. Suddenly the lightness had evaporated, and there was only death left—and perhaps murder.

"Augustus?" She looked at him long and steadily. "Do you mean do I know anyone who might hire lunatics to disinter the wretched man? No, I do not. He was not a person I cared for; no imagination, and therefore, of course, no sense of humor. But that is hardly a cause to dig him up—rather the opposite, I would have thought."

"So would I," Pitt agreed very softly. "In fact, every reason to wish him in his grave."

Vespasia's face changed. It was the only time he could recall her losing that magnificent composure.

"Good God!" She breathed out a long sigh. "You don't think he was murdered!"

"I have to consider it," he answered. "At least as a possibility. He was dug up twice now; that is more than coincidence. It may be insanity, but it is not random insanity. Whoever it is means Lord Augustus to remain unburied—for whatever reason."

"But he was so very ordinary," she said with exasperation and a touch of pity. "He was wealthy, but not exceptionally so; the title is not worth anything, and anyway, there is no one to inherit it. He was pleasing enough to look at, but not handsome, and far too pompous to have a romantic *affaire*. I really can think of—" She stood with a tired little gesture of her hands.

He waited. There was sufficient understanding between them that it would have been faintly insulting for him to have reasoned with her. She was as capable as he of seeing the nuances, the shadings of suspicion and fear.

"I suppose it is better that I tell you than you learn it from backstairs gossip," she said irritably, angry not with him but with the circumstances.

He understood. "And probably more accurate," he agreed.

"Alicia," she said simply. "It was an arranged marriage, as what else could it be between a sheltered girl of twenty and a comfortable, unimaginative man in his midfifties?"

"She has a lover." He stated the obvious.

"An admirer," she corrected him. "To begin with, no more than a social acquaintance. I wonder if you have any idea how small London Society really is? In time one is bound to meet practically everybody, unless one is a hermit."

"But now it is more than an acquaintance?"

"Naturally. She is young and has been denied the dreams of youth. She sees them parading in the ballrooms of London—what else do you expect her to do?"

"Will she marry him?"

She raised silver eyebrows very slightly, her eyes bright. There was a dry recognition of social difference in them, but whether there was amusement at it or not, he was not sure.

"Thomas, one does not remarry, or even allow oneself to be seen considering it, within a year of one's husband's death; whatever one may feel, or indeed do in the privacy of the bedroom. Provided, of course, that the bedroom is in someone else's house, at a weekend, or some such thing. But to answer your question, I should imagine it is quite likely, after the prescribed interval."

"What is he like?"

"Dark and extremely handsome. Not an aristocrat, but sufficient of a gentleman. He has manners enough, and most certainly charm."

"Money?"

"How practical of you. Not a great deal, I think, but he does not appear to be in need of it, at least not urgently."

"Lady Alicia inherits?"

"With the daughter, Verity. The old lady has her own money."

"You know a great deal about their affairs." Pitt disarmed it with a smile.

She smiled back at him. "Naturally. What else is there to occupy oneself with, in the winter? I am too old to have any *affaires* of interest myself."

His smile widened to a grin, but he made no comment. Flattery was far too obvious for her.

"What is his name, and where does he live?"

"I have no idea where he lives, but I'm sure you could find out easily enough. His name is Dominic Corde."

Pitt froze. There could not be two Dominic Cordes, not both handsome, both charming, both young and dark. He remembered him so clearly, his easy smile, his grace, his obliviousness of his young sister-in-law Charlotte, so painfully in love with him. It had been four years ago, before she met Pitt, at the start of the Cater Street murders. But do the echoes of first love ever die away? Doesn't something linger, perhaps more imagination than fact, the dreams that never came true? But painful. . . .

"Thomas?" Vespasia's voice invaded his privacy, drawing him back to the present: Gadstone Park and the disinterment of Augustus Fitzroy-Hammond. So Dominic was in love with Lady Alicia, or at least sought after her. He had seen her only twice, yet had gathered an opinion that she was utterly unlike Charlotte, far more a memory of Dominic's first wife, Charlotte's sister Sarah, who had been murdered in the fog. Pretty, rather pious Sarah, with the same fair hair as Alicia, the same smooth face. He could think only of Charlotte and Dominic.

"Thomas!" Vespasia's face swam up at him as he lifted

29

his head; she was leaning forward touched with concern now. "Are you quite well?"

"Yes," he said slowly. "You said 'Dominic Corde'?"

"You know him." It was a statement rather than a question. She had lived a long time, known many loves and hurts. Little escaped her understanding.

He knew she would recognize a lie. "Yes. He was married to Charlotte's sister, before she died."

"Good gracious." If she read anything more into it than that, she was far too tactful to say so. "So he is a widower. I don't recall his mentioning it."

Pitt did not want to talk about Dominic. He knew it would have to come, but he was not ready yet. "Tell me about the rest of Gadstone Park?" he asked.

She looked a little surprised.

He pulled a small, ironic face. "I can't imagine Alicia dug him up," he said, meeting her eyes. "Or Dominic?"

Her body relaxed, altering the line of the high lace neck. "No," she sighed wearily. "Of course not. They would be the last ones to wish him back. It would appear, unless the whole thing is fortuitous after all, that either one of them murdered Augustus or someone believes they did."

"Tell me about the other people in the Park," he repeated.

"The old lady is a fearful creature." Vespasia seldom minced words. "Sits upstairs in her bedroom all day devouring old love letters, and letters of blood and military vainglory from Waterloo and the Crimea. In her own eyes she is the last of a great generation. She savors over and over again every victory in her life, real or imagined, up to the last minute, so she can wring life dry before it is snatched away from her. She doesn't like Alicia, thinks she has no courage, no style." A sudden dry twist lit up her face. "I really don't know whether she would like her better or worse if she thought her capable of having murdered Augustus!"

Pitt hid a smile by turning it into a grimace. "What about the daughter, Verity?"

"Nice girl. Don't know where she gets it from; must be

30

her mother's side. Not especially good-looking, but quite a bit of life to her, underneath the well-drilled manners. Hope they don't marry her off before she has a little fun."

"How does she get on with Alicia?"

"Well enough, so far as I know. But you needn't look at her; she would have no idea where to employ a grave robber, and she could hardly do it herself!"

"But she might prompt someone else," Pitt pointed out. "Someone in love with her—if she thought her stepmother had murdered her father.

Vespasia snorted. "Don't believe it. Far too devious. She's a nice child. If she thought such a thing she would have come out and accused her, not gone around persuading someone to desecrate her father's grave. And she seems genuinely fond of Alicia, unless she's a far better actress than I take her for."

Pitt had to agree. The whole thing was preposterous. Perhaps, after all, it was the work of a lunatic and the fact that it was the same body both times only a grotesque mischance. He said as much to Vespasia.

"I tend to disbelieve in coincidences," she replied reluctantly, "but I suppose they do occur. The rest of the Park are ordinary enough, in their way. Lord St. Jermyn I cannot fault; neither can I like him, in spite of the fact that it is he who will sponsor our bill through Parliament. Hester is a good woman making the best of an indifferent situation. They have four children, whose names I cannot remember."

"Major Rodney is a widower. He was not at the interment, so you have not seen him yet. He fought in the Crimea, I believe. No one can recall his wife, who must have died thirty-five years ago. He lives with his maiden sisters, Miss Priscilla and Miss Mary Ann. They talk too much and are always making jam and lavender pillows, but are otherwise perfectly pleasant. There is nothing to say about the Cantlays. I believe they are precisely what they seem to be: civil, generous, and a little bored.

"Carlisle is a dilettante; plays the piano rather well, tried to get into Parliament and failed, a bit too radical. Wants to reform. Good family, old money."

"The only one of any interest is that appalling American who bought number seven, Virgil Smith. I ask you?" She raised her eyebrows as high as they would go. "Who on earth but an American would call a child Virgil? And with a name like Smith! He's as plain as a ditch, and with manners to suit. He has not the least idea how to conduct himself, which fork to eat with, or how to address a duchess. He talks to cats and dogs in the streets!"

Pitt had spoken to cats and dogs himself, and he found he was warming to the man immediately. "Did he know Lord Augustus?" he asked.

"Of course not! Do you imagine Lord Augustus kept the company of people like that? He had not the imagination!" Her face softened. "Fortunately, I am old enough for it not to matter anymore what company I am seen to keep, and I rather like him. At least he is not a bore." She looked at Pitt rather pointedly, and he knew that he himself was included in the same bracket of socially impossible people who redeem themselves by not being bores.

He could learn no more from her at present, so, after thanking her for her frankness, he took his leave. This evening he would have to tell Charlotte that Dominic Corde was involved, and he wanted to prepare himself.

Charlotte had not taken more than a cursory interest in the case of grave robbing. It did not concern anyone she knew, not like the murders at Paragon Walk the previous year. She had plenty to keep her busy in the house, and Jemima was consumed with curiosity every minute she was awake. Charlotte spent half her day in household duties, and the other half deciphering Jemima's questions and supplying answers to them. Time after time she could, with a flash of instinct, understand what Jemima meant and repeat the words over clearly to be imitated with solemn diligence.

By six o'clock when Pitt came home, cold and wet, she was tired herself and as glad as he to sit down. It was in the comfortable silence after dinner that he told her. He had debated how to phrase it, whether to lead up to it or simply be bold. In the end his own urgency overtook him.

"I went to see Aunt Vespasia today." He looked at her, then away again, into the fire. "About the grave robbing. She knows everyone in Gadstone Park."

Charlotte waited for him to continue.

Usually he was good at being evasive, coming to things in his own way, but this was too powerful; it forced itself to be said.

"Dominic is involved!"

"Dominic?" She was incredulous; it was too unbelievable, too unexpected to have sense. "What do you mean?"

"Dominic Corde is involved with the Fitzroy-Hammonds. Lord Augustus died a few weeks ago, and his corpse has been unburied twice and left to be found, once on the box of a hansom cab and once in his own pew in church. Alicia, his wife, now his widow, had an admirer, and has had for some time—Dominic Corde!"

She sat quite still, repeating his words over inside her head, trying to grasp them. She had not even thought of Dominic for months; now all her adolescent dreams flooded back, embarrassing in their gaucheness and their fervor. She felt the color burn up her face and wished Pitt had never known anything about it, that she had been less transparent in her infatuation when he had first met her in Cater Street.

Then she began to realize the enormity of it. He had said Dominic was involved. Did he really imagine Dominic had had something to do with disinterring the body? She could not imagine it—not because of the cruelty or the desecration of it, but because she did not believe Dominic had the heat of emotion or the courage in him to do such a wild thing.

"How involved?" she asked.

"I don't know." His voice was unusually sharp. "I should imagine he means to marry her!"

For once he had misunderstood her. "I mean how is he involved with digging up the body?" she corrected. "Surely you don't think he could have done it? Why should he?"

He hesitated, searching her eyes, trying to gauge what she was thinking, how much it mattered to her. He had seen the color in her face at the mention of Dominic's name, and it brought a coldness to him, an uncertainty he had not known for years, not since his father had lost his job and the family had left the great estate where he had been born and grown up.

"I don't imagine he did," he answered. "But I have to consider the possibility that Lord Augustus did not die as naturally as was supposed at the time."

The blood drained out of her face. "You mean murder?" Her tongue was dry. "You think Dominic might have murdered him? Oh, no—I don't believe it! I know him—he is not—" She could not think of a way to say it without cruelty, and less than justice.

"Not what?" he asked, the edge back in his voice. "Not capable of murder?"

"No," she said simply. "I don't think so; not unless he was very frightened, or perhaps in a fit of temper, by accident. But if he did, he would give himself away afterwards. He would never be able to live with it."

"He has such a delicate conscience?" Pitt said sarcastically.

She was hurt by the hardness in him. She had no idea why it should be. Had he remembered her youthful foolishness and been angered by it, found her silliness annoying, even after all this time? Surely he could not be so unforgiving of what had after all been no more than a girl's romanticism. She had tortured no one but herself with it. She remembered all that had happened at Cater Street very clearly. Even Sarah had been unaware of her feelings, and Dominic certainly had.

"We all have sides of ourselves we prefer not to acknowledge," she said quietly. "Sides we reason away with all sorts of arguments why it is wrong for others, but in our case quite justified. Dominic is as good at it as most, perhaps in some things better, but his were only the faults he was brought up to. He learned his values from other people, just as we all do. He could excuse himself easily enough for an *affaire* with a maid, because that is something most gentlemen accept; but nobody accepts murdering someone in order to marry his widow. There is no way Dominic could excuse that to himself, or to anyone else.

After he had done it, he would be terrified. That is what I meant."

"Oh." He sat quite still.

For several minutes there was no noise but the crackle of the fire.

"How was Aunt Vespasia?" she asked at length.

"The same as always," he replied politely. Then he wanted to say more, to establish contact again without exactly apologizing, because that would be to admit to the thoughts he had had. "She asked that you should call upon her sometime. She said that when I saw her at the interment, and I forgot to mention it."

"Will they inter him again?" she asked. "It seems a bit—ridiculous!"

"I suppose so. But I shan't let them do it immediately. The body is in police custody now. I want a postmortem."

"A postmortem! You mean cut him up?"

"If you must put it that way." Slowly he smiled, and she smiled back. Suddenly the warmth flooded into him again, and he sat grinning idiotically, like a boy.

"The family won't be pleased," she pointed out.

"They'll be furious," he agreed. "But I mean to—I have no choice now!"

3

I*T WAS INEVITABLE* the next day that Pitt should call on Alicia. No matter how distasteful it was, he must question her, obliquely, about Lord Augustus, about her relationship with him and with Dominic Corde. Then, of course, he would have to meet Dominic again.

They had not met since Pitt's wedding to Charlotte nearly four years ago. Then Dominic had been newly a widower, still numb from his fear in the Cater Street murders; and Pitt had been too amazed at his own success in winning Charlotte to be more than dimly aware of anyone else.

Now it would be different. Dominic would be over the shock and would have found a new life for himself away from the Ellisons and memories of Sarah. He was bound to marry again; he could not be more than thirty-two or -three, and eminently eligible. Even if he did not have it in mind himself, Pitt knew enough of society to know that some ambitious mother would grasp him for her unmarried daughter. It would merely be a competition as to who would succeed first.

He did not dislike Dominic for himself, only for his relationship with Charlotte and the dreams she had woven about him, and he felt guilty that he had to be the one to drag him again into the shadow of murder.

If indeed he could not clear up the affair before murder need be put into words?

It was a gray, sullen morning with a sky threatening snow when Pitt pulled the bell of number twelve Gadstone Park and the funereal butler let him in with a sigh of resignation.

"Lady Fitzroy-Hammond is at breakfast," he said wearily. "If you care to wait in the morning room, I will inform her that you are here."

"Thank you." Pitt followed him obediently, passing a small, elderly maid in a neat, white-lace-edged uniform. Her thin face sharpened as she saw him, and her eyes glittered. She turned around and retraced her steps upstairs, whisking across the landing and disappearing as he went into the silent, ice-chill morning room.

Alicia came in about five minutes later, looking pale and a little hurried, as if she had left the breakfast table without finishing her meal.

"Good morning, ma'am." He remained standing. The room was too cold to conduct any discussion, especially the relaxed, rather rambling exploration he needed now.

She shivered. "What more can there possibly be to speak of? The vicar has assured me he will take care of all the—arrangements." She hesitated. "I—I am not sure how it should be done—after all—there has already been a funeral—and—" She frowned and shook her head a little. "I don't know anything more to tell you."

"Perhaps we could talk somewhere more convenient?" he suggested. He did not wish to say, precisely, somewhere warmer.

She was confused. "Discuss what? I don't know anything else."

He spoke as gently as he could. "Desecration of a grave is a crime, ma'am. To disinter the same body twice seems unlikely to be merely an insane coincidence."

The blood drained out of her face. She stared at him, speechless.

"Could we go to some room where we may speak comfortably?" This time he made it rather more of guidance, as one would instruct a child.

Still without answering, she turned and led him to a smaller, very feminine withdrawing room at the side of the house. A fire was already burning strongly, and there was a radiance of warmth from it. As soon as they were inside she swung round. Her composure was regained.

"What is it you are supposing, Inspector? More than a madman? Something intentional?"

"I'm afraid so," he replied soberly. "Madness is not usually so—directed."

"Directed at what?" She closed the door and walked over to sit down on the settee. He sat opposite her, feeling the warmth ease out the muscles knotted with cold.

"That is what I must find out," he replied, "if I am to make sure it does not happen again. You said before that you knew of no enemy who would have wished your husband such harm or could conceivably have behaved in such a manner—"

"I don't!"

"Then I am left to consider what other motives there could be," he said reasonably. She was more intelligent than he had expected, calmer. He began to understand how Dominic might be very genuinely attracted to her; neither money nor position need be involved. He thought of what Vespasia had said about laughter and the dreams of youth, and he was angry at the restrictions, the insensitivities of a social convention that could have married her to a man like Augustus Fitzroy-Hammond and bred into her compliance with such a thing. "Or who else might be the intended victim," he finished.

"Victim?" she repeated, turning it over in her mind. "Yes, I suppose you are right. In a sense we are all victims of this—the whole family."

He was not prepared yet to ask her about Dominic. "Tell me something about his mother," he said instead. "She was in the church, wasn't she? Does she live here?"

"Yes. But I don't know what I can tell you."

"Could she be the one intended to be hurt, do you think?"

There was a small flicker over her face, like recognition,

even perhaps a momentary harsh, self-mocking humor. Or perhaps that was something he imagined because it was in his own feelings.

"Are you asking me if she has enemies?" She was looking at him very directly.

"Has she?" It was now no longer a secret between them; he understood, and she had seen it.

"Of course; no one can live to her age without earning enemies," she agreed. "But by the same token, most of them are dead. All the rivals from her youth, or the days of her social power, they are gone, or too old to care. I imagine most scores have been settled long ago."

There was too much truth in that to argue. "And the daughter, Miss Verity?" he went on.

"Oh, no." She shook her head immediately. "She has only been out for a Season. There is no spite in her, and she has done no one harm, even inadvertently."

He was not quite sure how to say the inevitable. Usually it was hard to frame the words that led to accusation, especially when the person could not see them coming; but he had grown accustomed to it over the years, as one lives with early rheumatism, knowing there will be pain now and again, moving to accommodate it, anticipating when the prick would come, growing used to it. But this time it was harder than usual. At the last moment he became oblique again.

"Could there not be envy?" he asked. "She is a charming girl."

Alicia smiled, and there was patience in it for his ignorance. "The only people to envy young ladies of society are other young ladies of society. Do you really imagine, Inspector, that one of them hired men to disinter her dead father?"

He felt foolish. "No, of course not." This time he abandoned tact; he was being clumsier with it than without. "Then if it is not the dowager Lady Fitzroy-Hammond, and it is not Miss Verity, could it be you?"

She swallowed and waited a second before replying. Her fingers were stiff on the carved wooden arm of the settee, grasping onto the fringe.

"I had not thought anyone hated me so much," she said gently.

He plunged in. He could not afford to let pity hold his tongue. She would not be the first murderess to be the supreme actor.

"There has been more than one crime committed from jealousy."

She sat perfectly still. For a while he thought she was not going to answer.

"Do you mean murder, Inspector Pitt?" she said at last. "It is horrible, sick and nightmarish, but it is not murder. Augustus died of heart failure. He had been ill for over a week. Ask Dr. McDuff."

"Perhaps someone wishes us to think it was murder?" Pitt kept his voice calm, almost unemotional, as if he were examining an academic problem, not talking of lives.

Suddenly she perceived what he was thinking. "You mean they are—digging Augustus up to make the police take notice? Do you think someone could hate one of us so much?"

"Is it not possible?"

She turned a little to look into the fire. "Yes—I suppose it is; it would be foolish to say it couldn't be. But it is a very frightening thought. I don't know who—or why."

"I'm told you are acquainted with a Mr. Dominic Corde." Now it was said. He watched the color rise up her cheeks. He had expected to dislike her for it, to disapprove; after all, she was newly widowed. Yet he did not. He found himself sorry for her embarrassment, even for the fact that she was probably in that uncertain stage of love when you can no longer deny your own feelings and are not yet sure of the other's.

She still looked away from him. "Yes, I am." She picked at the fringe of the settee. Her hands were very smooth, used to embroidery and arranging flowers. She was impelled to say more, not simply to leave the subject. "Why do you ask?"

Now he was more delicate. "Do you think someone else might be jealous of your friendship? I have met Mr. Corde; he is a most charming man, and eligible for marriage."

The color deepened in her face, and, perhaps feeling its heat, her embarrassment became more painful.

"That may be, Mr. Pitt." Her eyes came up sharply. He had not noticed before, but they were golden hazel. "But I am newly a widow—" She stopped. Possibly she realized how pompous it sounded. She began again. "I cannot imagine anyone being so deranged as to do such a thing because of a social envy, even over Mr. Corde."

He was still sitting opposite her, only a few feet away. "Can you think of any kind of sane reason for a person to do it, ma'am?"

There was silence again. The fire crackled and fell in sparks. He reached forward for the tongs and put on another piece of coal. It was a luxury to burn fuel without thought of price. He put on a second piece, and a third. The fire blazed up in yellow heat.

"No," she said gently. "You are quite right."

Before he could say anything else, the door swung open and a stout old lady in black came in, banging ahead of herself with a stick. She surveyed Pitt with disdain as he automatically stood up.

Alicia stood up also. "Mama, this is Inspector Pitt, from the police." She turned to Pitt. "My mother-in-law, Lady Fitzroy-Hammond."

The old lady did not move. She did not intend to be introduced to a policeman as if he were a social acquaintance, and certainly not in what she still considered her own house.

"Indeed," she said sourly. "I had assumed so. I imagine you have some duties to attend to, Alicia? The house does not grind to a halt because someone has died, you know. You cannot expect the servants to supervise themselves! Go and see to the menus for the day and that the maids are properly employed. There was dust on the window ledge in the upstairs landing yesterday. I soiled my cuff on it!" She drew in her breath. "Well, don't stand there, girl. If the policeman wants to see you again, he can call again!"

Alicia glanced at Pitt, and he shook his head fractionally. She accepted his dismissal with the civility and the respect

41

for the old that had been bred in her. After she was gone, the old lady waddled over to the settee and sat down, still holding her stick.

"What are you here for?" she demanded. She had on a white lace cap, and Pitt noticed that underneath it her hair was not yet dressed. He guessed she had heard his arrival reported by a maid and risen hurriedly in order not to miss him.

"To see if I can discover who disinterred your son," he replied baldly.

"What in goodness!—Do you imagine it was one of us?" Her disgust at his stupidity was immense, and she took care he should be aware of it.

"Hardly, ma'am," he answered levelly. "It is a man's job. But I think it very likely it was directed at one of you. Since it has happened twice, we cannot assume it coincidence."

She banged her stick on the floor. "You should investigate!" she said with satisfaction, her fat cheeks tight inside their skin. "Find out everything you can. A lot of people seem to be what they aren't. I would start with a Mr. Dominic Corde, if I were you." Her eyes never wavered from his face. "Much too smooth, that one. After Alicia's money, shouldn't wonder. Take a good look at him. Sniffing round here before poor Augustus was dead, long before! Turning her head with his handsome face and easy manners—stupid girl! As if a face were worth anything. Why, when I was her age I knew twenty just like him." She snapped her fingers sharply. "Courts of Europe are full of them; grow a crop of them every summer, just like potatoes. Good for a season, then they're gone. Rot! Unless they marry some rich woman who's taken in by them. You go and inquire into his means, see what he owes!"

Pitt raised his eyebrows. He would have given a week's pay to have been rude to her. Unfortunately, it would have been a lifetime's.

"Do you think he could have disinterred Lord Augustus?" he asked innocently. "I don't see why he should."

"Don't be such an idiot!" she spat. "If anything, he

42

murdered him! Or put that silly girl up to it! I dare say someone knows and dug up Augustus to show it.''

He faced her without blinking. ''Did you know, ma'am?''

She glared at him with stone-faced anger, while she decided which emotion to show.

''Dig up my own son!'' she said at last. ''You are a barbarian! A cretin!''

''No, ma'am.'' Pitt refused to rise to her bait. ''You mistake me. I meant, did you suspect that your son had been murdered?''

Suddenly she realized the trap, and her temper vanished. She looked at him with wary little eyes. ''No, I did not. Not at the time. Although now I am beginning to consider the possibility.''

''So are we, ma'am,'' Pitt stood up. He needed to learn everything he could, but venomous gossip from this old woman would only cloud the issue so early on. Murder was no more yet than a possibility, and there were still others left—hatred, or simply vandalism.

She snorted, held out her hand to be helped up, then remembered he was a policeman and withdrew it again, climbing to her feet unaided. She banged her stick on the floor.

''Nisbett!''

The ubiquitous maid appeared as if she had been leaning against the door.

''Show this man out,'' the old lady ordered, lifting her stick in the air to point. ''And then bring me a cup of chocolate up to my room. I don't know what's the matter with the world; it gets colder every winter. It never used to be like this. We knew how to heat our houses properly!'' She stumped out without looking at Pitt again.

Pitt followed Nisbett into the hallway and was about to go out when he heard voices in the withdrawing room to his left. One was a man's, not loud but very clear, with words precisely spoken. It brought back a tide of memory—it could only be Dominic Corde.

He gave Nisbett a flashing smile, leaving her startled and not a little alarmed, and turned sharply to the door, brushed it with his knuckles in the briefest of knocks, and strode in.

Dominic was standing with Alicia by the fireplace. They both looked round with surprise as he burst in. Alicia flushed, and Dominic made as if to demand an explanation; then he recognized Pitt.

"Thomas!" His voice rose a little in surprise. "Thomas Pitt!" Then his composure returned and he smiled, putting his hand out; it was genuine, and Pitt's dislike evaporated in spite of himself. But he could not afford to forget why he was here. There might be murder, and either one of these two, or even both, could be involved. Even if it were only grave robbing—then surely they were the intended victims of malice.

He took Dominic's outstretched hand. "Good morning, Mr. Corde."

Dominic was quite innocent, as he had always been. "Good morning. How is Charlotte?"

Pitt felt a strange mixture of elation, because Charlotte was his wife now, and resentment, because Dominic asked so easily, so naturally. But after all, he had lived in the same house with her all the years of his marriage to Sarah; he had seen her grow up from an adolescent to a young woman. And all the time it had never entered his head that Charlotte was infatuated with him.

But this was different; he was thirty now, surely more mature, wiser to his effect upon women? And this was Alicia, not his young sister-in-law.

"In excellent health, thank you," Pitt replied. He could not resist adding, "And Jemima is two years old and full of conversation."

Dominic was a little startled. Perhaps he had not thought of Charlotte with children. He and Sarah had not had any— instantly Pitt regretted his bragging. Already, with these few emotion-driven words, he had made detachment impossible, destroyed the professionalism he had intended to observe.

"I hope you're well?" He floundered a little. "This is a very wretched business about Lord Fitzroy-Hammond."

Dominic's face colored, then the blood drained away.

"Ghastly," he agreed. "I hope you can find whoever did it and have him put away. Surely he must be mad and not too hard to recognize?"

"Unfortunately, insanity is not like the pox," Pitt replied. "It doesn't give you a rash that can be seen by the eye."

Alicia stood silently, still absorbing the fact that the two men obviously knew each other and that it was no chance or merely formal acquaintance.

"Not by the untrained eye," Dominic agreed. "But you are not untrained! And haven't you doctors, or something?"

"Before you can do anything with a disease, you need to be familiar with it," Pitt pointed out. "And grave robbing is not something that happens more than once in a policeman's career."

"What about selling them for medical research, wasn't there a trade? I'm sorry, Alicia—" he apologized.

"Resurrectionists? That was quite a while ago," Pitt replied. "They get cadavers quite legally now."

"Then it can't be that." Dominic's shoulders slumped. "It's grisly. Do you think—no, it can't be. They didn't harm the body. It can't be necromancers or satanists or anything like that—"

Alicia spoke at last. "Mr. Pitt is obliged to consider the possibility that they did not choose Augustus by chance, but quite deliberately, either out of hatred for him or for one of us."

Dominic was not as surprised as Pitt would have expected. The thought occurred to him that perhaps she had already said as much before he came into the room. Perhaps that was even what they were discussing when he had broken in on them.

"I can't imagine hating anyone so much," Dominic said flatly.

It was Pitt's chance, and he took it. "There can be many reasons for hatred," he said, trying to make his voice lighter again, as though he were speaking impersonally. "Fear is one of the oldest. Although I have not yet been able to discover any reason why anybody should have feared Lord

45

Augustus. It might turn out he had a power I know nothing of, a financial power, or even a power of knowledge of something someone else would greatly prefer kept secret. He may have learned of something, even unintentionally.''

"Then he would have kept it so," Alicia said with conviction. "Augustus was very loyal, and he never gossiped."

"He might consider it his duty to speak if the matter were a crime," Pitt pointed out.

Neither Alicia nor Dominic spoke. They were both still standing, Dominic so close to the fire his legs must be scorching.

"Or revenge," Pitt continued. "People can harbor a desire for revenge, nursing it over the years till it becomes monstrous. The original offense need not have been grave; indeed, it may not have been a genuine offense at all, merely a success where the other failed, something quite innocent."

He drew in breath and came a little closer to what he really wanted to say.

"And of course there is greed, one of the commonest motives in the world. It may be that someone stood to benefit from his death in ways that are not immediately obvious—"

The blood ebbed out of Alicia's face and then rushed back in scarlet. Pitt had not meant anything quite so simple as inheritance, but he knew she thought he did. Dominic too was silent, shifting from one foot to the other. It may have been unease, or merely that he was too close to the fire and unable to move without asking Pitt to move also.

"Or jealousy," Pitt finished. "A desire for freedom. Perhaps he stood in the way of something someone else wished for desperately." Now he could not look directly at either of them, and he was aware they did not look at each other.

"Lots of reasons." He backed a little to allow Dominic away from the heat. "Any one of them possible, until we find otherwise."

Alicia gulped. "Are—are you going to investigate all of them?"

46

"It may not be necessary," he answered, feeling cruel as he said it and hating his job because already the suspicion was taking form in his mind and shaping like a picture in the fog. "We may discover the truth long before that."

It was no comfort to her, as indeed he had not intended it to be. She came forward a little, standing between Pitt and Dominic. It was a gesture he had seen a hundred times in all manner and walk of women: a mother defending an unruly child, a wife lying about her husband, a daughter excusing her drunken father.

"I hope you will be discreet, Inspector," she said quietly. "You may cause a great deal of unnecessary distress if you are not and wrong my husband's memory, not to mention those you imply may have had such motives."

"Of course," he agreed. "Facts may have to be inquired into, but no implications will be made."

She did not look as if she were able to believe him, but she said no more.

Pitt excused himself, and the footman made sure that he left this time.

Outside, the cold caught at him, seizing his body even through his layers of coat and jacket, chilling the skin and tying knots in the muscles of his stomach. The fog had blown away, and there was sleet on the wind. It sighed through the laurel and magnolia, and the rain blackened everything. There was no alternative now but to press for a postmortem of Augustus Fitzroy-Hammond. The possibility of murder could not be ignored, discreetly tucked away because it could hurt too many people.

He had previously discovered where to find Dr. McDuff, and he took himself straight there. The less time he had to think about it the better. He would face telling Charlotte when he had to.

Dr. McDuff's house was spacious and solid and conventional, like the man; it had nothing to wake the imagination, nothing to risk offending the complacent. Pitt was shown into yet another cold morning room and told to wait. After a quarter of an hour he was conducted to the study lined with leatherbound books, a little scuffed, where he stood before a vast desk to answer as a schoolboy might to a master. At least here there was a fire.

"Good morning," Dr. McDuff said dourly. He may have been comely enough in his youth, but now his face was wrinkled with time and impatience, and self-satisfaction had set unbecoming lines round his nose and mouth. "What can I do for you?"

Pitt pulled up the only other chair and sat down. He refused to be treated like a servant by this man. After all, he was only another professional like himself, trained and paid to deal with the less pleasant problems of humanity.

"You were the physician in attendance to the late Lord Augustus Fitzroy-Hammond up to the time of his death—" he began.

"Indeed," Dr. McDuff replied. "That is hardly a matter for the police. The man died of a heart attack. I signed the certificate. I know nothing about this appalling desecration that has taken place since. That is your affair, and the sooner you do something about it the better."

Pitt could feel the antagonism in the air. To McDuff he represented a sordid world beyond the grace and comfort of his own circle, a tide that must be forever held back with sandbags of discrimination and social distinction. If he were to get anything from him at all, it would not be by a head-long charge, but with deviousness and appeal to his vanity.

"Yes, it is an appalling business," he agreed. "I have not had to deal with anything like it before. I would value your professional opinion as to what manner of person might be affected with such an insane desire."

McDuff had opened his mouth to disclaim anything to do with it, but his professional standing had been called on. It was not what he had been expecting Pitt to say, and he was momentarily off guard.

"Ah." He sought to rearrange his thoughts rapidly. "Ah! Now, that's a very complex matter." He had been going to say he knew nothing about it either, but he never admitted ignorance outright; after all, his years of experience had given him immense wisdom, knowledge of human behavior in all its comedies and tragedies. "You are quite right; it is

48

an insanity to dig a man's corpse out of its grave. No question about it.''

''Do you know of any medical condition that would lead to such a thing?'' Pitt inquired with a perfectly sober face. ''Perhaps some sort of obsession?''

''Obsession with the dead?'' McDuff turned it over in his mind, casting about for something positive to say. ''Necrophilia is the term you are seeking.''

''Yes,'' Pitt agreed. ''Perhaps even an obsessive hatred or envy of Lord Augustus himself—after all, the wretched creature has dug him up twice! That hardly seems like coincidence.''

McDuff's face stiffened to even harder lines of dislike. It was his own world that was being threatened now, his social circle.

Pitt saw it and turned it into necessity. ''Naturally, your professional ethics would not permit you to mention names, Dr. McDuff,'' he said quickly. ''Even obliquely. But you can tell me, as a man of long experience in medicine, if there is any such condition—then I must search for myself to see if I can find its victim. It is the duty of both of us to see that Lord Augustus is decently buried and allowed to rest—and of course his unfortunate family. His widow— and his mother—''

Dr. McDuff remembered the purse strings.

''Of course,'' he said immediately. ''I will do everything I can—within the bounds of ethical discretion,'' he added. ''But I cannot readily think of any disease whatever which would produce such a repulsive form of madness. I will give the matter deep thought, and if you care to call again, I will have a more considered opinion.''

''Thank you very much.'' Pitt stood up and moved to the door; then, just before he opened it, he turned. ''By the way, there are some very unpleasant suggestions that Lord Augustus might have been murdered, and someone knows of it and is digging up his body to draw our attention to the fact—force us to investigate. I suppose his death was perfectly natural—expected?''

McDuff's face darkened. ''Of course it was perfectly

natural, man! Do you imagine I would have signed the certificate if it were not?''

"Expected?'' Pitt insisted. "He had been ill for some time?''

"A week or so. But in a man of sixty that is not unusual. His mother has a weak heart.''

"But she is still alive,'' Pitt pointed out. "And somewhat over eighty, I should judge.''

"That has nothing to do with it!'' McDuff snapped, his fist tightening on the desk top. "Lord Augustus's death was quite natural, and in a man of his years and health not unusual.''

"You did a postmortem?'' Pitt knew perfectly well he had not.

McDuff was too angry to think of that. The very idea outraged him. "I did not!'' His face mottled heavily with purple. "You have practiced too long in the back streets, Inspector. I would have you remember that my clients have no resemblance whatsoever to yours! There is no murder here, and no crime, except that of grave robbing; and doubt-less it is one from your world, not one from mine, who is to blame for that! Good day to you, sir!''

"Then I shall have to get a postmortem now,'' Pitt said softly. "I am obliged to tell you, I shall apply to the magistrate this afternoon.''

"And I shall oppose you, sir!'' McDuff banged his fist down. "And you may allow yourself to be quite certain his family will also! They are not without influence. Now please take yourself out of my house!''

Pitt went to his superiors with his request for a postmortem on Lord Augustus, and they received him with anxiety, saying they would have to consider such a thing and could not put it to a magistrate without due weighing of all its aspects. One could not do such things lightly or irrespon-sibly, and they must be sure they were justified before com-mitting themselves.

Pitt was angry and disappointed, but he knew that he should have been prepared for it. One did not disembowel the corpses of the aristocracy and question their deaths without the most dire compulsion, and even then one obtained a justification that could not be denied before venturing forth.

The following day McDuff had done his best. The answer was returned to Pitt in his office that there were no grounds for the application, and it would not be made. He went back to his own small room, not sure whether he was angry or relieved. If there were no autopsy, then it was unlikely there would ever be any murder proved; the certificate had been signed for a natural death from heart failure. And he had already seen enough of Dr. McDuff to believe it would take more than anything Pitt was capable of to make him reverse a professional opinion, and certainly not publicly. And if there were no murder, Pitt would still be obliged to make the motions of further investigations as to who had disinterred the body and left it so bizarrely displayed, but he did not for a moment hold any hope of discovering the answer. In time it would be overtaken by more urgent crimes, and Dominic and the Fitzroy-Hammonds would be left alone to get on with their lives.

Except, of course, that whoever had dug up Augustus might not give up so easily. If someone believed, or even knew, that there had been murder, he—or she—might have more ideas on how to bring it to attention. God knew what could be next!

And Pitt hated an open case. He liked Alicia; as far as his imagination stretched to a totally alien way of life, he even sympathized with her. He did not want to learn that she had either killed her husband or had been party to it. And for Charlotte's sake, he did not want it to have been Dominic.

For the time being there was nothing he could do. He turned his mind to a case of forgery he had been closing in on before Lord Augustus fell off the cab at his feet.

It was half-past five and, outside, as dark as an unlit cellar between the fog-wrapped gas lamps when a junior constable opened his door to say that a Mr. Corde had come to see him.

Pitt was startled. His first thought was that there had been some new outrage, that his extraordinary opponent was impatient and ready to prompt him again. It was a sick, unhappy feeling.

Dominic came in with his collar turned up to his ears and his hat on far lower than his usual rakish angle. His nose was red and his shoulders hunched.

"My God, it's a wretched night." He sat uncomfortably on the hard-backed chair, looking at Pitt with anxiety. "I pity any poor devil without a fire and a bed."

Instead of asking why Dominic had come, Pitt made the instinctive reply that was on his tongue. "There'll be thousands of them." He met Dominic's eyes. "And without supper either, within a stone's throw of here."

Dominic winced; he had never had much imagination when Charlotte had known him, but maybe the few years between had changed him. Or perhaps it was only distaste at Pitt's literal reply to what had been meant only as a passing remark.

"Is it true that you want to do a postmortem on Lord Augustus?" he asked, taking his gloves off and pulling a white linen handkerchief out of his pocket.

Pitt could not let a chance for truth slip away unused. "Yes."

Dominic blew his nose, and when he looked up his face was tight. "Why? He died of heart failure; it's in the family. McDuff will tell you it was all perfectly normal, even expected! He ate too much and seldom took any recreation. Men like that in their sixties are dying all the time." Dominic screwed up the handkerchief and shoved it in his pocket. "Can't you see what it will do to the family, especially Alicia? That old woman is pretty good hell to live with now; imagine what she will be like if there is a postmortem. She will blame it all on Alicia and say that such a thing would never have happened to Augustus if he had not married her. If Alicia were not more than thirty years younger than he, no one would think anything of it!"

"It's nothing to do with age," Pitt said wearily. He wished he could leave the affair, put it out of his mind as well as his duty. "It is because the body was dug up twice and left where we could not help but find it. Quite apart from the fact that that is a crime, we have to prevent it happening again. Surely you can see that?''

"Then bury him and put a constable on watch!" Dominic said with exasperation. "No one is going to dig him up with a policeman standing there looking at them. It can't be an easy job, or a quick one, moving all that earth and raising a coffin. They must do it at night and take a fair bit of equipment. Spades, ropes and things. And there must be more than one of them, it stands to reason.''

Pitt did not look at him. "One strong man could do it, with a little effort,'' he argued. "And he wouldn't need ropes; the coffin was left, only the actual corpse was taken. We could post a constable for a night or two, even a week, but sometime we'd have to take him away—and then he could go and do it again, if that was what he wanted.''

"Oh, God!'' Dominic shut his eyes and put his hands over them.

"Or else he'll do something else,'' Pitt added. "If he is determined to make somebody act.''

Dominic lifted his head. "Something else? Such as what, for God's sake?''

"I don't know,'' Pitt admitted. "If I knew, then perhaps I could prevent it.''

Dominic stood up, the blood high in his face now. "Well, I'll prevent a postmortem! There are plenty of people in the Park who will put their weight against it. Lord St. Jermyn, for one. And if necessary, we can hire somebody to keep a guard over the grave to see that the body rests in peace and decency. Nobody but a madman disturbs the dead!''

"Nobody but madmen do many things,'' Pitt agreed. "I'm sorry about it, but I don't know how to stop it.''

Dominic shook his head, moving slowly away. "It's not your fault, and not your responsibility. We'll have to do something—for Alicia's sake. Remember me to Charlotte— and Emily, if you ever see her. Goodnight.''

The door closed behind him, and Pitt stared at it, feeling guilty. He had not told him there was no postmortem because he had wanted to see what Dominic would say. And now he knew he felt worse than before. A postmortem might have cleared up forever any suspicion of murder. Perhaps he should have said that. But why had Dominic not seen that himself?

Or was he afraid it would show the very opposite? That there had been murder! Was Dominic guilty himself—or afraid for Alicia? Or only afraid of the scandal and all the dark, corroding suspicions, the old sores opened up that investigation always brings? He could not have forgotten Cater Street.

But if Dominic wanted the matter silenced, there was at least one other who did not. In the morning Pitt received a rather stiff letter from the old lady reminding him that it was his duty to discover who had disturbed Lord Augustus in his grave—and why! If there had been murder done, he was paid by the community to learn of it and avenge it.

He called her an exceedingly uncomplimentary name and put the sheet of paper down. It was ordinary white note-paper—perhaps she kept the deckle-edged for her social acquaintances. The thought flickered through his mind that maybe he should take it to his superiors and let them fight among themselves as to which was the more imperative for their careers and duty—the establishment's prohibition or the old lady's social weight.

He was still considering the matter, with the letter in his top drawer, when Alicia came, wrapped in furs to her throat. She caused a few surprised comments in the outer office, and the constable who preceded her to tell Pitt had eyes as round and bulbous as marbles.

"Good morning, ma'am." Pitt offered her the chair and waved the constable away. "I'm afraid I have nothing new to tell you, or I should have called to say so."

"No." She looked everywhere but at Pitt. He wondered whether she was simply avoiding him, or if she had any interest at all in the brownish walls and the austere prints on them, the boxes bulging with files. He waited, leaving her to find her own courage.

At last she looked at him. "Mr. Pitt, I have come to ask you not to continue with the matter of my husband's grave

54

being disinterred—'' That was a ridiculous euphemism, and she realized it, stammering a little awkwardly. ''I—I mean—the digging up of his body. I have come to the belief that it was someone deranged, vandals who knew no better. You will never catch them, and no good can be served by pursuing it.''

A sudden idea occurred to him. ''No, I may not catch him,'' he agreed slowly. ''But if I do not pursue it, then there may be great distress, not least to you yourself.'' He met her eyes squarely, and she was unable to look away without obviously avoiding him.

''I don't understand you.'' She shook her head a little. ''We shall bury him and if necessary hire a servant to keep guard for as long as need be. I see no way in which that can cause distress.''

''It may well be that it was merely a lunatic.'' He leaned a little forward. ''But I'm afraid not everyone will believe so.''

Her face pinched. He did not need to use the word ''murder.''

''They will have to think as they choose.'' She lifted her head and gripped her fur tighter.

''They will,'' Pitt agreed. ''And some of them will choose to think you have refused to allow a postmortem precisely because there is something to hide.''

Her face paled, and she knotted her fingers unconsciously in the thick pelts.

''Unkindness is surprisingly perceptive,'' he continued. ''There will be those who have remarked Mr. Corde's admiration for you, and no doubt those also who have envied it.'' He waited a moment or two, allowing her to digest the thought, with all its implications. He was preparing to add that there would be suspicion, but it was not necessary.

''You mean they will wonder if he was murdered?'' she said very softly, her voice dry. ''And they will say it was Dominic, or me myself?''

''It is possible.'' Now that he had come to it again, it was hard to say. He wished he could disbelieve it himself, but remembering Dominic and sitting here looking at her face, eyes hot and miserable, hands twisting at her collar, he knew that she was not sure beyond question even in her own heart.

"They are wrong!" she said fiercely. "I have done nothing to harm Augustus, ever, and I am sure Dominic—Mr. Corde—has not, either!"

It was the protest of fear, to convince herself, and he recognized it. He had heard just that tone so often before when the first doubt thrusts itself into the mind.

"Then would it not be better to allow a postmortem?" he said softly. "And prove that the death was natural? Then no one would consider the matter any further, except as an ordinary tragedy."

He watched as the fears chased each other across her face: first a catching at the hope he held out; then doubt; then the sick pain that it might prove the exact opposite and make murder unarguable, a fact.

"Do you think Mr. Corde might have killed your husband?" he said brutally.

She glared at him with real anger. "No, of course I don't!"

"Then let us prove that it was a natural death with a postmortem, which will put it beyond doubt."

She hesitated, still weighing the public scandal against the private fears. She made a last attempt. "His mother would not permit it."

"On the contrary." He could afford to be a little gentler now. "She has written to request it. Perhaps she wishes these voices silenced as much as anyone else."

Alicia pulled a face of derision. She knew as well as Pitt, who had read the letter, what the old lady wanted. And she also knew what the old lady would say, and go on saying until the day she died, if there were no postmortem. It was the deciding factor, as Pitt had intended it should be.

"Very well," she agreed. "You may add my name to the request and take it to whoever it is who decides such things."

"Thank you, ma'am," he said soberly. The victory had no pleasure in it. He had seldom fought so hard for something that tasted so bitter.

*　　*　　*

The postmortem was a gruesome performance. They were never pleasant, but this one, performed on a body that had now been dead for nearly a month, was grimmer than most.

Pitt attended because in the circumstances it was expected that someone from the police be there, and he wanted to know for himself each answer the minute it was obtained. It was a day when the cold seemed to darken everything, and the autopsy room was as bleak and impersonal as a mass grave. God knew how many dead had passed across its scrubbed table.

The pathologist wore a mask, and Pitt was glad of one, too. The smell caught at the stomach. They worked for hours, calmly and in silence but for brief instructions as organs were removed and handed over, samples taken to search for poisons. The heart was looked at with particular care.

At the end Pitt walked out, numb with cold, his stomach tight from nausea. He huddled his jacket round him and pulled his muffler up to his ears.

"Well?" he asked.

"Nothing," the pathologist replied dourly. "He died of heart failure."

Pitt stood silently. Half of him had wanted that answer, and yet the other half could not believe it, could see no sense in it.

"Don't know what brought it on," the pathologist went on. "Heart's not in a bad condition, for a man of his age. Bit fatty, arteries thickening a little, but not enough to kill him."

Pitt was obliged to ask. "Could it have been poison?"

"Could have," the pathologist answered. "Quite a lot of digitalis there, but his doctor says the old lady had it for her heart. He could have taken it himself. Doesn't look like enough to have done him any harm—but I can't say for certain. People don't all react the same way, and he's been dead awhile now."

"So he could have died of digitalis poisoning?"

"Possibly," the pathologist agreed. "But not likely.

57

Sorry I can't be more help, but there just isn't anything definite.''

Pitt had to be content. The man was professional and had done his job. The postmortem had proved nothing, except confirm to the world that the police were suspicious.

Pitt dreaded having to tell the news to his superiors. He treated himself to a hansom from the hospital back to the police station and got out in the rain at the other end. He ran up the steps two at a time and dived into the shelter of the entrance. He shook himself, scattering water all over the floor, then went in.

Before he reached the far side of the room and went up the stairs to break the news, he was confronted by the red face of a young sergeant.

''Mr. Pitt, sir!''

Pitt stopped, irritated; he wanted to get this over as soon as possible. ''What is it?'' he demanded.

The sergeant took a deep breath. ''There's another grave, sir—I mean another open one—sir.''

Pitt stood stock-still. ''Another grave?'' he said fatuously.

''Yes, sir—robbed, like the last one. Coffin—but no corpse.''

''And whose is it?''

''A Mr. W. W. Porteous, sir. William Wilberforce Porteous, to be exact.''

4

PITT DID NOT tell Charlotte about the second grave, nor indeed about the result of the postmortem. She heard about the latter two days later in the early afternoon. She had just finished her housework and put Jemima to bed for her rest when the doorbell rang. The woman who came in three mornings a week to do the heavy work had gone before midday, so Charlotte answered the door herself.

She was startled to see Dominic on the step. At first she could not even find words but stood stupidly, without inviting him in. He looked so little different it was as if memory had come to life. His face was just as she had remembered it, the same dark eyes, the slightly flared nostrils, the same mouth. He stood just as elegantly. The only difference was that it did not tighten her throat anymore. She could see the rest of the street, with its white stone doorsteps and the net twitching along the windows.

"May I come in?" he asked uncomfortably. This time it was he who seemed to have lost his composure.

She recollected herself with a jolt, embarrassed for her clumsiness.

"Of course." She stepped back. She must look ridiculous. They were old friends who had lived in the same house for years when he had been her brother-in-law. In fact, since he had apparently not remarried, even though Sarah had been dead for nearly five years, he was still a member of the family.

"How are you?" she asked.

He smiled quickly, trying to look comfortable, to bridge the immense gap.

"Very well," he replied. "And I know you are. I can see, and Thomas told me when I met him the other day. He says you have a daughter!"

"Yes, Jemima. She's upstairs, asleep." She remembered that the only fire was in the kitchen. It was too expensive to heat the parlor as well, and anyway, she spent too little time in there for it to matter. She led him down the passage, conscious of the difference between this, with its well-worn furniture and scrubbed board floors, and the house in Cater Street with five servants. At least the kitchen was warm and clean. Thank goodness she had blackened the stove only yesterday, and the table was almost white. She would not apologize; not so much for herself as for Pitt.

She took his coat and hung it behind the door, then offered him Pitt's chair. He sat down. She knew he had come for some reason, and he would tell her what it was when he had found the words. It was early for tea, but he was probably cold, and she could think of nothing else to offer.

"Thank you," he accepted quickly. She did not notice his eyes going round the room, seeing how bare it was, how every article was old and loved, polished by owner after owner, and mended where use had worn it down.

He knew her too well to play with gentilities. He could remember her sneaking the newspaper from the butler's pantry when her father would not allow her to read it. He had always treated her as a friend, a strong friend, rather than as a woman. It was one of the things that used to hurt.

"Did Thomas tell you about the grave robbing?" he asked suddenly and baldly.

She was filling the kettle at the sink. "Yes." She kept her voice level.

"Did he tell you much?" he went on. "That it was a man called Lord Augustus Fitzroy-Hammond, and that they dug him up twice and left him where he was bound to be found quickly—the second time in his own pew in church, where it would be his family who saw him?"

"Yes, he told me." She turned off the tap and set the kettle on the stove. She could not think what to offer him to eat at this time of day. He was bound to have lunched, and it was far too early for afternoon tea. She had nothing elegant. In the end she settled for biscuits she had made, sharp, with a little ginger in them.

He was looking at her, his eyes following her round the room, anxious. "They did a postmortem. Thomas insisted on it, even though I begged him not to—"

"Why?" She met his eyes and tried to keep all guile out of her face. She knew he had come for some kind of help, but she could not give it if she did not understand the truth, or at least as much of it as he knew himself.

"Why?" He repeated her question as if he found it strange.

"Yes." She sat down opposite him at the scrubbed table. "Why do you mind if they do a postmortem?"

He realized he had not told her about his connection with the family and assumed that that was why she was confused. She could see the thoughts crossing his mind and was surprised how easily she read them. In Cater Street he had seemed mysterious, private, and out of reach.

She allowed the mistake.

"Oh," he acknowledged his omission. "I forgot to explain—I know Lady Alicia Fitzroy-Hammond, the widow. I met her at a ball some little time ago; we became—" He hesitated, and she knew he was debating whether to tell her the truth or not; not from any sensitivity to old feelings, because he had never been aware of them, but from a habitual delicacy in discussing such things. One did not speak freely of a relationship with a recent widow, still less of another man's wife. Personal emotion of any sort was hinted at, rather than named.

She smiled very slightly, allowing him to flounder.

He met her eyes, and memory was too strong for him. "—friends," he finished. "In fact, I hope to marry her—when a decent time has passed."

She was glad she had been prepared for it; somehow it would have been a shock if it had come without any warning. Was her resentment for Sarah's memory, or for her own, a final shedding of girlhood dreams?

She forced her mind back to the disinterment. "Then why do you mind there being a postmortem?" she asked frankly. "Are you afraid it will uncover something wrong?"

His face colored, but he remained looking at her fixedly. "No, of course not! It is the suspicion! If the police demand a postmortem, that means they must have a strong belief there is something to discover. In any event, they were wrong."

She was surprised. Pitt had not told her it had been done. "You mean it is over?" she asked.

His eyebrows went up. "Yes. You didn't know?"

"No. What did they find?"

He looked angry and unhappy. "They made it worse than before. It made their suspicions obvious, without proving anything. Alicia consented to it because Thomas told her it would put an end to all the speculation. But the answer was equivocal. It could have been natural heart failure, or it could have been an overdose of digitalis. And an overdose could have been accidental—his mother keeps it for her heart—or it could have been murder."

Of course she knew he would say this, but now that he had, she did not know how to answer. She asked the obvious question.

"Is there any reason to suppose it was murder?"

"The damned corpse was dug up twice!" he said furiously, his helplessness breaking through in anger. "That isn't exactly common, you know! Especially in that sort of society. Good God, Charlotte, have you forgotten what suspicion of murder did to us in Cater Street?"

"It stripped off the facade, so we saw all the weak and ugly things we had learned to hide from ourselves and each other," she said quietly. "What are you afraid you will see here?"

He stared at her, something close to dislike in his face. She would have expected it to hurt her, and yet it did not, not closely, inside herself where real pain lived; rather, it was the distant ache one feels for someone unknown, whose misfortune one has seen before and known to expect.

"I'm sorry." She meant it, not as an apology but as an expression of regret, even sympathy. "I really am sorry, but I don't know of anything I can say or do to help."

His anger vanished. He was caught; he knew all the disillusion, the malice, and the fear that almost inevitably would follow, and he was afraid.

He was still looking for an escape. "Can't they leave it now?" he said quietly, his voice tight, his hands white on the wooden tabletop. "Alicia didn't kill him; I didn't; and the old lady wouldn't have, unless she gave him a dose accidentally, and it was too much for him." He looked up at Charlotte. "But no one can prove it; all they will do is raise a lot of doubts, make everyone look with suspicion at each other. Can't Thomas just leave it now? Then there'll be some hope that whoever did this wretched thing will give up, be convinced at last that there's nothing to it?"

She did not know what to say. She would like to have believed him and accepted that it was simply either a natural death or an accident. But why the disinterment—twice? And why was he afraid? Was it no more than the shadow of Cater Street indelible in the memory, or was there growing in him a fear that Alicia could have become so in love with him, so frustrated by her husband that she had taken a simple, easily grasped opportunity and given him a fatal dose of his mother's medicine? She looked at Dominic's handsome face and felt as she sometimes did towards Jemima.

"He may do." She wanted to comfort him; she had known him a long time, and he had been part of her life, part of the deepest of her emotions in those callow, vulnerable years before she met Pitt. Yet it would be both useless and stupid to lie. "But grave robbing is a crime," she said clearly. "And if there is a chance he can find who did it, he will have to continue."

"He won't find out!" He spoke with such conviction she knew it was for himself he insisted, not for her.

"Probably not," she agreed. "Unless, of course, they do it again? Or they do something else?"

It was a thought he had been trying to banish. Now she had brought it where it could not be denied.

"It's insane!" he said hotly. It was the easiest way to explain it, the only acceptable way. Insanity did not have to have reason; by its very nature any incongruity could be explained and wiped away.

"Perhaps."

He had finished his tea, and she collected his cup to remove it.

"Can't you ask Thomas?" He leaned forward a little, urgently, his face puckered. "Point out the harm it will do to innocent people? Please, Charlotte? There will be such injustice! We won't even have the chance to deny or disprove what has only been whispered, never said outright. When people whisper, lies become bigger and bigger as they are passed around—"

The injustice convinced her. For a moment she placed herself in Alicia's position, in love with Dominic; she could still remember how sharp that was, full of excitement and pain, wild hope and hot disillusion. And to be tied to a husband without imagination or laughter! Then if he died, and at last you were free? Suspicion reached out its ugly fingers and soils everything; no one says to you what they think; it is all smiles and sympathy to your face, polite smirks in the withdrawing room. The moment you are gone the acid overflows, creeping wider and wider, eating away the fabric of everything good. The gossips court you; old friends no longer call. She had seen enough of envy and opportunism before.

"I'll ask him," she agreed. "I can't say what he will do, but I'll ask."

His face lit up, making her feel guilty for having promised when she knew she could influence Pitt very little where his job was concerned.

"Thank you." Dominic stood up, as graceful as always now that his fear had gone. "Thank you very much!" He smiled, and the last few years slipped away—they could have been conspirators again in something trivial, like the filching of Papa's newspaper.

When Pitt came home she said nothing at first, allowing him to warm himself, to speak with Jemima and see her to bed, and then to eat his meal and relax before the fire. The kitchen was comfortable from the day-long heat of the stove. The scrubbed wood was pale, almost white, and the pans gleamed on the shelves. Flowered china on the dresser reflected the gaslight.

"Dominic came here today," she said casually.

She was sewing, mending a dress of Jemima's where she had trodden on the hem and toppled over. She did not notice Pitt stiffen.

"Here?" he asked.

"Yes, this afternoon."

"What for?" His voice was cool, guarded.

She was a little surprised. She stopped sewing, needle in the air, and looked up at him. "He said you'd done a postmortem on Lord whatever his name is—the man who fell off the cab after the theatre."

"So we did."

"And you didn't discover anything conclusive. He died of heart failure."

"That's right. Did he come here to tell you that?" His voice was a beautiful instrument, precise and evocative. It was rich with sarcasm now.

"No, of course not!" she said sharply. "I don't care what the wretched man died of. He was frightened that the suggestion of murder might cause gossip, whispering that would hurt a lot of people. It is very difficult to deny something that no one has said outright."

"Such as that Alicia Fitzroy-Hammond murdered her husband?" he asked. "Or that Dominic did himself?"

65

She looked at him a little coolly. "I don't think he was afraid for himself, if that is what you are trying to say." As soon as the words were out she thought better of them. She loved Pitt, and she sensed in him a vulnerability, even though she did not know what it was. But justice was strong, too, and the old loyalty to Dominic died hard, perhaps because she knew his weaknesses. Pitt was the stronger; she had no need to defend him. He could be hurt, but he would not hurt himself, crumble under pressure.

"He ought not be," Pitt said drily. "If Lord Augustus was murdered, Dominic is an obvious suspect. Alicia inherits a good deal, not to mention an excellent social position; she's in love with Dominic—and she's an extremely handsome woman."

"You don't like Dominic, do you?" She was listening not to his words, but to what she read in them.

He stood up and walked away, pretending to fiddle with the curtains. "Like and dislike have nothing to do with it," he answered. "I am speaking of his position; he is a natural suspect if Lord Augustus was murdered. It would be naive to imagine otherwise. We cannot always have the world as we would like it, and sometimes even the most charming people, people we have known and cared for, for years, are capable of violence, deceit, and stupidity." He let the curtains go and turned back to her because he had to know what she was feeling. He would not ask her what Dominic had meant under his words, how he had spoken, what he had left unsaid.

Her face was calm, but there was anger under the surface, and he was not sure exactly why. He had to press until he did, even if it hurt him in the end, because not knowing was worse.

"Don't talk to me as if I were a child, Thomas," she said quietly. "I know that perfectly well. I don't think Dominic killed him, because I don't think he would want to enough. But I think he is afraid that she did. That is why he came here."

His eyes narrowed a little. "What did he expect you to do?"

"Point out to you the injustice that might be done if you continue with an investigation, especially since you are not even sure if there has been any crime."

"You think I shall be unjust?" He was looking for a quarrel now. Better to hear it than leave it in the air, waiting.

She refused to reply, biting her tongue instead of telling him not to be idiotic. She would like to have said it, but she did not dare.

"Charlotte!" he demanded. "Do you think that because it is Dominic, I shall be unjust?"

She looked up from Jemima's dress, the needle still in her fingers. "It does not need anyone to be unjust for injustice to happen," she said a little tartly. Really, he was being stupid on purpose! "We all know what suspicion can do, and we have said as much. And in case you think otherwise, I told Dominic that you would do whatever was necessary, and I should have no influence upon you."

"Oh." He walked back across the room and sat down in his chair opposite her.

"But you still don't like Dominic," she added.

He did not answer. Instead, he pulled out the box where he kept the pieces he was making into a train for Jemima and began working on them skillfully with a knife. He had got enough of the answer he wanted. For tonight, he would prefer to leave it alone. She was still cross, but he knew it was not to do with Dominic, and that was all that mattered.

He carved at the wood with satisfaction, beginning to smile as it took shape.

The following day Charlotte determined to do something about the matter herself. She had not a really good winter dress, but she had one that, although it was very much last year's fashion, flattered her. Its cut fit her extremely well, especially now that her figure was quite back to its weight before Jemima's birth, in fact, if anything a little improved. The gown was the color of warm burgundy, complementary both to her hair and her complexion.

She remembered what Aunt Vespasia had said about a

suitable hour to call, and she spent the next day's house-keeping on a hansom cab to take her to Gadstone Park. She could not possibly be seen arriving on an omnibus, even if such a thing were to run anywhere near.

The parlormaid was surprised to see her but well trained enough to show it only slightly. Charlotte had no card to present, as most callers did in society, but she kept her chin in the air and begged the maid to be good enough to inform her mistress that Mrs. Pitt was here at her invitation.

She was more relieved than she had realized when the girl accepted this somewhat odd introduction and led her to an empty withdrawing room to wait, while Lady Cumming-Gould was apprised of the event. It was probably the word "invitation" that had decided it; after all, it was just possible Lady Cumming-Gould had invited her, the old lady being a trifle eccentric.

Charlotte was too tense to sit down. She stood with her hat and gloves still on and tried to affect an air of indifference, in case the maid should return before she heard her; anyway, it was good practice.

When the door opened it was Vespasia herself, dressed in dove gray and looking like a figure from a silversmith's dream. She was more magnificent in her seventies than most women ever are.

"Charlotte! How delightful to see you. For goodness' sake, girl, take off your hat and cloak! My house cannot possibly be as cold as that. Here. Eliza!" Her voice rang out in imperious disgust, and the maid appeared instantly. "Take Mrs. Pitt's cloak, and bring us something hot to drink."

"What would you like, m'lady?" The girl took the things obediently.

"I don't know," Vespasia snapped. "Use your imagination!" She sat down the moment the door was closed behind the maid and treated Charlotte to a detailed inspection. Finally she snorted and leaned back. "You look in excellent health. Time you had another child." She disregarded Charlotte's blush. "I suppose you've come about this disgusting business of the corpse? Old Augustus

Fitzroy-Hammond. He was always a nuisance; never knew when it was time to go, even when he was alive.''

Charlotte wanted to laugh; perhaps it was a relief from nervousness, especially after last evening's wretched, silly conversation with Pitt.

"Yes," she agreed warmly. "Dominic came to see me yesterday, you know. He is very afraid the continued investigation may cause a lot of unkind speculation.''

"No doubt," Vespasia said drily. "And most of it to the effect that either he or Alicia killed him—or both together.''

She had said it so immediately Charlotte's mind flew to the obvious. "Does that mean they have started already?''

"They are bound to have," Vespasia replied. "There is little enough else to talk about at this time of the year. At least half of Society is in the country, and those of us who are left are bored to stupidity. What more exciting than the rumor of a love *affaire* or a murder?''

"That's vicious!" Charlotte was angry at the callousness of it, the enjoyment of other people's tragedies, almost as if the gossipers were willing it to be true.

"Of course." Vespasia looked at her with amusement and regret under her hooded eyelids. "Nothing much changes; it is still bread and circuses. Why do you think they baited bears or bulls?''

"I'd hoped we had learned better," Charlotte replied. "We are civilized now. We don't throw Christians to the lions anymore.''

Vespasia raised her eyebrows, and her face was perfectly straight. "You are out of date, my dear, far out: Christians are passé now; it is Jews who are the fashion. They are the stuff for the circuses.''

Memories of delicate social cruelty came back to Charlotte. "Yes, I know. And I suppose if there isn't a Jew or a social climber to hand, then Dominic will do as well.''

The maid came in with a tray with hot chocolate in a silver pot and very small cakes. She set it in front of Vespasia and waited for acceptance.

"Thank you." Vespasia regarded it down her nose.

"Very good. I'll call if I wish for you again. For the time being, I am not at home."

"Yes, m'lady," and the girl departed, her face still wide open with surprise. Why in goodness' name should her ladyship treat this Mrs. Pitt, whom no one had ever heard of, with such extra-ordinary regard? She could hardly wait to regale the other servants with the news and discover if anyone knew the answer.

Charlotte sipped the chocolate; she had a weakness for it, but it was something she could not often afford.

"I suppose someone must think he was murdered," she said presently. "Or they would not keeping digging him up!"

"It seems the most likely explanation," Vespasia agreed with a frown. "Although I cannot for the life of me imagine who would do such a thing. Unless, of course, it is the old woman."

"What old woman?" For the moment Charlotte could not think whom she meant.

"His mother, the old dowager Lady Fitzroy-Hammond. Fearful old creature, lives in her bedroom most of the time, except Sundays, when she goes to church and watches everyone. She has ears like a ferret, although she affects to be deaf so people will not be discreet in front of her. She never comes anywhere near me; in fact, she took to her bed for a week when she heard I had come to live in the Park, because I am nearly as old as she is, and I can remember her perfectly well fifty years ago. She is forever recalling her youth and what a splendid time she had, the balls and the carriage rides, the handsome men and the love *affaires*. Only her memory has in it a great deal more than mine has, and a good deal more highly spiced. I recall her as a mouse-colored girl far too short in the leg for elegance, who married above herself, rather later than most. And winters were just as cold then, orchestras just as out of tune, and the handsome men just as vain and every bit as silly as they are now."

Charlotte smiled into her chocolate cup. "I'm sure she must hate you soundly, even if you never say anything at all about it. No doubt part of her remembers the truth. Poor Alicia. I suppose she is in a constant comparison, a moth to the memories of a butterfly?''

"Very well put." Vespasia's eyes glittered in appreciation. "If it were the old woman who had been killed, I would hardly have blamed her.''

"Did Alicia love Lord Augustus—I mean in the beginning?" Charlotte asked.

Vespasia gave her a long stare. "Don't be ingenuous, Charlotte. You are not so long out of society as that! I dare say she was fond enough of him; he had no intolerable habits, so far as I am aware. He was a bore, but no more so than many men. He was not generous, but neither was he mean. He certainly kept her well enough. He seldom drank to excess, nor was he indecently sober.'' She sipped at her chocolate and looked Charlotte straight in the eye. "But he was no match for young Dominic Corde, as I dare say you know for yourself!''

Charlotte felt the color sweep up her face. Vespasia could not possibly know of her infatuation with Dominic, unless Pitt had told her; or Emily? But they would not! Vespasia must know he had been her brother-in-law. Thomas would say so. She knew he liked Vespasia and would tell her that much of the truth.

Charlotte chose her words very slowly. To lie would be pointless and lose Vespasia's regard. She made herself look up and smile.

"No, I should imagine not," she answered lightly. "Especially if he was her father's choice rather than her own. There is nothing to put one off anything like not having chosen it yourself, even if you might have liked it well enough otherwise.''

Vespasia's smile lit up her face, going all the way to her eyes. "Then you did well, my dear. I'm sure Thomas Pitt was not your father's choice!''

Charlotte found herself grinning, a tide of memories coming back to her; although to be fair, Papa had not fought her nearly as hard as might have been expected. Perhaps he was glad enough she had at last made a choice at all? But she

71

had not come here merely to enjoy herself. She must get back to the purpose.

"Do you think the old lady could have hired someone to dig up Lord Augustus, just to spite Alicia?" she asked a little too bluntly. "Jealousy can be very obsessive, especially in someone who has nothing else to occupy herself with but the past. Perhaps she has even convinced herself it is true?"

"It may be true." Vespasia weighed it in her mind. "Although I doubt it. Alicia does not seem to have the desperation in her actually to have murdered the old fool, even for Dominic Corde. But then, one seldom knows what fires may burn underneath a comparatively passive exterior. And perhaps Dominic is greedier than we think, or more urgently pressed by creditors. He dresses extremely well. I should think his tailor's bill is no small matter."

The thought was ugly, and Charlotte refused to entertain it. She knew she might well have to eventually—but not yet, not until they had tried every other answer.

"What possibilities are there, apart from that?" she said cheerfully.

"None that I know of," Vespasia admitted. "I cannot imagine anyone else of his social acquaintance either hating him enough to kill him, or loving him enough to wish him avenged. He was not the sort of man to inspire passion of any sort."

Charlotte could not give up. "Tell me about the other people in the Park."

"There are several who would be of no interest to you; they are away for the winter. Of those who are here, I can see no reason why any should be involved, but you may as well consider them. Sir Desmond and Lady Cantlay you have already met; they are pleasant enough, quite harmless, I should have judged. If Desmond has anything more to him, he should be on the stage; he is the finest actor I have seen. Gwendoline may be a little bored, like many women of her station with everything provided for her and nothing to complain of, but if she took a lover it would most assuredly not have been Augustus, even had he unbent himself so

72

far as to be willing. He was a great deal more boring than Desmond.''

"Could it have anything to do with money?'' Charlotte was clutching at extremes.

Vespasia's eyebrows went up. "Not likely, my dear. Everyone in the Park has more than adequate means, and I don't believe anyone lives significantly beyond them. But if one is temporarily embarrassed, one goes to the Jews, not to Augustus Fitzroy-Hammond. And there are no fortunes to be inherited, except by the widow.''

"Oh.'' It was disappointing. As always, it led back to Dominic and Alicia.

"The St. Jermyns were well acquainted,'' Vespasia continued. "But I cannot conceive of any reason why they should wish him harm. In fact, Edward St. Jermyn is far too involved in his own affairs to have time or effort for anyone else's.''

"Romantic *affaires*?'' Charlotte's hopes rose.

Vespasia pulled a small, dry face. "Certainly not. He is a member of the House of Lords and has great ambitions for office. At the moment he is drafting a private member's bill to reform conditions in workhouses, particularly with regard to children. Believe me, Charlotte, it is very much needed. If you have any idea of the suffering of children in such places, that may well affect them all their lives— He will achieve a great thing if he succeeds, and a good deal of regard throughout the country.''

"Then he is a reformer?'' Charlotte said eagerly.

Vespasia looked at her down her long nose. She sighed a little wearily. "No, my dear, I fear he is no more than a politician.''

"You are being unkind! That is quite cynical!'' Charlotte accused.

"It is quite realistic. I have known Edward St. Jermyn for some time, and his father before him. Nevertheless, it is an excellent bill, and I am giving it every support I can. Indeed, we were discussing it when Thomas came here last week. I see he did not mention it.''

"No.''

"He seemed to feel strongly about it; in fact, I felt it was hard for him to be civil. He looked at my lace and Hester's silk as if it had been a crime in itself. He must see a great deal more of poverty than any of us imagine, but if we did not buy the clothes, how would the seamstresses get even the few pence they do?" Her face tightened, and for the first time all the wit was gone out of her voice. "Although Somerset Carlisle says that even sewing eighteen hours a day, till their fingers bleed, they still do not earn enough to live. Many of them are driven to the streets, where they can make as much in a night as they would in a fortnight on the sweatshop floor."

"I know," Charlotte said quietly. "Thomas seldom speaks of it, but when he does I cannot rid myself of the visions it brings for nights afterwards: twenty or thirty men and women huddled together in a room, probably below the street, with no air and no sanitation, working, eating, and sleeping there, just to make enough to cling to life. It is obscene. God alone knows what a workhouse must be like, if they still prefer the sweatshop. I feel so guilty because I do nothing—and yet I go on doing nothing!"

Vespasia's face warmed to her honesty. "I know, my dear. Yet there is very little we can do. It is not an isolated instance, or even a hundred instances; it is a whole order of things. You cannot relieve it by charity, even had you the means. It needs law. And to initiate laws, you must be in Parliament. That is why we need men like Edward St. Jermyn."

For some time they sat silently; then at last Charlotte brought herself back to the thing that she could accomplish, or at least could try. "That doesn't answer why Lord Augustus was dug up, does it?"

Vespasia took the last cake. "No, not in the least. Nor do I think the other people in the Park will enlighten the situation. Somerset Carlisle never showed anything for Augustus beyond the courtesy required of good manners; he, like St. Jermyn, is far too occupied with the bill. Major Rodney and his two sisters are very retiring. They are maiden ladies and will assuredly remain so. They busy themselves with domestic chores, largely of a refined nature, such as fine sewing and the making of endless preserves, and I think rather a lot of homemade wine from quite dreadful ingredients like parsnips and nettles. Perfectly appalling! Not that I have tasted it above once! Major Rodney has left the army now, of course, and collects butterflies, or something small that crawls around on dozens of legs. He has been writing his memoirs of the Crimea for the last twenty years. I had no idea so much had happened out there!"

Charlotte hid a smile.

"And there is a portrait artist," Vespasia continued, "Godolphin Jones, but he has been absent for some little while, in France, I believe, so he could not have dug up Augustus. And I can think of no possible reason why he should wish to.

"The only other person," she concluded, "is an American called Virgil Smith! Quite outrageous, of course. Society will abhor him if he is brazen enough to remain here next Season, but then on the other hand he is laden with money from something quite uncouth, like cattle, out in wherever it is he comes from, so they will not be able to refrain from courting him at the same time. It should be greatly entertaining. Except that I hope the poor creature does not get too hurt. He really is very good-natured and seems to be quite without airs, which is such a change. Of course, his manners and his appearance are both disasters, but money covers a multitude of sins."

"And kindness even more," Charlotte pointed out.

"Not in Society!" Vespasia stared at her. "Society is all to do with what seems, and nothing to do with what is. That is one of the reasons you will find it uncommonly difficult to discover whether Augustus was killed, by whom, or why—and still less if anybody cares!"

While Charlotte was sitting in Vespasia's carriage being driven home, feeling self-conscious but utterly pampered, turning over in her mind the fruits of the journey, or rather the lack of them, in the churchyard of St. Margaret's two gravediggers were standing in the rain for a moment's respite from the long and heavy duty of preparing the earth to receive Augustus Fitzroy-Hammond yet again.

"I dunno, 'Arry," one of them said, wiping the drop off the end of his nose. "I'm beginning to think as I could make me livin' purely out o' this, just buryin' 'is lordship. No sooner does we 'ave 'im down there as some great fool goes an' digs 'im up again!"

"I know what you mean," Harry sniffed. "I dreams about this, I does! Spend me life goin' in an' out o' this bleedin' grave. You should 'ear what my Gertie says about it! She says it's only them wot's murdered as won't rest, an' I tell you, Arfur, I'm beginnin' to think as she's right! I don't suppose this is the last time we'll be in an' out of 'ere!"

Arthur spat and took up his spade again. The next blow hit the coffin lid. "Well, I'll tell you this, 'Arry, it's the last time I will! I don't want no truck wiv murder, or them w'ot's been murdered. I don't mind buryin' nice decent corpses what 'ave died natural. I'll bury as many of them as you like. But there's two things as really gets me. One is babies—I 'ate buryin' kids—and the other is them w'ot's been murdered. An' I already buried this one twice! If'n 'e don't stay there this time, they needn't ask me to do 'im again—'cos I shan't! Enough's enough. Let the rozzers find out 'oo done 'im in, then maybe 'el'll stay there, that's w'ot I say."

"Me too," Harry agreed vehemently. "I'm a patient man, God knows I am. In this line you gets to see a lot o' death, you gets to know w'ot's important and w'ot ain't. We all comes to this in the end, and some folks as forgets that might do better if they remembered. But my patience is wore out, and I won't stand by for no murder. I agree wiv yer, let the rozzers bury 'im theirselves next time. Do 'em good, it would."

They had cleaned the earth off the lid of the coffin and climbed out of the grave again for the ropes.

"I suppose they'll want this thing all cleaned up fit to look at?" Arthur said with heavy disgust. "They'll 'ave another service for 'im, like as not. They must be fair sick o' payin' their last respecs."

"Only it ain't last—is it?" Harry asked drily. "It's second to last, or third, or fourth? Who knows when 'e'll stay there? 'Ere, take the other end o' this rope, will you?''

Together they eased the ropes under the coffin, heaving on its weight, and worked in silence except for grunts and the occasional expletive till it was laid on the wet earth beside the gaping hole.

"Gor, that bleedin' thing weighs a ton!" Harry said furiously. "Feels like it 'ad a load o' bricks in it. You don't suppose they put suffink else in there, do you?"

"Like w'ot?" Arthur sniffed.

"I dunno! You want to look?"

Arthur hesitated for a moment; then curiosity overcame him, and he lifted one of the corners of the lid. It was not screwed and came up quite easily.

"God all-bloody-mighty!" Arthur's face under the dirt went sheet-white.

"W'ot's the matter?" Harry moved toward him instinctively, stubbing his toe on the coffin corner. "Damn the flamin' thing! W'ot is it, Arfur?"

" 'E's in 'ere!" Arthur said huskily. His hand went up to his nose. "Rotten as 'ell, but 'e's 'ere all right."

" 'E can't be!" Harry said in disbelief. He came round to where Arthur was standing and looked in. "You're bloody right! 'E is 'ere! Now w'ot in 'ell's name do you make o' that?"

Pitt was considerably shaken when he heard the news. It was preposterous, almost incredible. He did up his muffler, pulled his hat down over his ears, and strode out into the icy streets. He wanted to walk to give himself time to compose his mind before he got there.

There were two corpses—because the corpse from the church pew was still in the mortuary. Therefore one of them was not Lord Augustus Fitzroy-Hammond. His mind went back over the identification. The man from the cab outside the theatre had been identified only by Alicia. Now that he thought about it, she had been expecting it to be her husband. Pitt himself had as much as told her it was. She had only glanced at him and then looked away. He could hardly

77

blame her for that. Perhaps her eyes had seen only what had been told them, and she had not actually examined him at all?

On the other hand, the second corpse, the one in the church pew, had been seen not only by Alicia but by the old lady, the vicar, and lastly by Dr. McDuff, who one would presume was reasonably used to the sight of death, even if not three weeks old.

He crossed the street, splashed with dung and refuse from a vegetable cart. The child who normally swept the crossing had bronchitis and was presumably holed up somewhere in one of the innumerable warrens behind the facade of shops.

Therefore the most reasonable explanation was that the second corpse was Lord Augustus, and the first was someone else. Since the grave of Mr. William Wilberforce Porteous had also been robbed, presumably it was his corpse they had buried in St. Margaret's churchyard!

He had better make arrangements for the widow to see it—and properly this time!

It was half-past six and the wind had dropped, leaving the fog to close in on everything, deadening sound, choking the breath with freezing, cloying pervasiveness, when Pitt drove in a hansom cab with a very stout and painfully corseted Mrs. Porteous, flowing with black, toward the morgue where the first corpse was now waiting. They were obliged to travel very slowly because the cabby could not see more than four or five yards in front of him, and that only dimly. Gas lamps appeared like baleful eyes, swimming out of the night, and vanished behind them into the void. They lurched from one to the next, as alone as if it had been an ocean with no other ship upon it.

Pitt tried to think of something to say to the woman beside him, but rack his brains as he might, there seemed nothing at all that was not either trivial or offensive. He ended by hoping his silence was at least sympathetic.

When the cab finally stopped, he got out with inelegant haste and offered her his hand. She weighed heavily upon it, a matter of balance rather than degree of distress.

78

Inside, they were greeted by the same cheerfully scrubbed young man with his glasses forever sliding down his nose. Several times he opened his mouth to remark on the extraordinariness of the circumstance, never having had the same corpse twice in this manner, then cut himself off halfway, realizing that his professional enthusiasm was in poor taste and might be misunderstood by the widow—or Pitt, for that matter.

He pulled back the sheet and composed his face soberly.

Mrs. Porteous looked straight at the corpse, then her eyebrows rose and she turned to Pitt, her voice level.

"That is not my husband," she said calmly. "It's nothing like him. Mr. Porteous had black hair and a beard. This man is nearly bald. I've never seen him before in my life!"

5

Since the unnamed corpse was in the morgue, there was no reason why Augustus should not be reinterred. Of course, it would have been ludicrous to have yet another ceremony, but it was felt indecent not at least to observe the occasion in some manner. It was a show of sympathy for the family, and perhaps of respect not so much for Augustus as for death itself.

Alicia naturally had no choice but to go; the old lady decided first that she was too unwell because of the whole miserable affair, then later that it was her duty to pay a final farewell—and please God it was final! She was attended, as always, by Nisbett, in dourest black.

Alicia was in the morning room waiting for the carriage when Verity came in from the hall. She was pale, and the black hat made her look even younger. There was an innocence about her that had often caused Alicia to wonder what her mother had been like, because Verity possessed a quality that had nothing to do with Augustus, and she was as unlike the old lady as a doe is unlike a weasel. It was an odd thought, but in the darkness of the night Alicia had even talked to the dead woman as if she had been a friend, someone who could understand loneliness, and dreams that were fragile but so very necessary. In Alicia's mind, that first wife who had died at thirty-four had been very like herself.

Because of her, the ridiculous conversation in the dark, she could almost feel as if Verity were her own daughter, although there was only a handful of years between them.

"Are you sure you wish to come?" she asked now. "No one would misunderstand if you preferred not to."

Verity shook her head a little. "I'd love not to come, but I can't leave you to do it alone."

"Your grandmother is coming," Alicia replied. "I shan't be alone."

Verity gave a dry little smile; it was the first time Alicia had seen it. She had grown up a lot since her father's death, or perhaps she had only now felt the freedom to show it.

"Then I shall definitely come," she said. "That is worse than alone."

At another time Alicia might have made some protest as a matter of form, but today the hypocrisy seemed emptier than ever. It was a time for substance, and form was irrelevant.

"Thank you," she said simply. "It will be much less unpleasant for me if you are there."

Verity gave a sudden, flashing smile, almost conspiratorial; then, before Alicia could make an answer, they both heard the old woman's stick banging in the hall as she came toward them. Nisbett opened the door wide, right back on its hinges, and the old woman stood in the entrance, glaring. She examined both of them closely, every article of their clothing from black hats and veils to black polished boots, then nodded.

"Well, are you coming then?" she demanded. "Or do you mean to stand there all morning like two crows on a fence?"

"We were waiting for you, Grandmama," Verity replied instantly. "We would not leave you to come alone."

The old lady snorted. "Huh!" She looked venomously at Alicia. "I thought perhaps you were waiting for that Mr. Corde you are so fond of! Not here this time, I see. Perhaps he is afraid for his skin! After all, you seem to bury husbands more often than most!'' She grabbed at Nisbett's arm and went out, whacking the door lintel with her stick as if it might have moved out of her way were it more aware of its duty.

"It would hardly be appropriate for Mr. Corde to have come." Alicia could not help defending him, explaining, even though the old lady was out of hearing and Verity had said nothing but lowered her eyes. "It is a very private affair," she added. "I expect no one but the family, and perhaps a few of those who knew Augustus well."

"No, of course not," Verity murmured. "It would be silly to expect him." Nevertheless there was a ring of disappointment in her voice, and as Alicia followed her outside and into the black-draped carriage, she could not help wondering why Dominic had not at least sent a message. Good taste would keep him from coming himself; that was simple to explain. Since he loved Alicia, it would be a little brazen to turn up yet again to an interment, but it would have been so easy to have sent a small message, just a sympathy.

A coldness jarred through Alicia which had nothing to do with the wind and the drafty carriage. Perhaps she had read too much into his flatteries, the soft looks, the seeking after her company? She would have sworn, a few days ago, that he loved her, and she loved him with all the excitement, the laughter ready to burst open at the silliest things, the sharing of very private thoughts and sudden understandings. But maybe it was only she who felt like that and had put her own joy into his heart quite falsely? After all, he had not actually said as much—she had assumed out of delicacy for her position, first as a married woman, then as a very recent widow. Maybe he had not said so quite simply because it was not true? Many people loved to flirt; it was a kind of game, an exercise of skills, a vanity.

But surely Dominic was not like that? His face swam before her memory, the dark eyes, the fine brows, the curve of his mouth, the quick smile. The tears welled up and slid down her cheeks. At any other time she would have been mortified, but she was sitting in a dark carriage on a wet, bitter day, on the way to bury her husband. No one would remark her weeping, and anyway, under her veil it would take a careful eye even to notice it.

The carriage lurched to a stop, and the footman opened the door, letting in a blast of icy air. The old lady got out first, holding her stick across their legs so they could not precede her. The footman helped Alicia. It was raining even harder, and the water ran round the brim of her hat and fell off the front, blowing into her face.

The vicar spoke to the old lady, then held out his hand to Alicia. He was never a cheerful man, but he looked unusually wretched today. Far inside herself she half smiled, but it would not reach her lips. She could hardly blame the man, even though she did not like him. After all, it was an occasion for which he probably had no precedent, and he was at a loss to know what to say. He had stock phrases of piety for all the foreseeable events—baptisms, deaths, marriages, even scandals—but who could expect to bury the same man three times in as many weeks?

She could have laughed, albeit a little hysterically, but she saw in the distance the slim, elegant figure of a man, and for a moment her heart lurched. Dominic? Then she realized it was not; the shoulders were squarer, leaner, and there was something different about the way he stood. It was Somerset Carlisle.

He turned as she picked her way through the puddles on the path and offered her his arm.

"Good morning, Lady Fitzroy-Hammond," he said gently. "I'm so sorry this should be necessary. Let us hope they get it over with as quickly as possible. Perhaps the rain will cut the vicar's desire to expound." He smiled very slightly. "He's going to be as wet as a fish if he stands out here for long!"

It was a pleasing thought; to remain here by the grave while the vicar droned on imperviously would be the final wretchedness. The old woman looked like a sodden black bird, feathers ruffled, her whole stance bristling with anger. Verity stood with her head down and her eyes lowered so no one could read her face; whether it was out of grief for her father or because in mind she was not attending at all, Alicia could only guess, but she imagined the latter.

Lady Cumming-Gould, of all people, had also elected to attend. Her dignity was as superb as always. Indeed, but for her deep lavender mourning, she might have been at a garden party, rather than standing by a yawning grave in a winter churchyard in the rain.

Major Rodney was there, shifting unhappily from foot to foot, blowing water off his moustache, obviously acutely embarrassed by the whole business. Only knowledge of duty could have brought him. He kept darting furious glances at his sisters, who had presumably nagged him into coming. They huddled together, round-eyed, like little animals woken from hibernation and longing to return home.

The only other person was Virgil Smith, enormous in a heavy coat and bareheaded. She could not help noticing how thick his hair was and how it had been cut level at the bottom of his ears. Really, someone should find him a decent barber!

The vicar began to speak, then became increasingly unhappy with what he was saying, stopped, and began again quite differently. There was no other sound but the rain, swirling in blusters, and the far rattle of branches in the wind. No one else spoke.

Finally he became desperate and finished at a positive shout: "—commit the body of our brother—Augustus Albert William Fitzroy-Hammond—to the ground"—he took a deep breath, and his voice rose to a shriek—"until he come forth at the resurrection of the just, when the earth yields up her dead. And may the Lord have mercy on his soul!"

"Amen!" came the response with infinite relief.

They all turned and made with indecent haste for the shelter of the lychgate.

When they were crammed together underneath it, the old lady suddenly made a startling announcement. "There will be a funeral breakfast for anyone who cares to come." She issued it rather as a challenge, a defiance to them to dare not to.

There was a moment's silence, then a murmur of thanks. Hastily they stepped out into the rain again and splashed through the water now running down the paths and climbed into their respective carriages, sitting wrapped in wet clothes, trouser legs and skirt hems sodden, while the horses clopped back through the Park. On any other occasion they would have trotted, but it would be unthinkable for one to hurry leaving a funeral.

Back at home again, Alicia found the servants prepared to receive, although she had given no such instructions. Once, in the hall, she caught Nisbett's eye and saw in it a gleam of satisfaction. It explained a great deal. One day she would deal with Nisbett; that was a promise.

In the meantime she must force herself to behave as was expected of her. The old lady might have invited them, but she was the hostess because this had been Augustus's house, so now it was hers. She welcomed them in and thanked them for coming, ordered the footmen to bank up the fires and dry out as much clothing as possible, and then led the way into the dining room where the cook had prepared an array of suitable dishes. It was hardly the day for cold food, even as rich as game pies and salmon, but at least someone had thought to provide hot, mulled wine. She doubted it was the old lady; probably Milne, the butler. She must remember to thank him.

Conversation was stilted; no one knew what to say. All the sympathies had already been expressed; to say they were sorry yet again would be so jarring as to be offensive. Major Rodney made some mumbled remark about the weather, but since it was midwinter, it was hardly a subject for surprise. He began on some reminiscences about how many men had frozen to death on the heights Sevastopol, then trailed off into clearing his throat as everybody looked at him.

Miss Priscilla Rodney commented on the excellence of the chutney that was served with one of the pies but blushed when Verity thanked her, because they both knew that Priscilla made infinitely better herself. It was not the cook's strength; she was far more skilled with soups and sauces.

She always put too much pepper in pickles, and they bit like a cornered rat.

Lady Cumming-Gould seemed satisfied merely to observe. It was Virgil Smith who rescued them with the only viable conversation. He was staring at a portrait of Alicia over the fireplace, a large, rather formal study set against a brown background which did not flatter her. It was one of a long succession of family portraits going back over two hundred years. The old lady's hung in the hallway, looking very young, like a memory from a history book, in an empire dress from the days just after Napoleon's fall.

"I surely like that picture, ma'am," he said, staring up at it. "It's a good likeness, but I guess it don't flatter you with that color behind it. I sort of see you inside, with all green and the like behind you, trees and grass, and maybe flowers."

"You cannot expect Alicia to trail out to some countryside to sit for a portrait!" the old lady snapped. "You may spend your days in the wilderness where you come from, Mr. Smith, but we do not do so here!"

"I didn't exactly have the wilderness in mind, ma'am." He smiled at her, completely ignoring her tone. "I was thinking more of a garden, an English country garden, with willow trees with all of those long, lacy leaves blowing in the wind."

"You cannot paint something blowing!" she said tartly.

"I reckon a real good artist could." He was not to be cowed. "Or he could paint it so as you could feel as though it was."

"Have you ever tried to paint?" She glared at him. It would have been more effective had she not been forced to stare upwards, but she was nearly a foot shorter than he, and even her voluminous bulk could not make up for the difference.

"No, ma'am." He shook his head. "Do you paint, yourself?"

"Of course!" Her eyebrows shot up. "All ladies of good breeding paint."

A sudden thought flashed into his face. "Did you paint that picture, ma'am?"

She froze to glacial rigidity. "Certainly not! We do not paint commercially, Mr. Smith!" She invested the idea with the same disgust she might have had he suggested she took in laundry.

"All the same, you know"—Somerset Carlisle eyed the picture critically—"I think Virgil is right. It would have been a great deal better against green. That brown is quite muddy and deadens the complexion. All the tones are spoiled."

The old lady looked from him to Alicia, then back at the picture. Her opinion of Alicia's complexion was plain.

"No doubt he did the best he could!" she snapped.

Miss Mary Ann joined in the conversation, her voice lifting helpfully.

"Why don't you have it done again, my dear? I am sure in the summer it would be quite delightful to sit in the garden and have one's portrait painted. You could ask Mr. Jones; I am told he is quite excellent."

"He is expensive," the old lady said witheringly. "That is not the same thing. Anyway, if we get any more pictures done, it ought to be of Verity." She turned to look at Verity. "You probably are as good-looking now as you will ever be. Some women improve a little as they get older, but most don't!" She flashed a glance back at Alicia, then away again. "We'll see this man Jones—what is his name?"

"Godolphin Jones," Miss Mary Ann offered.

"Ridiculous!" the old lady muttered. "Godolphin! Whatever was his father thinking of? But I am not paying an exorbitant price, I warn you."

"You don't need to pay at all," Alicia finally responded. "I shall pay for it, if Verity would like a portrait. And if she would prefer someone other than Godolphin Jones, then we will get someone else."

The old lady was momentarily silenced.

"Godolphin Jones seems to be away at the moment, anyway," Vespasia observed. "I am informed he is in France. It seems to be the obligatory thing for artists to do. One can ˉ

hardly call oneself an artist in society if one has not been to France.''

"Gone away?'' Major Rodney sputtered in his drink and sneezed. "For how long? When is he due back?''

Vespasia looked a trifle surprised. "I have no idea. You might try sending to his house if it is important to you, although from what my own servants say, they have no idea either. Being unreliable seems also to be part of the professional character.''

"Oh, no!'' Major Rodney said hastily, grabbing a game pastry and dropping it. "No, not at all! I was merely trying to be helpful!'' He picked up the pasty again, and it fell apart on the tablecloth. Virgil Smith handed him a napkin and a plate, then helped him scoop it up with a knife.

The old lady made a noise of disgust and turned to look the other way. "I suppose he is a competent artist?'' she said loudly.

"He fetches a very high price,'' Miss Priscilla replied. "Very high, indeed. I saw the portrait of Gwendoline Cantlay, and she told me what she had paid for it. I must say, I thought it a great deal, even for a good likeness.''

"And that is about all it is.'' Carlisle's mouth turned down. "A good likeness. It catches something of her character; it would be hard for a likeness not to, but it is not art. One would not wish for it unless one was fond of Gwendoline herself.''

"Is that not the purpose of a portrait?'' Miss Mary Ann inquired innocently.

"A portrait, perhaps,'' Carlisle agreed. "But not of a painting. A good painting should be a pleasure to anyone, whether they know the subject or not.''

"Overrated,'' the old lady nodded. "And overpaid. I shall not pay him that much. If Gwendoline Cantlay did, then she is a fool.''

"Hester St. Jermyn paid something similar,'' Miss Priscilla said with her mouth full. "And I do know dear Hubert paid a good deal for the picture Mr. Jones painted of us, didn't you, dear?''

Major Rodney colored painfully and treated her to a look of something close to loathing.

"I've seen the one of Lady Cantlay." Virgil Smith screwed up his face. "I wouldn't buy it if it were on sale. It seems kind of—heavy—to me. Not like a lady should look."

"What do you know about such things?" the old lady snapped derisively. "Do you have ladies wherever it is you come from?"

"No, ma'am, I don't reckon you would call them ladies," he said slowly. "But I've seen a few over here. I think Miss Verity is surely a lady and deserves a portrait that says so."

Verity blushed with pleasure and treated him to one of her rare smiles. Alicia found herself suddenly liking him very much, in spite of his manners and his plain face.

"Thank you," Verity said quietly. "I think I shall like to have a portrait done, in the summer, if Alicia does not mind?"

"Of course not," Alicia agreed. "I shall make inquiries to find someone." She was aware of Virgil Smith looking at her. She was a handsome woman and she was used to admiration, but there was something more personal in his gaze, and she found it uncomfortable. She wanted to break the silence, and she rushed to find something to say. She turned to Vespasia. "Lady Cumming-Gould, can you recommend anyone who might paint Verity pleasingly? You must have been painted many times yourself."

Vespasia looked a trifle pleased. "Not lately, my dear. But I will ask among my acquaintances, if you wish. I am sure you can do better than Godolphin Jones. I believe he is very highly regarded by some, or so the price he fetches would indicate, but I agree with Mr. Smith; he is somewhat heavy-handed, a little fleshy."

The old lady glared at her, opened her mouth, met Vespasia's unflinching stare, and closed it again. Her eyes swept over Virgil Smith as if he had been an unpleasant stain on the carpet.

"Precisely," Carlisle said with satisfaction. "There is an

abundance of portrait painters about. Just because Godolphin lives in the Park, that is not a reason to patronize him, if you prefer someone else."

"Gwendoline Cantlay had two pictures done," Miss Priscilla offered. "I cannot imagine why."

"Perhaps she likes them?" Miss Mary Ann suggested. "Some people must, or they would not pay so very much money."

"Art is very much a matter of taste, isn't it?" Alicia looked from one to the other.

The old lady snorted. "Naturally. Good taste—and bad taste! Only the vulgar, who know no better, judge anything as a matter of money." Once more her eyes darted to Virgil Smith and away again. "Time is the thing—whatever has lasted, that is worth something! Old paintings, old houses, old blood."

Alicia felt embarrassed for him, as if she were both receiving the hurt herself, and at the same time responsible for it because the old lady was part of her family.

"Pure survival alone is hardly a mark of virtue." She surprised herself by speaking so vehemently and with something that could only be regarded as insolence by the old lady, but she wanted to contradict her so badly it was like a bursting in her head. "After all, disease survives!"

Everyone was staring at her, the old lady with a look as if her footstool had risen up and smitten her.

Somerset Carlisle was the first to react. "Bravo!" he said cheerfully. "An excellent argument, if somewhat eccentric! I'm not sure Godolphin would appreciate it, but it just about sums up the relationship between art, survival, and price."

"I don't understand." Miss Priscilla squinted painfully. "I don't see the relationship at all."

"That is precisely what I mean," he agreed. "There is none."

The old lady banged her stick on the ground. She had been aiming at Carlisle's foot and missed. "Of course there is!" she snapped. "Money is the root of all evil! Bible says so. Do you argue with that?"

"You misquote." Carlisle was not daunted, and he did

90

not move his feet. "What it says is that 'the love of money is the root of all evil.' Things are not evil; it is the passions they stir in people that may be."

"A piece of sophistry," she said with disgust. "And this is not the place for it. Go to your club if you have a taste for that kind of conversation. This is a funeral breakfast. I would oblige you to remember that!"

He bowed very slightly. "Indeed, ma'am, you have my sympathies." He turned to Alicia and Verity. "And you also, of course."

Suddenly everyone remembered this was the third time they had attended such an affair, and Major Rodney excused himself rather loudly in the awkwardness that followed. He took his sisters by the arms and almost propelled them out into the hallway, where the footman had to be sent for to bring their coats.

Vespasia and Carlisle followed; Virgil Smith hesitated a moment by Alicia.

"If there is anything I can do, ma'am?" He looked uncomfortable, as if he wanted to say something and could not find the words.

She was aware of the kindness in him, and it made her also feel a little clumsy. She thanked him more hastily than she meant to, and with a faint color in his face, he followed the others out.

"I see your Mr. Corde didn't come!" the old lady said spitefully. "Other fish to fry, maybe?"

Alicia ignored her. She did not know why Dominic had sent no word, no flowers or letter of sympathy. It was something she did not want to think about.

On the morning of the interment Dominic had been in two minds as to what to do. He had got up and dressed, intending to go, as a support to Alicia in a time which was bound to be extremely trying for her. Verity was too young and too vulnerable herself to afford much comfort, and he knew the old lady would, if anything, make matters worse. No one would find his attendance odd; it was a mark of respect. After all, he had been invited to the original funeral.

Then as he stared at himself in the mirror, making the final adjustment to his appearance, he remembered his visit to Charlotte. He had never been inside a house of working people before, not something on a level with a tradesman's house, like Pitt's. All things considered, it was odd how comfortable he had felt, and how little Charlotte had changed. Of course, it would have been different if he had stayed there long! But for that hour or so, the surroundings had been unimportant.

But what Charlotte had said was a totally different matter. She had asked him if he thought Alicia capable of murdering her husband in all but as many words. Charlotte had always been frank to the point of tactlessness; he smiled even now to recall some of the more socially disastrous incidents.

The image smiled back at him from the mirror.

Of course, he denied it—Alicia would never even think of such a thing! Old Augustus had been a bore; he talked endlessly and fancied himself an expert on the building of railways, and since his family had made money in their construction perhaps he was. But it was hardly a subject to pontificate on interminably over the dinner table. Dominic had never met a woman yet who cared in the slightest about railway construction, and very few men!

But that does not move to murder! Actually to kill someone, you have to care desperately over something, whether it is hate, fear, greed, or because they stand in the way between you and something you hunger for—he stopped, his hand frozen on his collar. He imagined being married to some sixty-year-old woman, twice his age, boring, pompous, with all her dreams in the past, looking forward to nothing more than a sinking into slow, verbose old age—a relationship without love. Perhaps one day, or one night, the need to escape would become unbearable, and if there were a bottle of medicine on the table, what would be simpler than to dose a little too much? How easy just to step it up a fraction each time, until you got the amount that was not massive but just precisely enough to kill?

But Alicia could never have done that!

92

He pictured her in his mind, her fair skin, the curve of her bosom, the way her eyes lit up when she laughed—or when she looked at him. Once or twice he had touched her more intimately than mere courtesy required, and he felt the quick response. There was a hunger underneath her modesty. There was something about her, perhaps a mannerism, a way of holding her head, that reminded him of Charlotte; he was not sure how. It was indefinable.

And Charlotte cared enough to kill! That he was as sure of as his own reflection in the glass. Morality would stop her—but never indifference.

Was it possible Alicia really had killed Augustus—and the old lady knew it? If that were so, then he was bound up in it, the catalyst for the motive.

Slowly he undid the tie and took off the black coat. If that were so, and it could be—it was not completely impossible—then it would be better for everybody, especially Alicia, if he did not go today. The old lady would be waiting for it, waiting to make some stinging remark, even to accuse outright!

He would send flowers—tomorrow; something white and appropriate. And then perhaps the day after he would call. No one would find that odd.

He changed from the black trousers into a more usual morning gray.

He did send the flowers the next morning and was appalled at the price. Still, as the icy wind outside reminded him, it was the first day of February, and there was hardly a thing in bloom. The sun was shining fitfully, and the puddles in the street were drying slowly. A barrow boy whistled behind a load of cabbages. Today funerals and thoughts of death seemed far away. Freedom was a precious thing, but every man's gift, not something that needed fighting for.

He walked briskly round to his club and was settled behind his newspaper when a voice interrupted his half thought, half sleep.

"Good morning. Dominic Corde, isn't it?"

Dominic had no desire for conversation. Gentlemen did

not talk to one in the morning; they knew better, most especially if one had a newspaper. He looked up slowly. It was Somerset Carlisle. He had met him only two or three times, but he was not a man one forgot.

"Yes. Good morning, Mr. Carlisle," he replied coolly. He was lifting his paper again when Carlisle sat down beside him and offered him his snuffbox. Dominic declined; snuff always made him cough. To sneeze was acceptable; lots of people sneezed when taking snuff, but to sit coughing with one's eyes running was merely clumsy.

"No, thank you."

Carlisle put the snuff away again without taking any himself.

"Much pleasanter day, isn't it," he remarked.

"Much," Dominic agreed, still holding onto the paper.

"Anything in the news?" Carlisle inquired. "What's happening in Parliament?"

"No idea." Dominic had never thought of reading about Parliament. Government was necessary; any sane man knew that, but it was also intensely boring. "No idea at all."

Carlisle looked as nonplussed as courtesy would allow. "Thought you were a friend of Lord Fleetwood?"

Dominic was flattered; friend was perhaps overstating it a little, but he had met him lately, and they had struck up an acquaintance. They both liked riding and driving a team. Dominic had perhaps less courage than Fleetwood, but far more natural skill.

"Yes," he identified guardedly, because he was not sure why Carlisle asked.

Carlisle smiled, sitting back in the chair easily and stretching his legs. "Thought he'd have talked politics with you," he said casually. "Could be quite a weight in the House, if he wished. Got a following of young bloods."

Dominic was surprised; they had never discussed anything more serious than good horses, and of course the occasional woman. But come to think of it, he had mentioned a number of friends who had hereditary titles; whether they ever attended was quite another thing. Half the peers in England went nowhere nearer the House of Lords than the closest club or party. But Fleetwood did have a large circle, and it was not an exaggeration to say that Dominic was now on the fringes of it.

Carlisle was waiting.

"No," Dominic replied. "Horses, mostly. Don't think he cares much about politics."

Carlisle's face flickered only very slightly. "Dare say he doesn't realize the potential." He raised his hand and signaled to one of the club servants and, when the man arrived, looked back at Dominic. "Do join me for luncheon. They have a new chef who is quite excellent, and I haven't tried his specialty yet."

Dominic had intended having a quiet meal a little later, but the man was pleasant enough, and he was a friend of Alicia's. Also, of course, an invitation should never be turned down without sound reason.

"Thank you," he accepted.

"Good." Carlisle turned to the servant with a smile. "Come for us when the chef is ready, Blunstone. And get me some of that claret again, same as last time. The bordeaux was awful."

Blunstone bowed and departed with murmurs of agreement.

Carlisle allowed Dominic to continue with his newspaper until luncheon was served; then they repaired to the dining room and were halfway through a richly stuffed and roasted goose garnished with vegetables, fruit, and delicate sauce when Carlisle spoke again.

"What do you think of him?" he inquired, eyebrows raised.

Dominic had lost the thread. "Fleetwood?" he asked.

Carlisle smiled. "No, the chef."

"Oh, excellent." Dominic had his mouth full and found it hard to reply gracefully. "Most excellent. I must dine here more often."

"Yes, it's a very comfortable place," Carlisle agreed, looking round at the wide room with its dark velvet curtains, Adam fireplaces on two sides with fires burning warmly in each. There were Gainesborough portraits on the blue walls.

It was something of an understatement. It had taken Dominic three years to get himself elected as a member, and he disliked having his achievement taken so lightly.

"Rather more than comfortable, I would have said." His voice had a slight edge.

"It's all relative." Carlisle took another forkful of goose. "I dare say at Windsor they dine better." He swallowed and took a sip of wine. "Then, on the other hand, there are thousands in the tenements and rookeries within a mile of here who find boiled rats a luxury—"

Dominic choked on his goose and gagged. The room swum before him, and for a moment he thought he was going to disgrace himself by being sick at the table. It took him several seconds to compose himself, wipe his mouth with his napkin, and look up to meet Carlisle's curious eyes. He could not think what to say to him. The man was preposterous.

"Sorry," Carlisle said lightly. "Shouldn't spoil a good meal by talking politics." He smiled.

Dominic was completely unguarded. "P-politics?" he stammered.

"Most distasteful," Carlisle agreed. "Much pleasanter to talk about horseracing, or fashion. I see your friend Fleetwood has adopted that new cut of jacket. Rather flattering, don't you think? I shall have to see if I can get my tailor to do something of the sort."

"What in hell are you talking about?" Dominic demanded. "You said 'rats.' I heard you!"

"Perhaps I should have said 'workhouses.' " Carlisle chose the words carefully. "Or pauper-children laws. So difficult to know what to do. Whole family in the workhouse, children in with the idle or vagrant, no education, work from waking to sleeping—but better than starvation, which is the alternative, or freezing to death. Have you seen the sort of people that get into the workhouses? Imagine how they affect a child of four or five years old. Seen the disease, the ventilation, the food?"

Dominic remembered his own childhood: a nurse, recalled only hazily, mixed in his mind with his mother, a governess, then school—with long summer holidays; rice pudding, which he loathed, and afternoon teas with jam, especially raspberry jam. He remembered songs round the piano, making snowballs, playing cricket in the sun, stealing plums, breaking windows, and receiving canings for insolence.

"That's ridiculous!" he said sharply. "Workhouses are supposed to be temporary relief for those who cannot find legitimate work for themselves. It is a charitable charge on the parish."

"Oh, very charitable." Carlisle's eyes were very bright, watching Dominic's face. "Children of three or four years old in with the flotsam of society, learning hopelessness from the cradle onwards; those that don't die of disease from rotten food, poor ventilation, cross infection—"

"Well, it should be stopped!" Dominic said flatly. "Clean the places up!"

"Of course," Carlisle agreed. "But then what? If they don't go to schools of some sort, they never learn even to read or write. How can they ever get out of the circle of vagrant to workhouse, and back again? What can they do? Sweep crossings summer and winter? Walk the streets as long as their looks last and then turn to the sweatshops? Do you know how much a seamstress earns for sewing a shirt, seams, cuffs, collars, buttonholes, and four rows of stitching down the front, all complete?"

Dominic thought of the prices of his own shirts. "Two shillings?" He hazarded a guess, a little on the mean side, but then Carlisle had suggested as much.

"How extravagant!" Carlisle said bitterly. "She would have to sew ten for that!"

"But how do they live?" The goose was going cold on Dominic's plate.

Carlisle turned his hands up. "Most of them are prostitutes at night, to feed their children; and then when the children are old enough, they work as well—or else it is all back to the workhouse, and there's your cycle again!"

"But what about their husbands? Some of them have husbands, surely?" Dominic was still looking for rationality, something sane to explain it.

"Oh, yes, some of them do," said Carlisle. "But it's cheaper to employ a woman than a man; you don't have to pay her much, so the men don't get the work."

"That's—" Dominic searched for a word and failed to find one. He sat staring at Carlisle over the congealing goose.

"Politics," Carlisle murmured, picking up his fork again. "And education."

"How can you eat that?" Dominic demanded; it was repulsive to him now, an indecency, if what Carlisle said was true.

Carlisle put it into his mouth and spoke round it. "Because if I were not to eat every time I think of sweated labor, uneducated children, the indigent, sick, filthy, or destitute, I should never eat at all—and what purpose would that serve? Parliament. I ran for it once and failed. My ideas were remarkably unpopular with those who have the vote. Sweated labor doesn't vote, you know—female, mostly, too young, and too poor. Now I have to try the back door— House of Lords, people like St. Jermyn, with his bill, and your friend Fleetwood. They don't give a damn about the poor, probably never really seen any, but an eye to a cause—great thing, a cause."

Dominic pushed his plate away. If this were true, not a piece of melodramatic luncheon conversation designed to shock, then something ought to be done by people like Fleetwood. Carlisle was perfectly right.

He drank the end of the wine and was glad of its clean bite; he needed to wash his mouth out after the taste that had been on his tongue. He wished to God he had never seen Somerset Carlisle; the man was uncouth to invite him to a meal and then discuss such things. They were thoughts that were impossible to get rid of.

Pitt's superiors had meantime directed his attention to a case of embezzlement in a local firm, and he was returning to the police station after a day of questioning clerks and reading endless files he did not understand when he was met at the door by a wide-eyed constable. Pitt was cold and tired, and his feet were wet. All he wanted was to go home and eat something hot, then sit by the fire with Charlotte and talk about anything, as long as it was removed from crime.

"What is it?" he said wearily; the man was practically wringing his hands with anxiety and pent-up apprehension.

"It's happened again!" he said hoarsely.

Pitt knew, but he put off the moment. "What has?"

"Corpses, sir. There's been another corpse. I mean one dug up like, not a new one."

Pitt shut his eyes. "Where?"

"In the park, sir. St. Bartholomew's Green, sir. Not really a park, just a stretch o' longish grass with a few trees and a couple o' seats. Found on one o' the seats, 'e was, sitting up there like Jackie, bold as you like—but dead, o' course, stone dead. And 'as been for a while, I'd say."

"What does he look like?" Pitt asked.

The constable screwed up his face.

" 'Orrible, sir, downright 'orrible."

"Naturally!" Pitt snapped; his patience was worn thin to transparency. "But was he young or old, tall or short; come on, man! You're a policeman, not a penny novelist! What kind of a description is ' 'orrible'?"

The constable blushed crimson. " 'E was tall and corpulent, sir, with black 'air and black whiskers, sir. And 'e was dressed in an 'and-me-down sort o' coat; didn't fit 'im none too good, not like a gentleman's would, sir."

"Thank you," Pitt said ungraciously. "Where is he?"

"In the morgue, sir."

Pitt turned on his heel and went out again. He walked the few blocks to the morgue, head bent against the rain, mind turning over furiously every conceivable answer to the disgusting and apparently pointless happenings. Who on earth was going around digging up random corpses—and above all, why?

When he reached the morgue, the assistant was as buoy-

99

ant as ever, in spite of a streaming cold. He led Pitt over to the table and whipped off the cloth with the air of a muscle-hall magician producing a clutch of rabbits.

As the constable had said, the corpse was a robust middle-aged man with black hair and whiskers.

Pitt grunted. ''Mr. William Wilberforce Porteous, I presume?'' he said irritably.

6

THERE WAS NOTHING for Pitt to do but go home, and after thanking the attendant he turned and went back out into the rain. It took him half an hours' steady walking before he at last rounded the corner into his own street and five minutes later was sitting in front of the stove in the kitchen, the fender open to let out the heat, his trousers rolled up and his feet in a basin of hot water. Charlotte was standing next to him with a towel.

"You're soaking!" she said exasperatedly. "You must get a new pair of boots. Where on earth have you been?"

"The morgue." He moved his toes slowly in the water, letting the ecstasy ripple through him. It was hot and tingling, and it eased out the numbness with a caress almost like pain. "They found another corpse."

She stared at him, the towel hanging from her hands. "You mean one that had been dug up again?" she said incredulously.

"Yes; dead three or four weeks, I should say."

"Oh, Thomas." Her eyes were dark and horrified. "What sort of person digs up the dead and leaves them sitting on cabs and in churches? Why? There isn't any sanity in it!" Her face suddenly went white as a new thought occurred to her. "Oh! You don't think it could be different

101

people, do you? I mean, if Lord Augustus was murdered, or someone thinks he was, and they dug him up to bring your attention to it—then whoever killed him, or fears to be suspected of it, digs up these other people they don't even know to obscure the real murder?"

He looked at her slowly, the hot water forgotten. "You know what you are saying?" he asked, watching her face. "That means Dominic, or Alicia, or both of them."

For several moments she said nothing. She handed him the towel and he dried his feet; then she took the basin and poured the water away down the sink.

"I don't think I believe that," she said with her back still toward him. There was no distress in her voice that he could hear, just doubt, and a little surprise.

"You mean Dominic wouldn't commit murder?" he asked. He tried to make it impersonal, but the edge was still there, sharp with old fears.

"I don't think so." She wiped round the basin and put it away. "But even if he did kill someone, I'm pretty sure he wouldn't think to dig up other corpses and leave them around to hide it. Not unless he has changed more than I think people do."

"Maybe Alicia changed him," he suggested, but he did not believe that himself. He waited for her say it could have been Alicia with someone else. She had money enough to pay; but Charlotte said nothing.

"They found him in the park." He held out his hand for his dry socks, and she passed them off the airing rack, then winched it back up to the ceiling. "Sitting on a bench," he added. "I think, from the description, it is the body from the grave that was robbed last week, Mr. W. W. Porteous."

"Does he have anything to do with Dominic and Alicia or anyone in Gadstone Park?" she asked, going back to the stove. "Would you like some soup before your dinner?"

She lifted the lid, and the delicate odor of the steam caught his nostrils.

"Yes, please," he said immediately. "What is for dinner?"

"Meat and kidney pudding." She took a dish and a ladle

102

and gave him a generous portion of soup, full of leeks and barley. "Mind, it's very hot."

He smiled up at her and took it, balancing it on his knee. She was right; it was very hot. He put a tea towel under it to protect himself.

"Nothing at all, as far as I know," he replied.

"Where did he live?" She sat down again opposite him and waited for him to finish the soup before getting out the pie and vegetables. It had taken her awhile to learn how to cook economically and well, and she liked to watch the results of her efforts.

"Just off Resurrection Row," he replied, holding up the spoon.

She frowned, puzzled. "I thought that was rather a—a shabby area?"

"It is. Worn down, and a little seedy. There are at least two brothels that I know of; all discreetly covered up, but that's definitely what they are. And there's a pawnshop where we have found rather more than the usual number of stolen goods."

"Well that can't have anything to do with Dominic, and certainly not Alicia!" Charlotte said with conviction. "Dominic might have been to such a place; even gentlemen get up to the oddest things—"

"Especially gentlemen!" Pitt put in.

She let the jibe pass. "—but Alicia would never even have heard of it."

"Wouldn't she?" He was genuinely not sure.

She looked at him patiently, and for a moment they were both aware of the social gulf between their backgrounds.

"No." She shook her head minutely. "Women whose parents have social pretensions, real or imaginary, are far more protected—even imprisoned—than you know. Papa never allowed me to read a newspaper. I used to sneak them from the butler's pantry, but Emily and Sarah didn't. Papa considered anything controversial or in the least scandalous or distressing to be unsuitable for young ladies to know—and one should never mention them in discussion—"

"I know that—" he started.

"You think he was unusual?" She shook her head again, harder. "But he wasn't! He was no stricter or more protective than anyone else. Women can know about illness, childbirth, death, boredom, or loneliness, but not anything that could be argued about—real poverty, endemic disease, or crime—and most of all—not about sex. Nothing disturbing must be considered, especially if one might feel moved to question it, or try to change it!"

He looked at her with surprise; he was seeing a side of her thoughts he had never recognized before.

"I didn't know you were so bitter about it," he said slowly, reaching out to put the soup dish on the table.

"Aren't you?" she challenged. "Do you know how many times you come home and tell me about tragedy you've seen that need never happened? You've taught me at least to know there are rookeries behind the smart streets where people die of starvation and cold; where there is filth everywhere, and rats, and disease; where children learn to steal to survive as soon as they can walk. I've never been there, but I know they exist, and I can smell them on your clothes when you come back in the evening. There is no other smell like it."

He thought of Alicia in her silks and innocence. Charlotte had been like that when he met her.

"I'm sorry," he said quietly.

She opened the door with a cloth and took out the pudding. "Don't be," she said sharply. "I'm a woman, not a child, and I can stand knowing just as well as you can! What are you going to do about this Mr. Porteous?" She took a knife and cut into the pudding; the thick suet crust was brown, and the gravy bubbled through it when she took out a slice. Rookeries or no rookeries, he was hungry at the smell of it.

"Make sure he is Porteous," he replied; "then, I suppose, see what he died of and who knows anything about him."

She dished up the carrots and cabbage. "If that corpse is Mr. Porteous, then who is the first corpse, the one from the cab?"

"I've no idea." He sighed and took his plate from her. "He could be anybody!"

In the morning Pitt turned his attention to the unidentified corpse. There would be no solution to the whole business that did not include him, at least his name and the manner of his death. Perhaps he was the one who had been murdered, and Lord Augustus was the blind, the diversion. Or conceivably they had been involved in something together.

But what venture could possibly include Lord Augustus Fitzroy-Hammond and Mr. William Wilberforce Porteous from Resurrection Row—and lead to murder? What about the man in the cab? And who was the other party to it, the one who dug them all up?

The first step was to discover the precise manner of death of the corpse from the cab. If it had been murder, or could have been, then that shed a totally new light on the disinterment of Lord Augustus. If, on the other hand, it had been natural, then since he had been burned, was it a lawful burial in a graveyard? Where was the empty grave, and why had it not been reported? Presumably it had been filled in again and left to appear like any other new grave.

But normal deaths are certified by a doctor. Once the nature of death was known, then the investigation could begin of all recorded deaths from that cause over the period. In time, they would narrow it down, the correct one would be found. They would have a name, a character, a history.

As soon as he reached the police station, he called his sergeant to take over the matter of the embezzlement and went upstairs to request permission for a postmortem on the unidentified corpse. No one demurred. Since it was not Lord Augustus, after all, and no one else had come forward to claim him, in the circumstances murder must be considered. Permission was granted immediately.

Next was the rather unpleasant job of making sure that the new corpse in the morgue was indeed W. W. Porteous, although he had little doubt about it. He put on his hat and coat again and went outside into the intermittent drizzle, and took an omnibus to Resurrection Row. He walked a hundred yards, turned to the right, and looked for number ten where Mrs. Porteous lived.

It was one of the larger houses, a little faded on the outside, but with prim white curtains at the windows and a whitened step. He pulled the bell and stood back.

"Yes?" A stout girl in black stuff dress and starched apron opened the door and stared at him inquiringly.

"Is Mrs. Porteous in?" Pitt asked. "I have information regarding her late husband." He knew that if he said he was from the police the servants would have it all over the street within the day, and it would grow in scandal with each retelling.

The girl's mouth fell open. "Oh! Oh, yes sir; you'd better come in. If you wait in the parlor, I'll tell Mrs. Porteous you're here, sir. What name shall I say?"

"Mr. Pitt."

"Yes, sir." And she disappeared to inform her mistress.

Pitt sat down. The room was crammed with furniture, photographs, ornaments, an embroidered sampler saying "Fear God and do your duty," three stuffed birds, a stuffed weasel under glass, an arrangement of dried flowers, and two large, shining, green potted plants. He felt intensely claustrophobic. It gave him the rather hysterical feeling that it was all alive and, when he was not looking, creeping closer and closer to him, hungry and defensive against an alien in their territory. Eventually he preferred to stand.

The door opened and Mrs. Porteous came in, as robustly corseted as before, her hair perfect, her cheeks rouged. Her bosom was decorated with rows and rows of jet beads.

"Good morning, Mr. Pitt," she said anxiously. "My maid says you have some news about Mr. Porteous?"

"Yes, ma'am. I think we have found him. He is in the morgue, and if you would be good enough to come and identify him, we can be sure, and then in due course we can have him reinterred—"

"I can't have a second funeral!" she said in alarm. "It wouldn't be proper."

"No, naturally," he agreed. "Just an interment, but first let us be sure it is indeed your husband."

She called for the maid to fetch her coat and hat, and followed Pitt outside into the street. It was still raining lightly, and in Resurrection Row they hailed a hansom and rode in silence to the morgue.

Pitt was beginning to feel an antiseptic familiarity with the place. The attendant still had a cold and his nose was now bright pink, but he greeted them with a smile as wide as decorum before a widow allowed.

Mrs. Porteous looked at the corpse and did not require either the chair or the glass of water.

"Yes," she said calmly. "That is Mr. Porteous."

"Thank you, ma'am. I have some questions I must ask you, but perhaps you would prefer to discuss them in a more comfortable place? Would you like to go home? The cab is still waiting."

"If you please," she accepted; then, without looking at the attendant, she turned and waited for Pitt to open the door for her outside into the rain, preceded him down the path and back into the cab again.

Seated in the parlor of her own house, she ordered hot tea from the maid and faced Pitt, hands folded in her lap, jet beads glistening in the lamplight. On a day as dark as this, it was impossible to see clearly inside without the lamps lit.

"Well, Mr. Pitt, what is is you wish to ask me? That is Mr. Porteous; what else is there to know?"

"How did he die, ma'am?"

"In his bed! Naturally."

"From what cause, ma'am?" He tried to make it clear without being offensive or distressing her more than was necessary. Her remarkable bearing might well hide deep emotion underneath.

"A complaint of digestion. No doubt it had a name, but I do not know it. He had been ill for some time."

"I see. I'm sorry. Who was his doctor?"

Her arched eyebrows rose. "Dr. Hall, but I cannot see why you wish to know. Surely you do not suspect Dr. Hall of violating the grave?"

"No, of course not." He did not know how to explain that he was questioning the cause of death. Obviously the

107

whole train of thought had not occurred to her. "It is just that in order to find who did, we need all the information possible."

"Do you expect to find out?" She was still perfectly composed.

"No," he admitted frankly, meeting her eyes with something like a smile. There was no answer in her face, and he looked away, feeling a little foolish. "But it is not the only case," he went on in a more businesslike tone. "And anything they have in common might help."

"Not the only case?" She was startled now. "You mean you think Mr. Porteous's grave robbing is connected to those others everyone is talking about? You ought to be ashamed, allowing such things to happen here in London, to respectable people! Why aren't you doing your job, I should like to know?"

"I don't know whether there is a connection, ma'am," he said patiently. "That is what I am trying to establish."

"It's a lunatic," she said firmly. "And if the police can't catch a lunatic, I don't know what the world is coming to! Mr. Porteous was a very respectable man, never mixed with fast society, every penny he had was earned, and he never put a wager in his life."

"Perhaps there is no connection, apart from the time he died," Pitt said wearily. "Lord Augustus was a respectable man, too."

"That's as may be," she said darkly. "They didn't find Mr. Porteous in that Gadstone Park, did they?"

"No, ma'am, he was sitting on a bench in St. Bartholomew's Green."

Her face paled. "Nonsense!" she said sharply. "Mr. Porteous would never be in such a place! I cannot believe it, you know what kind of people frequent it. You must be mistaken."

He did not bother to argue; if it mattered to her to cling onto the distinction, even after death, then allow her to. It was a curious divergence. He remembered the rather worn clothes with the corpse. He had been buried very much in his second best. Perhaps at the last moment she had felt the

108

best black all such men kept for Sundays to be too good to consign to the oblivion of the tomb. At least at that time she would expect it to be oblivion.

He stood up. "Thank you, ma'am. If I need to ask anything else, I shall call on you."

"I shall make arrangements to have Mr. Porteous put away again." She rang the bell for the maid to show him out.

"Not yet, ma'am." He wanted to apologize because he knew the outrage before it came. "I'm afraid we shall have to do some more investigation before we can allow that."

Her face mottled with horror, and she half rose in her chair.

"First you allow his grave to be desecrated and his body to be left in a park where public—'women'—offer themselves, and now you want to investigate him! It is monstrous! Decent people are no longer safe in this city. You are a disgrace to your—" She had wanted to say "uniform"; then she looked at Pitt's jumble of colors—hat still dripping in his hands, muffler end trailing down his front—and gave up. "You are a disgrace!" she finished lamely.

"I'm sorry." He was apologizing not for himself but for the whole city, for the entire order that had left her with nothing but need and the trimmings of being respectable.

He spoke to the doctor and discovered that Porteous had died of cirrhosis of the liver, and had most assuredly visited the benches of St. Bartholomew's Green before some grotesque chance had placed his corpse under its shade to be solicited by a prostitute to whom even the dead were no horror or surprise.

He left, wondering what had been the stuff of lives that ended like this: what failures; what bolstered-up loneliness, what constant small retreats.

Dominic put Somerset Carlisle and the disgraceful luncheon from his mind. He was looking forward to seeing Alicia again. The reinterment was over, and from now on, provided decent mourning was observed, at least outwardly, they could begin to think of the future. He would not wish to offend her sensibilities by speaking too quickly or cause her any embarrassment, but he could certainly call to pay his respects and spend a little time in her company. And in a few weeks she could afford to be seen out, not at theatres or parties, but at church with the family or during a carriage ride to take the air. He did not mind if Verity came also, for appearances; in fact, he liked her very well for her own sake. She was easy to talk to, once she felt comfortable with him and, although she was modest, she had her own opinions and quite a dry sense of humor with which to express them.

Altogether he was feeling in a very pleasant mood when he arrived at Gadstone Park on Thursday morning and presented his card to the maid.

Alicia received him with delight, almost relief, and they spent a totally happy hour talking trivialities, and meaning everything else. Just to be in each other's company was sufficient; what was said was immaterial. Augustus was forgotten; empty graves and wandering corpses did not even stray into their minds.

He left a little before luncheon, walking briskly back across the Park, coat collar turned up against the north wind, finding it exciting and sharpening rather than bitter. He saw a figure coming the other way. There was something familiar about the step, the rather lean shoulders, that made him hesitate, even consider for a moment taking a sidecut across the grass, even though it was rough and wet. But he was not even sure who the person was. It was far too tidy for Pitt, too elegant, and not quite tall enough. Pitt's coat always flapped, and his hat sat at a different angle on his head.

It was not until he was close enough to see the face, too close courteously to go another way, that he recognized Somerset Carlisle.

"Good morning," he said without slackening his stride. He had no wish whatever to speak with the man.

Carlisle stood in his path. "Good morning," he said, then turned and fell in step beside him. Short of being appallingly rude, there was nothing Dominic could do but make some attempt at conversation.

"Pleasant weather," he remarked. "At least this wind should keep the fog away."

"Good day for a walk," Carlisle agreed. "Gets one an appetite for luncheon."

"Quite," Dominic replied. Really, the man was a confounded nuisance. He seemed to have no idea when he was intruding, and Dominic had no desire to be reminded of their previous meal together.

"Nice leisurely meal by a good fire," Carlisle went on. "I should thoroughly enjoy a soup, something savory and delicate."

There was no way to avoid it. Dominic owed the man a meal, and obligations must be honored if one wished to remain in society. Such a gaffe would quickly be remarked, and word spread like fire.

"An excellent idea," he said with as much heart as he could muster. "And perhaps a saddle of mutton to follow? My club is not far, and I should be delighted if you would consent to dine with me."

Carlisle smiled broadly, and Dominic had an uncomfortable feeling he saw something funny in the affair. "Thank you," he said easily. "I should enjoy that."

The meal fulfilled none of Dominic's fears, in fact it was extremely pleasant. Carlisle did not mention politics at all and proved an agreeable companion, talking neither too little nor too much. When he did speak he was cheerful, and occasionally witty.

Dominic thoroughly enjoyed it and determined to repeat it as soon as opportunity arose. He was thinking along these lines when he found himself outside again, where the wind was sharper and beginning to carry a fine rain. Carlisle hailed a cab immediately, and, to Dominic's astonishment, fifteen minutes later he was deposited in a filthy back street where precarious houses huddled together like a lot of drunken men supporting each other before the final collapse.

"Where in God's name are we?" he demanded, alarmed and confused. The street was swarming with children, noses running, clothes dirty; women sat in areaways, hands blue

111

with cold, presiding over rows of worn-looking shoes; and light glimmered from below-street rooms. The whole air was pervaded with a stale, sour smell he could not identify, but it clung to the back of the nose, and he seemed to swallow it with every breath. "Where are we?" he said again with mounting fury.

"Seven Dials," Carlisle replied. "Dudley Street, to be precise. Those people are secondhand shoe sellers. Down there"—he pointed to the rooms below pavement level—"they take old shoes or stolen ones; remake them out of the bits that are worth saving, and then sell the botched-up results. In other places they do the same with clothes; unpick them and use whatever fabric is still good for a little while longer. Someone else's remade wool is better than new cotton, which is all they could buy. No warmth in cotton."

Dominic shivered. It was perishing out in this ghastly street, and he was white with rage at Carlisle for having brought him here.

Either Carlisle was oblivious to it, or he simply did not care.

"Call back that cab!" Dominic snarled. "You had no right to bring me here! This place is—" He was lost for words. He stared around him, appalled at it; the weight of the buildings seemed to overpower him. The squalor was everywhere, and the smell of dirt, old clothes, grime of soot and oil lamps, unwashed bodies, yesterday's cooking. On top of the roast it was almost too much for his stomach.

"A preview of hell," Carlisle said quietly. "Don't speak so loudly; these people live here; this is their home. I dare say they don't like it any more than you do, but it's what they have. Show your disgust, and you may not get out of here as immaculately as you came in—in any sense. And this is only a foretaste; you should see Bluegate Fields down by the docks or Limehouse, Whitechapel, St. Giles. Walk with me. We've got about three hundred yards to go, along that way." He pointed down a side street. "Over the square at the end of that is the local workhouse. That's what I want you to see; this is only incidental. Then perhaps the Devil's Acre, below Westminster?"

Dominic opened his mouth to say he wanted to leave, then saw the children's faces gaping up at him: young bodies, young skins, and eyes as old as the roués' he had seen with the prostitutes in the night houses of the Haymarket. It was the weary avariciousness in them that frightened him more than anything else; that and the smell.

He saw one urchin, chased by another in play, pass close to Carlisle, and, in a movement as smooth as a weasel, extract his silk handkerchief from his pocket and move on.

"Carlisle!"

"I know," Carlisle said quietly. "Don't make a fuss. Just follow me." And he moved almost casually over the street, onto the pavement on the other side, then down the alleyway. At the far side of the square beyond, he stopped at the large, blind wooden door and knocked. It was opened by a stout man in a green frock coat. The sour expression on his face changed to one of alarm, but before he could speak, Carlisle stepped inside, forcing him back.

"Morning, Mr. Eades. Comes to see how you are today."

"Well, thank you. Yes, very well, sir." Eades said defensively. "You are too kind, sir. You pay too much attention. I'm sure your time is valuable, sir."

"Very," Carlisle agreed. "So don't let us waste it. Any of your children gone to the schools since the last time I was here?"

"Oh, yes! As many as we had at the time of intake, sir, you may be sure."

"And how many is that?"

"Ah, well now; I don't have the precise figures to my mind; you must recall, people come and go here, as the necessity finds them. If they are not here on the day of intake, which you must know is only once a fortnight, then, naturally, they don't go!"

"I know that as well as you do," Carlisle said tartly. "I also know they check out the day before the intake, and back in again the day after."

"Now, sir, that ain't my fault!"

"I know it isn't!" Carlisle's voice was raw with anger at his own impotence. He strode past Eades and down the airless, dank corridor to the great hall, and Dominic was obliged to follow him or be left alone in the stone passage, his flesh standing out with cold.

The room was large and low, gaslit; one stove burned in the corner. About fifty or sixty men, women, and children sat unpicking old clothes, sorting the rags, and cutting and piecing them together again. The air was so fetid it caught in Dominic's throat, and he had to concentrate to prevent himself from vomiting. Carlisle seemed to be used to it. He stepped over the rags and approached one of the women.

"Hello, Bessie," he said cheerfully. "How are you today?"

The woman smiled, showing blackened teeth, and mumbled something in reply. She had a large, shambling figure, and Dominic would have judged her to be about fifty. He did not understand a word of her speech.

Carlisle led him on a few yards to where half a dozen children sat unpicking old trousers, some of them no more than three or four years old.

"Three of these are Bessie's." He looked at them. "They used to work at home, before putting the new railway through caused the slum clearance, and the house their room was in was demolished. Her husband and older children made match boxes at tuppence ha' penny for a hundred and forty-four, and out of that they found their own twine and paste. Bessie herself worked in the Bryant and Mays match factory. That's why she speaks so oddly—phossy jaw—a necrosis of the jaw caused by the phosphorus in the matches. She's three years older than Alicia Fitzroy-Hammond—you wouldn't think it, would you?"

It was too much. Dominic was bewildered and appalled. "I want to get out of here," he said quietly.

"So do we all." Carlisle embraced the room in a gesture. "Do you know third of London lives no better than this, either in the rookeries or the workhouses?"

"What can anybody do?" Dominic said helplessly. "It's—it's so—vast!"

Carlisle spoke to one or two more people; then he led Dominic back out into the square again, bidding Mr. Eades a tart farewell on the doorstep. After the thick air inside, even the gray drizzle seemed cleaner.

"Change some of the laws," Carlisle replied. "The meanest ledger clerk who can write or add is a prince compared with these. Get pauper children educated and apprenticed. There's little you can do for their parents, except charity; but we can try for the children."

"Possibly." Dominic had to walk sharply to keep up with him. "But what is the point in showing me? I can't change laws!"

Carlisle stopped. He passed a few pence to a child begging and saw him immediately hand them over to an old man.

"Fancy sending your grandchild out to beg for you," Dominic muttered.

"He's more likely no relation." Carlisle kept on walking. "He probably bought the child. Children make better beggars, especially if they are blind or deformed. Some women even cripple them on purpose; gives them a better chance of survival. To answer your question, you can talk to people like Lord Fleetwood and his friends, persuade them to go to the House and vote."

Dominic was horrified. "I can't tell them about this sort of thing! They'd—" He realized what he was saying.

"Yes," Carlisle agreed. "They would be disgusted and offended. Most distasteful. Not the sort of subject a gentleman embarrasses others with. I think I rather spoiled your luncheon the other day. You don't get the same pleasure out of roast goose when you think about something like this, do you? And yet how far do you think it is from Gadstone Park church pews to Seven Dials?" They turned the corner into another street and saw a cab at the far end. Carlisle increased his pace, and Dominic had almost to trot to keep up with him. "But if I can court a cold-blooded sod like St. Jermyn," Carlisle continued, "to get a bill introduced, I think you can manage a little discomfort with Fleetwood, can't you?"

Dominic spent a wretched evening and woke the next morning feeling no better. He told his valet to have all his clothes cleaned, and if the smell would not come out, then to give them away to whosoever would take them. But nothing so simple would get rid of the pictures from his mind. Part of him hated Carlisle for obliging him to see things he would much rather not ever have known of. Of course, he had always appreciated in his head that there was poverty, but he had never actually seen it before, one did not really see the faces of beggars in the streets; they were simply faces, there—like lamp posts or railings. One was always about some business of one's own and too occupied to think of them.

But worse than the sight was the taste of it in his mouth, the smell that stayed at the back of the throat and tainted everything he ate. Perhaps it was guilt?

He had arranged to take Alicia on an errand she had some little distance away, and he had taken a carriage for the occasion. He called for her at a quarter-past ten, and she was ready, waiting for him, although of course she did not allow it to be obvious, in fact, might even have imagined he did not see it. Possibly she forgot he had been married and was acquainted with at least some of women's habits.

She was dressed in black and looked particularly fine, her hair bright and her skin flawless, with the delicacy of alabaster. Everything about her was impeccably clean. It was impossible to equate her in any way with the woman in the workhouse.

She had been talking to him, and he was not listening. "Dominic?" she said again. "Are you unwell?"

He needed to share the turmoil inside him; indeed, he could not keep his mind upon anything else. "I met your friend Carlisle yesterday," he said harshly.

She looked surprised, surely at his tone rather than the information. "Somerset? How was he?"

"We had luncheon together; then he tricked me into going with him into the most awful place I have ever seen in my life! I have never imagined anything so wretched—"

"I'm sorry." Her voice was full of concern. "Were you hurt? Are you sure you are well now? I can easily put off this call; it is not urgent."

116

"No, I wasn't hurt!" His voice was uglier than he meant it to be, but it would not stay in his control. Confusion and anger were boiling up inside him. He wanted someone to explain it away, to give back the ignorance that had been so much easier.

She obviously did not understand. She had never seen a workhouse in her life. She had never been permitted to read newspapers, and she did not handle money. The house-keeper kept the accounts, and her husband had paid the bills. The nearest she had ever come to poverty was a restriction in her dress allowance when her father had suffered a reverse in his investments.

He wanted to explain what he had seen and, above all, how he felt about it; but the only words for it were unseemly, and anyway, they described things that were completely beyond anything she could imagine. He gave it up and sank into silence.

After they returned from the visit he dropped her off at Gadstone Park, and then, feeling miserable and dissatisfied, he sent the carriage away and sat in front of his own fire for an hour. Finally he got up again and called a hansom.

Charlotte had put the matter of the corpses from her mind. Indeed, she had far too much of her own to do to interest herself in most of Pitt's cases, and the identity of a corpse that had, so far as anyone knew, died quite naturally was not of concern to her. Jemima had sat in a puddle and required a complete change of clothing. She was now busy with a larger laundry then usual, and ironing was not quite one of her favorite chores.

She was startled when the doorbell rang because she was not expecting anyone. People seldom called in the middle of the day; they all had their own duties and meals to prepare. She was even more surprised when she saw Dominic standing on the step.

"May I come in?" he asked before she had time to speak.

She opened the door wider.

"Yes, of course. What's wrong? You look—" She

117

wanted to say "miserable" but decided "unwell" would be more tactful.

He passed her into the hall, and she closed the door and led the way to the kitchen again. Jemima was building bricks in her playpen in the corner. Dominic sat down on the wooden chair in front of the table. The room was warm, and the washed wood smelled good. There were sheets hanging from the airing rail on the ceiling, and he looked with curiosity at the rope and pulleys for hauling it up and down. The flatiron was warming on the stove.

"I've interrupted you," he said without moving.

"No, you haven't." She smiled and picked up the iron to continue. "What's the matter?"

He was irritated with himself for being so transparent. She was treating him like a child, but at the moment he wanted the reassurance enough to shelve the resentment.

"A man called Carlisle took me to see a workhouse yesterday, somewhere in Seven Dials. There were fifty or sixty people in one room, all unpicking clothes to remake them. Even children. It was foul!"

She remembered the anger she had felt when Pitt had first told her about the slums and tenements when she lived in Cater Street and thought herself terribly knowledgeable because she looked at the newspapers. She had been shocked, angry that she had not known before, and angry most of all with Pitt because he had know all the time and had chosen to disturb her world with ugliness and other people's pain.

There was nothing comforting to say. She went on ironing the shirt. "It is," she agreed. "But why did he take you—this Mr. Carlisle?"

The reason was at once the best and the worst side to it.

"Because he wants me to speak to a friend of mine in the House of Lords and see if I can influence him to be there when St. Jermyn's bill is put up."

She remembered what Aunt Vespasia had said, and it was immediately understandable. "And are you going to?"

"For heaven's sake, Charlotte!" he said exasperatedly. "How on earth do you go up to a fellow you only know because of racing horses and things, and say to him, 'By the

118

way, I'd like you to take your seat in the House when they put up St. Jermyn's bill because the workhouses really are awful, and the children need educating, you know! There ought to be a law to support and educate pauper children in London, so be a good chap and get all your friends to vote for it! It's impossible! I can't do it!''

"That's a pity." She did not look up from her ironing. She was sorry for him; she knew how nearly impossible it was to engage people in thoughts they do not like, especially those that make them uncomfortable and threaten their pleasures by questioning the order of things. But she was not going to tell him he had no obligation, or that it was up to someone else. Not that he was likely to have accepted it if she had. He had seen and smelled the streets of Seven Dials, and no words would wipe out that memory.

"A pity!" he said furiously. "A pity! Is that all you can say? Has Thomas ever told you what those places are like? It's indescribable—you can taste the filth and despair."

"I know," she said calmly. "And there are worse places than workhouses, places inside the rookeries that even Thomas won't describe."

"He's told you?"

"Something, not all."

He screwed his face up and stared down at the white wood of the table. "It's awful!"

"Would you like some luncheon?" She folded the shirt and put it away, then folded the ironing board also. "I'm going to have some. It's just bread and soup, but you are welcome, if you wish."

Suddenly the gulf opened, and he realized he had been speaking to her as if they were both still in Cater Street, with the same material possessions. He had forgotten his world was as different now from hers as hers was from Seven Dials. He was momentarily embarrassed for his clumsiness. He watched her as she took two clean plates out of the cupboard and set them on the table, then the bread out of the bin, a board and a knife. There was no butter.

"Yes, please," he answered. "Yes, I would."

She took the lid off the stockpot on the stove and ladled out enough to fill the two plates.

"What about Jemima?" he asked.

She sat down. "She's had hers. What are you going to do about Mr. Carlisle?"

He ignored the question. He knew what the answer would be, but he did not want to admit it yet.

"I tried to tell Alicia about it." He took a mouthful of the soup. It was surprisingly good, and the bread was fresh and crusty. He had not known Charlotte could make bread. Still—she must have had to learn.

"That was unfair." She looked at him steadily. "You can't tell people in words and expect them to understand, or feel the way you do."

"No—she didn't. She brushed it aside as so much conversation. She seemed like a stranger, and I thought I knew her so well."

"That's not fair either," she said. "It's you who have changed. What do you suppose Mr. Carlisle thought of you?"

"What?"

"Were you very impressed by what he said? Didn't he have to take you to Seven Dials to see it for yourself?"

"Yes, but that's—" He stopped, remembering his reluctance, disinterest. But he was nothing to Carlisle; whereas he and Alicia loved each other. "That's—"

"Different?" Charlotte raised eyebrows. "It's not. Caring for someone doesn't alter it. Knowing might—" Straightaway she was sorry for saying it. Enchantment was such an ephemeral thing, and familiarity had so little to do with it. "Don't blame her," she said quietly. "Why should she know about it, or understand?"

"No reason," he admitted, and yet he felt a void between himself and Alicia and realized how much of his feeling for her depended on the color of her hair, the curve of her cheek, a smile, and the fact that she responded to him. But what was inside her, in the part he could not reach?

Could there be even the simple removal of an object that

stood between her and what she wanted, a little movement of the hand with a bottle of pills—and murder?

At the top of Resurrection Row was a cemetery, hence its name. A tiny chapel stood in the center; in a wealthier area it would have been a crypt or family tomb, but here it was only the pretension to one. Marble angels perched on a few of the better tombstones; here and there, there was a distant cross, but most of them rose bare and a little crooked with age. Subsidence in the earth from frequent digging caused them to lean askew, and half a dozen skeletal trees had not been removed. It was an unlovely place at any time, and on a damp February evening it boasted only one virtue, privacy. For a seventeen-year-old maid of all work like Dollie Jenkins, who was in the process of courting a butcher's boy with excellent prospects, it was the only place in which she could give him just sufficient encouragement without losing her employment.

Arm in arm they walked in through the gates, whispering together, giggling under their breath; it was hardly decent to laugh out loud in the presence of the dead. After a little while they sat down, close together, on one of the tombstones. She allowed it to be known that she would not resent a little show of affection, and he responded enthusiastically.

After some fifteen minutes, she felt the situation was getting out of hand, and he might well end up taking liberties and afterwards think the worse of her for it. She pushed him away and saw, to her consternation, a figure sitting perched on one of the other gravestones, knees crossed, high stovepipe hat askew.

" 'Ere, Samuel!'' she hissed. "There's an old geezer sittin' over there spyin' on us!''

Samuel got to his feet in awkward haste. "Dirty old goat!'' he said loudly. "Go on! Get away wiv' yer. Peepin' Tom! Afore I thump yer!''

The figure did not move; indeed, he ignored Samuel completely, not even raising his head.

Samuel strode over to him. "I'll teach yer!'' he shouted.

"I'll box your ears for yer right proper. Go on, get out of 'ere, yer dirty old toad!" He seized the man by the shoulder and made as if to swing his fist at him.

To his horror the man swayed and toppled over sideways, his hat rolling onto the ground. His face was blue in the faint moonlight, and his chest was a most peculiar flat shape.

"Oh, God almighty!" Samuel dropped him and leapt away, falling over his own feet. He scrambled up again and backed toward Dollie, clutching onto her.

"What is it?" she demanded. "What 'ave you done?"

"I ain't done nuffin! 'E's dead, Doll—'e's as dead as anybody in 'ere. Somebody's gorn an' dug 'im up!"

The news was conveyed to Pitt the following morning.

"You'll never believe it!" the constable said, his voice squeaking up to top C.

"Tell me anyway." Pitt was resigned.

"They've found another one. Courting couple found him last night."

"Why shouldn't I believe it?" Pitt said wearily. "I'd believe anything."

"Because it was Horrie Snipe!" the constable burst out. "As I live and breathe, it was—sitting up on a gravestone in Resurrection Cemetery in his old stovepipe hat. He was run over three weeks ago, by a muck cart, and buried a fortnight—and there 'e was, sitting on a tombstone all by 'isself in the moonlight."

"You're right," Pitt said. "I don't believe it. I don't want to believe it."

"It's 'im, sir. I'd know Horrie Snipe anywhere. He was the busiest procurer the Row ever had."

"So it seems," Pitt said drily. "But for this morning, I still refuse to believe it."

7

On MONDAY Charlotte received a handwritten note from Aunt Vespasia, inviting her to call that morning and be prepared to stay for some little while, in fact, over luncheon and into the afternoon. No reason was given, but Charlotte knew Aunt Vespasia far too well to imagine it was idle. A request at such short notice, and stating such a specific time and duration, was not casual. Charlotte could not possibly ignore it; apart from good manners, curiosity made it absolutely imperative she go.

Accordingly, she took Jemima over the street to Mrs. Smith, who was always more than willing to tend her with great affection, in return for a little gossip as to the dress, manners, and especially foibles of the society that Charlotte kept. Her own resulting importance in the street, as Charlotte's confidante, was immeasurable. She was also quite genuinely a kind woman and enjoyed helping, especially a young woman like Charlotte who was obviously ill prepared by her own upbringing to cope with the realities of life such as Mrs. Smith knew them.

Having been rather rash with the housekeeping in buying bacon three days in a row, instead of making do with oatmeal or fish as usual, Charlotte was obliged to catch the omnibus to its nearest point to Gadstone Park, instead of hiring a hansom, and then walk in rising sleet the rest of the way.

She arrived on the doorstep with wet feet and, she feared, a very red nose: not in the least the elegant image she would wish to have presented. So much for bacon for breakfast.

The maid who answered was too sensitive to her mistress's own eccentricities to allow her thoughts to be mirrored in her face. She was becoming inured to any kind of surprise. She moved Charlotte into the morning room and left her standing as near to the fire as she dared without risking actually setting herself alight. The heat was marvelous; it brought life back into her numb ankles, and she could see the steam rising from her boots.

Aunt Vespasia appeared after only a few moments. She glanced at Charlotte, then took out her lorgnette. "Good gracious, girl! You look as if you came by sea! Whatever have you done?"

"It is extremely cold outside," Charlotte attempted to explain herself. She moved a little forward from the fire; it was beginning to sting with its heat. "And the street is full of puddles."

"You appear to have stepped in every one of them." Vespasia looked down at her steaming feet. She was tactful enough not to ask why she had walked in the first place. "I shall have to find something dry for you, if you are to be in the least comfortable." She reached out for the bell and rang it sharply.

Charlotte half thought of demurring, but she was wretched with cold, and if she was to be there for some time, it would be quite worth it to borrow something warm and dry.

"Thank you," she accepted.

Vespasia gave her a look of sharp perception; she had seen the edge of argument and quite possibly understood. When the maid came, she treated the whole matter quite lightly.

"Mrs. Pitt has unfortunately been splashed, and quite soaked, on her journey here." She did not even bother to look at the girl. "Go and have Rose put out dry boots and stockings for her, and that blue-green afternoon gown with

124

the embroidery on the sleeve. Rose will know which one I mean.''

"Oh, dear." The girl looked at Charlotte with sympathy. "Some of those hansom drivers don't look in the least where they're going, ma'am. I'm ever so sorry. Cook only took a step down the road the other day, and two of them lunatics passed, seein' as they could race each other, and she was fair covered in mud. Said something awful, she did, when she got 'ome again. I'll find something dry for you straight-away." She whisked out of the door, bound on an errand of mercy, and hoping eternal punishment for cab drivers in general and careless ones in particular.

Charlotte smiled broadly. "Thank you, that was remark-ably tactful of you."

"Not at all." Vespasia dismissed it. "I am holding a small soirée this afternoon, very small indeed." She fluttered her hand slightly to indicate how very minor it was. "And I would like you to be here. I'm afraid this wretched business of Augustus is not going well."

Charlotte was not immediately sure what she meant. Her mind flew to Dominic. Surely there could be no one who genuinely suspected him—

Vespasia saw her look and read it with an ease that made Charlotte blush, thinking if she were so transparent now, how truly painful she must have been in the past.

"Oh, I'm sorry," she said hastily. "I had hoped people would put it from mind, now that he is reinterred. It does seem as if he was only the unfortunate victim of some insane creature who is tearing up graves all over the place. There have been two more, you know—apart from Lord Augustus and the man in the cab!"

She had the satisfaction of seeing Vespasia's eyes widen in surprise. She had told her something she not only did not know but had not foreseen.

"Two more! I heard nothing of it. When, and who?"

"No one you would know," Charlotte replied. "One was an ordinary man who lived near Resurrection Row—"

Vespasia shook her head. "Never heard of it. It sounds most insalubrious. Where is it?"

"About two miles away. Yes, it isn't very pleasant, but nothing like a slum, just a back street, and of course there is a cemetery—there would be, with such a name. That is where the other corpse was found—in the graveyard."

"Appropriate," Vespasia said drily.

"Yes, but not sitting up on a tombstone, and with his hat on!"

"No," Vespasia agreed, pulling a painful face. "And who was he?"

"A man called Horatio Snipe. Thomas would not tell me what he did, so I presume it must be something disreputable—I mean worse than merely a thief or a forger. I suppose he kept a house of women, or something like that."

Vespasia looked down her nose. "Really, Charlotte," she snorted. "But I dare say you are right. However, I don't think it will help. Suspicion is a strange thing; even when it is proved to be entirely unjustified, the flavor of it stays on: rather like something disagreeable one has disposed of—the aroma remains. People will forget even what it was they suspected Alicia or Mr. Corde of having done—but they will remember that they did suspect them."

"That is quite unjust!" Charlotte said angrily. "And it is unreasonable!"

"Of course," Vespasia agreed. "But people are both unjust and unreasonable without the slightest awareness or intention of being either. I hope you will stay to the soirée; that is principally why I invited you today. You have something of a perception of people. I have not forgotten you understood what had really happened in Paragon Walk before any of the rest of us. Perhaps you can see something in this that we do not—"

"But in Paragon Walk there had been a murder!" Charlotte protested. "Here there has been no crime—unless you think Lord Augustus was murdered?" It was a horrible thought and she had not accepted it, nor did she now. She meant it as a criticism, a shock rather than a question.

Vespasia was not shaken. "Most probably he died quite naturally," she replied, as if she had been discussing something that happened every day. "But one must face the possibility that he did not. We know a great deal less about people than we like to imagine. Maybe Alicia is as simple as she seems, a pleasant girl of good family and more than usual good looks, whose father married her advantageously; and she was, if not pleased by it, at least not imaginative or rebellious enough to object, even in her own mind.

"But, my dear, it is also possible that, as her marriage became more and more tedious, and she began to realize it would never be otherwise and could well last another twenty years, the thought became unbearable. And then when Dominic Corde came along and at precisely the same time an opportunity presented itself quite easily to be rid of her husband, in an instant she took it. It would be very easily done, you know, merely a small movement of the hand, a drop, two drops too much, nothing more: no evidence, no lies as to where she had been or with whom. She could almost forget it, wipe it from memory, convince herself it had not happened."

"Do you believe that?" Charlotte was afraid. Even in front of the fire she became conscious of coldness again, of her feet being wet. Outside, the sleet clattered against the glass of the windows.

"No," Vespasia said quietly. "But I do not deny its possibility."

Charlotte stood still.

"Go and change out of those wet boots," Vespasia ordered. "We will take luncheon in here, and you may tell me about your child. What is it you have called her?"

"Jemima," Charlotte answered obediently, standing up.

"I thought your mother's name was Caroline?" Vespasia raised her eyebrows in surprise.

"It is," Charlotte agreed. She turned at the door and gave her a dazzling smile. "And Grandmama's name is Amelia. I don't care for that either!"

The soirée was informal, and there was a great deal more conversation than listening to the music, which Charlotte rather regretted, since it was good and she was fond of the piano. She had never played it well herself, but both Sarah

127

and Emily had, and this young man's gentle touch brought back memories of childhood and Mama singing.

Dominic was surprised to see her, but either he did not notice the excellence of Vespasia's gown on her, or he was too sensitive to comment on it, knowing that in her circumstances it would have to be borrowed.

Charlotte had not seen Alicia before, and her curiosity had been mounting from the time the first guest, who was Virgil Smith, arrived. As Vespasia had said, he was remarkably plain. His nose was anything but aristocratic; it appeared less like marble than warm wax, put on with a careless hand. His haircut might have been executed with a pair of shears round the edge of a basin, but his tailor was exemplary. He smiled at Charlotte with a warmth that lit up his eyes and spoke to her in an accent she would have loved to mimic, as Emily could have, to retail it to Pitt. But she had no skill in the art.

Sir Desmond and Lady Cantlay did not remember her or, if they did, chose not to acknowledge it. She could hardly blame them; when a corpse lands in the street in front of one, one does not recall the faces of the passersby, even those who offer assistance. They greeted her with the well-bred, mild interest of acquaintances who have nothing in common, so far as they know, except the place in which they meet. Charlotte watched them go and wondered nothing about them, except if they suspected Dominic or Alicia of having entertained murder.

Major Rodney and his sisters held no involvement for her either, and she murmured polite nonsenses to them that reminded her of standing beside her mother and Emily at endless parties when she was single, trying to sound as if she were totally absorbed by Mrs. So-and-so's most recent illness or the prospects of Miss Somebody's engagement.

She had already built in her mind very clearly how she expected Alicia to look: fair skin and hair that curled quite naturally—unlike her own—medium height and with soft shoulders, a little inclined to plumpness. Afterward she realized she was creating a vague picture of Sarah again.

When Alicia came she was utterly different. It was not so

much a matter of description; she did have fair skin, and her hair waved so softly and asymmetrically it must surely be natural. But she was as tall as Charlotte, and her body was quite slim, her shoulders almost delicate. Far more than that, there was a completely different look in her eyes. She was nothing like Sarah at all.

"How do you do?" Charlotte said after only a second's hesitation. She did not know whether she had expected to like her or not, but she was startled by the reality. In her own mind, because Dominic was in love with her, she had created a shadow of Sarah. She was unprepared for a different and independent person. And she had forgotten that to Alicia she would be a stranger and, unless Dominic had told her of Sarah and their relationship, one of no importance.

"How do you do, Mrs. Pitt?" Alicia replied, and Charlotte knew instantly that Dominic had not told her; there was no curiosity in her face. Alicia took a step away, saw Dominic, and stood perfectly still for a moment. Then she turned to Gwendoline Cantlay and complimented her on her gown.

Charlotte was still considering her own instinctive understanding of the moment when she realized she was being spoken to.

"I understand you are an ally of Lady Cumming-Gould?"

She looked round at the speaker. He was lean, with winged eyebrows and teeth that were a little crooked when he smiled.

Charlotte scrambled to think what he could mean. "Ally?" It must have something to do with the bill Aunt Vespasia was concerned with, to get children out of workhouses and into some sort of school. He would be the man who had driven Dominic to the street in Seven Dials and shown him the workhouse that had upset him so profoundly. She looked at him with more interest. She could understand Thomas's care for such things; his daily life brought him the results of its tragedies, every sort of victim. But why did this man care?

"Only in spirit," she said with a smile. Now she knew who he was, she felt assured; perhaps in all the room he was the one who discomfited her least. "A supporter; nothing so useful as an ally."

"I think you underrate yourself, Mrs. Pitt," he replied.

It stung her to be patronized. The cause was too real for trivia and meaningless flattery. She found herself resenting it, as if he did not consider her worthy of the truth.

"You do me no favor by pretending," she said rather sharply. "I am not an ally. I have not the means."

His smile widened. "I stand rebuked, Mrs. Pitt, and I apologize. Perhaps I was precipitate, making the wish the fact."

It would be churlish of her not to accept his apology. "If you can make it a fact, I shall be delighted," she said more gently. "It is a cause worthy of anyone's effort."

Before he could reply, they were introduced to more people. Lord and Lady St. Jermyn came in, and Charlotte found herself presented. Her first impressions of people were frequently wrong: most often the people she afterwards came to like, she felt nothing toward at first; but she could not imagine ever being anything but uncomfortable in the presence of Lord St. Jermyn. There was something about his mouth that repelled her. He was in no way ugly, rather the opposite, but there was a way his lips met that stirred half a memory, half imagination in her that was unpleasant. She heard her voice replying some inanity and felt Carlisle's eyes on her. He had every right to reproach her with the very dishonesty for which she had just criticized him.

A little later Alicia joined them, with Dominic at her elbow. Charlotte watched them and thought how well they looked together, a perfect complement. Odd how that thought would have hurt and bewildered her a few years ago, and now it gave her no feeling at all except anxiety, in case the picture broke and there was nothing behind its perfection strong enough to stand an injury to the balance, an assault.

The conversation turned back to the bill. St. Jermyn was talking to Dominic.

"I hear from Somerset that you are a friend of young Fleetwood? With him on our side we would have an excellent chance. He has considerable influence, you know."

"I don't know him very well." Dominic was nervous, beginning to disclaim. Charlotte had seen him twist a glass stem like that in Cater Street; she realized now how many times. She had never been conscious of it before.

"Well enough," St. Jermyn said with a smile. "You are a good horseman, and an even better judge of an animal. That's all it takes."

"I believe you have a fine stable yourself, sir." Dominic was still trying not to be pushed.

"Racing." St Jermyn waved his hand. "Fleetwood prefers a good carriage pair; likes to drive himself, and that's where you excel. Heard you even beat him once." He smiled, curling his long mouth down at the corners. "Don't make a habit of it! He won't like it more than the occasional time."

"I was driving to win, not to please Lord Fleetwood," Dominic said a little tartly. His eyes flickered over to Charlotte, almost as if he were aware of her thoughts and of what she herself would have said.

"That is a luxury we cannot afford." St. Jermyn was not pleased, but he ironed it out of his face the moment after Charlotte had seen it, and a second later there was no trace at all. She judged that Dominic had not even noticed. "If we want Fleetwood's help, it would not be clever to beat him too often," St. Jermyn finished.

Dominic drew breath to retort, but Charlotte spoke before he did. He was not quick to anger, in fact, most agreeable; he seldom took a hard position on any issue, but on the rare occasions that he did, she could not recall his ever having changed it. It would be easy for him to commit himself now and then be unable to move when he regretted it.

"I don't believe Mr. Corde will do that," she said, forcing herself to smile across at St. Jermyn. "But surely Lord Fleetwood will take more notice of a man who has beaten him at least once? To come second to him hardly marks one from the crowd, or earns his interest."

Dominic flashed her one of his beautiful smiles, and for an instant she remembered how she used to feel about

131

him; then the present returned, and she was staring at St. Jermyn.

"Quite," Dominic agreed. "I would like him to see the workhouse in Seven Dials, as I did. It would not be a sight he would forget in a hurry."

Alicia was looking puzzled, a slight frown on her face. "What is so dreadful about the workhouse?" she asked. "You said there was poverty, but no legislation is going to get rid of that. Workhouses at least provide people with food and shelter. There have always been rich and poor, and even if you were to alter it with some miracle, in a few years, or less, it would all be the same again—wouldn't it? If you give a poor man money, it does not make him a rich man for long—"

"You are more perceptive than perhaps you intend," Carlisle said with a lifting of his brows. "But if you feed the children and keep them clean from disease and despair, so they survive into adulthood without stealing to live, and give them some sort of education, then the next generation is not quite so poor."

Alicia looked at him, absorbing the idea, realizing that he was very serious.

"God! If you'd seen it!" Dominic said sharply. "You wouldn't be standing here discussing academic niceties; you would want to get out there and do something!" He looked across at Charlotte. "Wouldn't they?"

A look of pain shot across Alicia's face, and she moved almost imperceptibly away from him. Charlotte saw it and knew exactly what she felt, the sudden sense of alienation, of being shut out of something important to him.

Charlotte looked at him hard, making her voice clear and light. "I should imagine they would. It has certainly affected you that way. You are totally changed. But I hardly think it is a suitable place to take Lady Fitzroy-Hammond, from what I have heard. My husband would not permit me to go there."

But Dominic would not be told, nor read her hint.

"He doesn't need to take you," he said heatedly. "You already know about such places and the people in them, and you care. I can remember you telling me about it years ago; but I didn't really understand what you meant then."

"I don't think you were listening to me!" she said quite honestly. "It has taken you a long time to believe. You must permit others a little time as well."

"There isn't time!"

"Indeed, there isn't, Mrs. Pitt," St. Jermyn said, raising his glass. "My bill comes up in a few days. If we are to get it through, we will have to have our support then. There isn't any time to waste. Corde, I'd be most obliged if you'd tackle Fleetwood tomorrow, or the day after at the latest?"

"Of course," Dominic said firmly. "Tomorrow."

"Good." St. Jermyn patted him on the shoulder, then drained his glass. "Come on, Carlisle, we'd better go and talk to our hostess; she knows simply everyone, and we need that."

A flicker of distaste crossed Carlisle's face for an instant and was gone almost before Charlotte was sure of it, and he moved to keep up with St. Jermyn. They walked together past the Misses Rodney and Major Rodney, holding a glass in his hand and looking anxiously over their heads as if searching for someone, or possibly fearing someone.

There was an uncomfortable silence; then Virgil Smith appeared. He looked a little doubtfully at Charlotte; then his face softened and he spoke to Alicia. It was only some common remark, quite trivial, but there was a gentleness in his voice that jarred Charlotte away from thoughts of poverty or parliamentary bills, and even suspicions of murder. It was sad, and perhaps unnoticed by anyone else, but she was quite sharply aware that Virgil Smith was in love with Alicia. Probably she had eyes only for Dominic and was not in the least conscious of it, and perhaps he would know its futility and never tell her. In those few seconds Charlotte became one person with Alicia in her mind and memory, reliving her own infatuation with Dominic, finding again the miseries and wild hopes, the silly self-deceptions, all the virtues she read into him, and how little she really knew him. She had done them both a disservice with her dreams, saddling him with virtues he had never claimed to possess.

133

She would not have seen Virgil Smith either, with his unsculpted face and his impossible manners, and certainly never known or wanted to know that he loved her. It would have embarrassed her. But perhaps she would have been the loser for it.

She excused herself and went to talk to Vespasia and Gwendoline Cantlay and saw more than once a look of unease pass over Gwendoline's face as she recognized Charlotte vaguely, struggling to place her and failing. She was not sure if she knew her socially, and whether she ought to acknowledge it. With a faint malice, Charlotte allowed her to search; the satisfaction of telling her would not be as great and might possibly embarrass Aunt Vespasia. She might not care in the least if they all knew she kept company with policemen's wives—but, on the other hand, she might prefer to select whom she told, and how!

It was late, with one or two guests departed and the gray afternoon already beginning to close in, when Charlotte found herself comparatively alone, near the entrance to the conservatory, and saw Alicia coming toward her. She had been expecting this moment; in fact, if Alicia had not chosen it, she would have contrived it herself.

Alicia had obviously been rehearsing in her mind just how she could begin; Charlotte knew it, because it was what she would have done.

"It has been a most pleasant afternoon, hasn't it?" Alicia said quite casually as she drew level with Charlotte. "So considerate of Lady Cumming-Gould to arrange it in such a way that it is not inappropriate for me to come. Mourning seems to go on for so long, it only makes the bereavement worse. It allows no one diversion in order to relieve one's mind from thoughts of death, or from loneliness."

"Quite," Charlotte agreed. "I think people do not realize the added burden it is, on top of the loss one has already sustained."

"I did not know before today that Lady Cumming-Gold was an aunt of yours," Alicia continued.

"I think that is rather more than the truth," Charlotte smiled. "She is the great-aunt of my brother-in-law, Lord

134

Ashworth." Then she said what she intended to tell Alicia ever since the conversation with Lord St. Jermyn. "My sister Emily married Lord Ashworth a little while ago. My older sister, Sarah, was married to Dominic before she died; but then I'm sure you knew that—" She was, in fact, quite sure that she did not, but she wanted to allow Alicia room to pretend that she had.

Alicia disguised her confusion with a masterly effort. Charlotte affected not to have noticed.

"Yes, of course," Alicia pretended. "Although he has been so taken up with this business of Mr. Carlisle's lately that I have not talked with him much. I should be obliged if you could tell me a little more about it. You seem to be in their confidence, and I confess myself most dreadfully ignorant."

Charlotte surprised herself by lying. "Actually, I think it is rather more Aunt Vespasia's confidence I am in." She kept her voice quite light. "She is very concerned with it, you know. Mr. Carlisle seems to speak to her on the subject, perhaps to gain her assistance in persuading others with seats in the House to go and support them—" She glanced at Alicia and saw the memory of St. Jermyn's remark flicker across her face. "She does know a great many people. I have never seen a workhouse myself, naturally, but from what they have said, it is a most appalling distress which should be alleviated. And if this bill will provide maintenance and education for pauper children in the metropolis and remove them from the effects of living in the constant company of the vagrant of all sorts, I for one would hope and pray it will be passed."

Alicia's face softened with relief. "Oh, so do I," she agreed intensely. "I must think if I know anyone who could help; there must be some of Augustus's family or friends."

"Oh, could you?" Charlotte was not playacting this time; she cared about both Dominic and Alicia because they were individual people she could understand; but perhaps if she were honest, the bill was far more important than a simple murder, whatever tragedy brought it about or followed in its wake.

Alicia smiled. "Of course. I shall begin as soon as I get home." She held out her hand impulsively. "Thank you, Mrs. Pitt. You have been so kind, I feel as if I know you already. I hope you don't consider that an impertinence?"

"I consider it the greatest compliment," Charlotte said sincerely. "I hope you will feel so in the future."

Alicia kept her word. Upon arriving home, the first thing she did after giving her cloak to the maid and changing into dry boots was to go to her writing room and take out her address book. She had very carefully composed and written four letters before going upstairs to change for the evening meal.

Verity was not home, having gone to visit a cousin for a few days, and there was no one at the table except the old lady and herself. She missed Verity, because she both enjoyed her company and would have liked to share with her the new project she had found and her thoughts on Mrs. Pitt, whom Alicia had changed from disliking intensely, because of Dominic's obvious regard for and closeness to her, to liking her now as much; she was quite different from Alicia's imagining.

"Did you enjoy your tea party?" the old lady asked, spearing a large portion of fish with her fork and putting it whole into her mouth. "No one commented it odd that you should be out so soon after your husband's burial? I suppose they were too polite!"

"It is over five weeks since he died, Mama-in-law," Alicia replied, removing the bone from her fish delicately. "And it was a soirée, not a tea party."

"Music as well! Very unsuitable. All love songs, I suppose, so you could gape at Dominic Corde and make a fool of yourself. He won't marry you, you know! He hasn't the stomach for it. He thinks you poisoned Augustus!"

The full meaning of what she had said broke on Alicia only slowly. At first she was angry with the suggestion that she had disgraced herself at the soirée. Only after she had opened her mouth to deny it did she realize what the old lady had said about Dominic. It was ugly and utterly wrong! Of course he would never think anything so evil of her!

"Won't be able to prove it, of course," the old lady went on, eyes bright. "Won't say anything—just be a little cooler every time you see him. Notice he didn't call round the last few days! No more carriage rides—"

"It hasn't been the weather," Alicia said hotly.

"Never stopped him before!" The old lady took another mouthful of fish and spoke round it. "Seen him come here at Christmas when there was snow in the streets! Don't make a fool of yourself, girl!"

Alicia was too angry to be polite any more. "Last week you were saying you killed Augustus himself!" she snapped. "If he did it, how could he be thinking I did? Or do you imagine we both did it quite independently? If that is the case, then you should be delighted to see us marry—we deserve each other!"

The old lady glared at her, pretending to have her mouth too full to speak, while she thought of a suitable reply.

"Perhaps he thinks you did it?" Alicia went on, gathering impetus with the idea. "After all, the digitalis is yours, not mine! Maybe he is afraid to come and live here in the same house with you?"

"And why should I poison my own son, pray?" The old lady swallowed her mouthful and immediately put in more. "I don't want to marry some handsome young philanderer!"

"It's as well," Alicia snapped. "Since you don't have the least opportunity." She was appalled at herself, but years of good behavior had finally snapped, and it was a marvelous feeling, exhilarating, like riding too fast on a good horse.

"Neither do you, my girl!" The old lady's face was scarlet. "And you're a fool if you imagine you have. You've poisoned your husband for nothing!"

"If you think me a poisoner"—Alicia looked straight into her old eyes—"I am surprised you dine so voraciously at the same table with me and yet pursue my enmity so hard. Are you not afraid for yourself?"

The old lady choked, and her face went livid white. Her hand flew to her throat.

Alicia laughed with real and bitter humor. "If I were going to poison anyone, it would have been you in the beginning, not Augustus; but I am not, which you know as well as I do, or you would have thought of it long ago. You would have had Nisbett tasting everything before you put it in your mouth! Not that I wouldn't cheerfully have poisoned Nisbett, too!"

The old lady coughed and went into a spasm.

Alicia ignored her. "If you have had sufficient of that fish," she said coldly, "I'll have Byrne bring in the meat!"

Pitt knew nothing about the soirée. He was determined to find the identity of the corpse from the cab, and as soon as he received the result of the postmortem he snatched it from the delivery boy and tore it open. He had worn himself out speculating what it might be, something exotic and individual, damning to someone, to account for the extraordinary circumstances. If it were not connected to some crime or scandal, why should anyone perform the grisly and dangerous job of disinterring him and leaving him on the box of a hansom cab? Naturally, they had traced the cab, only to find it had been removed while its owner had been refreshing himself a little too liberally at a local tavern. Not an entirely uncommon occurrence and, on a January night, one for which Pitt had considerable sympathy. Only policemen, cabbies, and lunatics frequented the streets all night long in such weather.

He read the piece of paper from the envelope. It was as ordinary as possible—a stroke. It was a common and utterly natural way to die. There were no marks of violence on the body; in fact, nothing to comment on at all. He had been a man of late middle years, in generally good health, well nourished and well cared for, clean, a little inclined to overweight. In fact, as the morgue attendant had said, precisely what one might expect a dead lord to look like.

Pitt thanked the boy and dismissed him; then put the paper into the drawer of his desk, jammed his hat on his head, tied his muffler up to his ears, and, taking his coat off the stand, went out the door.

There was no open grave. That was perhaps the most sinister part about it; he had three graves and four bodies: Lord Augustus, William Wilberforce Porteous, Horrie Snipe—and this unknown man from the cab. Where was his grave, and why had the grave robber chosen to fill it in again so carefully that it remained hidden?

The other graves had all been within a fairly small perimeter. He would begin looking in the same area. Obviously he could not search all the recent graves for an empty one—he would have to question all the doctors who might have certified a death from stroke within the last four to six weeks. He might be able to narrow it down until he had a mere one or two who could then be taken to see the very unpleasant remains still lying at the morgue.

It took him until the afternoon of the following day before, tired, cold, and very ragged of temper, he climbed the stone stairs to the office of one Dr. Childs.

"He doesn't see patients this time o' the day!" his housekeeper said sharply. "You'll have to wait. 'E's just 'avin' 'is tea!"

"I'm not a patient." Pitt made an effort to control his voice. "I am from the police, and I will not wait." He met the woman's eyes and stared until she looked away.

"I'm sure I don't know what you want 'ere," she said with a lift of her shoulder. "But I suppose you 'ad better come in. Mind you wipe your feet!"

Pitt followed her in and disturbed a somewhat startled doctor sitting with his boots off in front of the fire, crumpet in his hand and butter on his chin.

Pitt explained his errand.

"Oh," the doctor said immediately. "Bring another cup, Mrs. Lundy. Have a crumpet, Inspector—yes, that would be Albert Wilson, I imagine. Warm yourself, man, you look perished. Mr. Dunn's butler, poor fellow. Still, don't know why I say that, very quick way to go. Dare say he never knew anything about it. Your boots are wet, man; take 'em off and dry your socks out. Can't bear this weather.

Why do you want to know about Wilson? Perfectly normal death. No relation and nothing to leave, anyway. Just a butler, good one, so I hear, but perfectly ordinary fellow. That's right, make yourself comfortable. Have another crumpet; watch the butter, runs all over the place. What's the matter with Wilson?" He raised his eyebrows and looked at Pitt curiously.

Pitt warmed to him as much as to the fire. "There was a disinterred corpse found on the box of a hansom cab outside the theatre about three weeks ago—"

"Good God! You mean that was poor old Wilson?" The doctor's eyebrows shot up almost to his hairline. "Now, why on earth should anybody do that? Your case, is it? Thank you, Mrs. Lundy; now pour the inspector a cup of tea."

Pitt took the tea gracefully and waited till the house-keeper was reluctantly out of the room.

"Terrible curious woman." The doctor shook his head at her departing back. "But it has its uses—knows more about my patients than they ever tell me. Can't cure a man if you know only half of what's wrong with him." He watched the steam rise from Pitt's socks. "Shouldn't walk around with wet feet. Not good for you."

"Yes, it is my case." Pitt could not help smiling. "And the odd thing is, there's no open grave left. Albert Wilson was buried, I presume?"

"Oh, certainly! Of course he was. I can't tell you where, but I'm sure Mr. Dunn could."

"Then I shall ask him," Pitt replied without moving. He bit into another crumpet. "I'm greatly obliged to you."

The doctor reached for the teapot.

"Think nothing of it, my dear fellow. Professional duty. Have some more tea?"

Pitt went to the Dunns' and learned the name of the church, but there was no use going to look for graves in the dark. It was the following morning when he found the grave of Albert Wilson, butler deceased, and obtained permission to open it. By eleven o'clock he was standing beside the gravediggers, watching as they took out the last of the black earth from the coffin lid. He passed the ropes down, waited as they poked them under the box and tied them, then stood back as they climbed out and began to haul. It was an expert job, a matter of balance and leverage. They seemed to find it heavy, finally laying it on the wet earth beside the cavity with a sigh of relief.

"That were rotten 'eavy, guv," one of them said soberly. "It didn't 'ardly feel like it were empty to me."

"Not me." The other shook his head and stared at Pitt accusingly.

Pitt did not reply but bent and looked at the fastenings on the lid. After a moment he fished in his pocket and pulled out a screwdriver. Silently, he started to work, moving round the coffin till he had all the screws in his hands. He put them in the other pocket, then inserted the blade between the lid and the box and lifted it up.

They were right. It was not empty. The man lying in it was slight, with thick red hair. He wore a loose-fitting white shirt, and there was paint on his fingers, thin, watercolor paint, such as an artist uses.

But it was the face that held Pitt. His eyes were closed, but the skin was bloated and puffy, the lips blue. Under the surface of the skin were dozens of tiny pinprick red marks where the capillaries had burst. But the most obvious of all were the dark bruises on the throat.

Here at last was the one who had been murdered.

8

SO MUCH HAD already centered on Gadstone Park it did not take Pitt long to discover the identity of the man buried in Albert Wilson's grave. There had been only one artist mentioned—Godolphin Jones. It was but a short step to see if this was his body.

Pitt put down the lid again and stood up. He called over the constable waiting at the end of the path and told him to have the body taken immediately to the morgue; he himself would repair to Gadstone Park and fetch a butler or footman to look at it. He thanked the gravediggers and left them angry and confused, staring at the earth-stained coffin, while he tied his muffler still tighter, pulled his hat forward to keep the drizzle off his face, and went out into the street.

It was a short, grim business. It was a distinctive face, even under the puffing and the marks, and the butler needed only one look.

"Yes, sir," he said quietly. "That is Mr. Jones." Then he hesitated. "Sir—he"—He swallowed hard—"he does not look as if he met with a natural death, sir?"

"No," Pitt said gently. "He was strangled."

The man was very pale, indeed. The morgue attendant reached for the glass of water.

"Does that mean he was murdered, sir? And there will be an investigation?"

"Yes," Pitt answered. "I'm afraid it does.

"Oh, dear." The man sat down on the chair provided. "How very unpleasant."

Pitt waited for a few minutes while the man collected his composure again; then they both went back to the hansom that was waiting and returned to Gadstone Park. There was a great deal to be done. No other event so far had included Godolphin Jones in any way. He had had no apparent relationship with Augustus Fitzroy-Hammond, or with Alicia or Dominic. In fact, he did not figure in anything that had been mentioned, not even the bill that Aunt Vespasia was so concerned with. No one had claimed any acquaintance with him beyond professional, or the merest sort that one has with any person who lives in the immediate neighborhood.

Charlotte had said Aunt Vespasia thought his paintings a little muddy and highly priced, but that was no cause for personal dislike, far less murder. If one did not like paintings, one simply did not purchase them. And yet he had been popular and, if his house was anything to judge by, of very considerable means.

The house was the place to begin. Possibly it was where he had been murdered, and if that could be established, it was a point from which to pursue time and witnesses. At the very least he would discover the last occasion Godolphin Jones was there, if he was seen leaving, who had called upon him, and when. Servants frequent knew a great deal more about their masters than their masters would have chosen to believe. Discreet and well-judged questioning might elicit all sorts of information.

And, of course, a thorough search must be made of his belongings.

Pitt, in company with a constable, began the long task.

The bedroom yielded nothing. It was orderly, a little consciously dramatic for Pitt's taste, but clean and unremarkable in every other way. It held all the usual effects: washstand, mirror, chests of drawers for underwear and socks. Suits and shirts were kept in a separate dressing

143

room. There were several guest bedrooms, unoccupied and out of use.

Nor did any of the downstairs rooms offer anything unusual until they came to the studio. Pitt opened the door and stared inside. There was nothing posed or indulgent about this room; the floor was uncarpeted, the windows enormous and taking up the most part of two walls. There was a clutter of odd pieces of statuary in one corner, and what looked like a white garden chair. A Louis Quinze chair was half draped with a length of pink velvet, and an urn lay on its side on the floor. On the wall beside the door were shelves stacked with brushes, pigments, chemicals, linseed oil, spirits, and several bundles of rags. On the floor underneath were a number of canvases, and in the center of the room an easel with two palettes beside it and a half-worked canvas propped on the pegs. There was nothing else immediately visible, except a shabby rolltop desk and a hard-backed kitchen chair beside it.

"Artist," the constable said obviously. "Reckon to find anything here?"

"I hope so." Pitt walked in. "Otherwise there's nothing left but questioning the servants. You start over there." He pointed and began to go through the canvases himself.

"Yes, sir," the constable replied, dutifully climbing over the urn to begin and knocking the chair off its balance. It fell over and rolled onto its side with a clatter, carrying a vase of dried flowers with it.

Pitt refrained from comment. He already knew the constable's opinion of art and artists.

The canvases were mostly primed but unused. There were only two with paint on, one with background and outline of a woman's head, the other almost completed. He sat them up and stepped back to consider them. They were, as Vespasia had said, a little muddy in color, as if he had used too many pigments in the mixing, but the balance was good and the composition pleasing. He did not recognize the almost completed one, nor the one on the easel, but probably the butler would know who they were, and no doubt Jones himself kept a record, for financial purposes if nothing else.

The constable knocked over a piece of pillar and swore under his breath. Pitt ignored him and turned to the desk. It was locked, and he was obliged to fiddle for several minutes with a wire before getting it open. There were few papers inside, mostly bills for artist's supplies. The household accounts must be kept somewhere else, probably by the cook or the butler.

"There's nothing 'ere, sir," the constable said hopelessly. "Couldn't rightly tell if there's been a struggle in among this lot or not, seein' as it's such a mess, anyway. I suppose it's bein' a hartist, like?" He did not approve of art; it was not an occupation for a man. Men should do a job of work, and women should keep house, a neat and tidy house, if they were any good at it. "They all live like this?" He eyed the room with disdain.

"I've no idea," Pitt replied. "See if you can find any blood. There was a hell of a bruise on his head. Whatever he hit it on is bound to have traces." And he resumed his search of the desk, picking up a bundle of letters. He read through them quickly; they were of no interest that he could see, all to do with commissions for portraits, detailing poses desired, colors of gowns, dates for sittings that might be convenient.

Next, he came to a small notebook with a series of figures which could have been anything, and after each figure a tiny drawing, either an insect or a small reptile. There was a lizard, a fly, two kinds of beetle, a toad, a caterpillar, and several small hairy things with legs. All of them were repeated at least half a dozen times, except the toad, which appeared only twice and toward the end. Perhaps if Jones had lived, the toad would have continued?

"Found something?" The constable climbed over the urn and the chair and came across, his voice lifting hopefully.

"I don't know," Pitt answered. "It doesn't look like much, but maybe if I understood it—"

The constable tried to lean over his shoulder, found it too high, and peered over his elbow instead.

"Well, I dunno," he said after a minute. "Was 'e interested in them kind o' things? Some gentlemen is—who

145

don't 'ave anythin' better to do wiv their time. Though why anybody wants to know about spiders and flies is a mystery to me."

"No." Pitt shook his head, frowning. "They're not naturalist drawings; they are all repeated at fairly regular intervals, and exactly the same. They are more like hieroglyphics, a sort of code."

"What for?" The constable screwed up his face. "It ain't a letter, or anything."

"If I knew what for, I should know the next step," Pitt said tartly. "These figures are set out in groups like either dates or money, or both."

The constable lost interest. "Maybe that was 'is way of doin' 'is accounts, to keep out nosy 'ousekeepers, or the like," he suggested. "There's nothing much over there, just a lot o' things like you see in paintings, bits o' plaster made up to look like stone, colored bits o' cloth, things like that. Ain't no blood. And they're all in such a mess you can't tell whether they been knocked like that, or 'e just threw 'em there, anyway. Seems like hartists is just naturally untidy. Looks as if 'e took photographs as well, as there's one o' them cameras over there."

"A camera?" Pitt straightened up. "I haven't seen any photographs, have you?"

"No, sir, now as you mention it, I 'aven't. Do you think 'e sold them?"

"He would hardly sell all of them," Pitt answered, puzzled. "And there weren't any in the rest of the house. Now, I wonder where they are?"

"Maybe 'e never used it," the constable suggested. "It's in among all them things 'e put in 'is pictures; maybe that's what it's for, part of a picture."

"Doesn't seem the sort of thing you'd put in a picture." Pitt climbed carefully over the chair and the urn and the pillars till he came to the black camera on its tripod. "And it's far from new," he observed. "So he hadn't just bought it, unless he got it secondhand. But we can find out from his past clients if anyone had a portrait painted with a camera in it, or if anyone commissioned such a thing for the future."

"It ain't a pretty thing." The constable caught his feet in a piece of the velvet cloth and swore vociferously. Then he noticed Pitt's face. "Beg pardon, sir." He coughed in a mixture of embarrassment and irritation. "But maybe 'e took photographs o' people 'e was goin' to paint, so 'e could know what they looked like when they wasn't 'ere, like?"

"And then destroyed them, or gave them away afterwards?" Pitt considered it. "Possible, but I would have thought he'd want to see them in color. After all, an artist works in color. Still, it could be." He started to examine the camera, pressing the pieces experimentally. He had never worked one himself, although he had seen them used by police photographers a few times and had begun to appreciate their possibilities. He knew the imprint of the picture was made on a plate, which then had to be developed. It took him a little fiddling before he got the plate out of this one, carefully, keeping it wound in the black cloth away from the light, because he was not used to it and did not know how fragile it might be.

"What's that?" the constable asked dubiously.

"The plate," Pitt replied.

"Anything on it?"

"I don't know. Have to have it developed. Probably not, or he wouldn't have left it in there, but we might be lucky."

"Probably only some woman 'e was painting." The constable dismissed it.

"He may have been murdered because of some woman he was painting," Pitt pointed out.

The constable's face lit up hopefully. " 'Avin' an *affaire*? Well, now that's a thought. Bit free with the posin', you reckon?"

Pitt gave him a dry, humorous look.

"Go and get the servants one by one," he ordered. "Starting with the butler."

"Yes, sir." The constable obeyed, but he was obviously turning over in his mind the limitless possibilities that had just dawned on him. He did not like effeminate men who made a great deal too much money by puddling around in smocks and painting pictures of people who ought to know better, but it was a good deal more interesting than the usual run-of-the-mill tragedies he saw. He did not want to be bothered with servants. He retired reluctantly.

The butler came in a few moments later, and Pitt invited him to sit down in the garden chair, while he himself sat in the one that had been beside the desk.

"Who was your master painting when he left?" he asked straightaway.

"No one, sir. He had just finished a portrait of Sir Albert Galsworth."

That was a disappointment; not only someone Pitt had never heard of, but also a man.

"What about the picture on the floor?" he asked. "That's a woman."

The butler walked over and looked at it.

"I don't know, sir. She appears to be a lady of quality by her clothes, but as you see, the face has not yet been filled in, so I cannot say who it may be."

"Has no one been coming here for sittings?"

"No, sir, not that I am aware of. Perhaps she was due and had put it off until a more convenient time?"

"What about this one?" Pitt showed him the other, more nearly completed canvas.

"Oh, yes, sir. That is Mrs. Woodford. She did not care for the picture; she said it made her look lumpish. Mr. Jones never finished it."

"Was there ill feeling?"

"Not on Mr. Jones's part, sir. He is used to—certain persons'—vanity. An artist has to be."

"He wasn't prepared to alter it to suit the lady?"

"Apparently not, sir. I believe he had already made considerable adjustments to suit the lady's view of herself. If he went too far, he would compromise his reputation."

Pitt did not argue; it was academic now.

"Have you seen this before?" He pulled out the note-book and let it fall open.

The butler glanced at it, and his face went blank. "No, sir. Is it of importance?"

"I don't know. Was Mr. Jones a photographer?"

The butler's eyebrows shot up. "A photographer? Oh, no, sir, he was an artist. Sometimes watercolors and sometimes oil, but certainly not photographs!"

"Then whose camera is that?"

The butler looked startled. He had not noticed the contraption. "I really have no idea, sir. I have never seen it before."

"Could someone else have borrowed his studio?"

"Oh, no, sir. Mr. Jones was most particular. Beside, if they had, I should have known. There have been no strangers here; in fact no caller has been inside this house since Mr. Jones—left."

"I see." Pitt was confused. The thing was becoming ridiculous. He wanted a mystery, something to investigate, but this was nonsensical. The camera had to have come from somewhere and belong to someone. "Thank you," he said, standing up again. "Will you make me a list of all the people you can remember who came here to have their pictures painted, starting with the latest and going back as far as you can remember, with the best recollection you have as to dates?"

"Yes, sir. Has Mr. Jones no accounts you can check?"

"If he has, they are not here."

The butler forbore from comment and retired to send in the next servant. Pitt interviewed them all, one by one, and learned nothing that seemed important. It was early afternoon when he had finished, and still time to visit at least one of the other houses in the Park. He chose the latest on the butler's list of portraits—Lady Gwendoline Cantlay.

Obviously she had not heard the news. She received him with surprise and a hint of irritation.

"Really, Inspector, I see no purpose to be served by pursuing this unfortunate subject. Augustus is buried, and there has been no further vandalism. I suggest you now leave his family to recover as well as they may and do not refer to the matter again. Haven't they been through enough?"

"I have no intention of raising the matter again, ma'am,"

he said patiently. "Unless it should become necessary. I'm afraid I am here over something quite different. You were acquainted with the artist, Mr. Godolphin Jones, I believe?"

Did he imagine it, or was there a tightening of her fingers in her lap, a faint flush across her cheeks?

"He painted my picture," she agreed, watching him. "He has painted many pictures and came highly recommended to me. He is a well-known artist, you know, and very much praised."

"You think highly of him, ma'am?"

"I—" she drew in her breath—"I don't really know sufficient to say. I am obliged to rest upon other people's opinions." She looked at him with a touch of defiance. Again her hands were tight in her lap, crunching the fabric of her dress. "Why do you ask?"

At last she had come to it. He had a sudden sense of anxiety, as if the knowledge might affect her more than he was prepared for.

"I'm very sorry to have to tell you, ma'am," he began, unusually awkwardly for him. He had done this often before, and the words were practiced. "But Mr. Jones is dead. He had been murdered."

She sat perfectly still, as if she did not understand. "He is in France!"

"No, ma'am, I'm sorry, but he is here in London. His body has been identified by his butler. There is no mistake." He looked at her, then round the room to see where the bell was to call a maid, in case she should require assistance.

"Did you say murdered?" she asked slowly.

"Yes, ma'am. I'm sorry."

"Why? Who would murder him? Do you know? Are there any clues?" She was agitated now. He would have sworn it came to her as a complete shock, but she had changed. She was frightened, and it was not hysterical or nameless; she knew what she was frightened of. Pitt would have given quite a lot if he could have known also.

"Yes, there are several clues," he said, watching her, her face, her neck, her hands grasping the arms of the chair.

Her eyes widened. "May I ask what they are? Perhaps if

I knew, I could help. I knew Mr. Jones a little, naturally, having sat for the portrait."

"Of course," he agreed. "There are unfinished canvases that the butler does not recognize as ladies who ever called at the house for sittings, or any other purpose. And there is a camera—"

He was quite sure her surprise was genuine. "A camera! But he was an artist, not a photographer!"

"Exactly. And yet one presumes it was his. It is very improbable someone else's camera would be there in his studio. The butler is quite positive he has not permitted anyone else to use it."

"I don't understand," she said simply.

"No, ma'am, neither do we, as yet. I take it Mr. Jones never took photographs of you, say to work from when you were not available?" ·

"No, never."

"Perhaps I could see the portrait, if you still have it?"

"Of course, if you wish." She stood up and led him to the withdrawing room where a large portrait of her sat over the mantelpiece."

"Excuse me." He went forward and began to study it carefully. He did not like it much. The pose was quite good, if rather stylized. He recognized several of the props from the studio, especially a piece of pillar and a small table. The proportions were correct, but the colors lacked something, a certain clarity. They seemed to have been mixed with a permanent undertone of ocher or sepia, giving even the sky a heavy look. The face was definitely Gwendoline's; the expression was pleasant enough, and yet there was no charm in it.

He began to study the background and was just about to leave it when he noticed in the bottom left-hand corner a small clump of leaves quite clearly drawn with a beetle on one of them, distinct and stylized, precisely like one of those he had seen in the notebook at least four or five times.

"May I ask you what it cost, ma'am?" he said quickly.

"I cannot see what that has to do with Mr. Jones's murder," she said with marked coolness. "And I have already said he is an artist of excellent repute."

Pitt was aware he had mentioned a subject socially crass. "Yes, ma'am," he acknowledged. "You did say so, and I have already heard that from others. Nevertheless, I have good reason for asking, even if only for comparison's sake."

"I do not wish half London to be familiar with my financial arrangements!"

"I shall not discuss it, ma'am; it is purely for police use, and then only should it be relevant. I would prefer to find it out from you rather than press your husband, or—"

Her face hardened. "You are overstepping your office, Inspector. But I do not wish you to disturb my husband with the affair. I paid three hundred and fifty pounds for the picture, but I don't see what possible use that can be to you. It is quite a usual price for an artist of his quality. I believe Major Rodney paid something the same for his portrait, and that of his sisters."

"Major Rodney has two pictures?" Pitt was surprised. He would not have imagined Major Rodney as a man who cared for, or could afford, such an indulgence in art.

"Why not?" she asked, eyebrows raised. "One of himself, and one of Miss Priscilla and Miss Mary Ann together."

"I see. Thank you, ma'am. You have been very helpful."

"I don't see how!"

He was not quite sure of himself, but at least there were other places to search, and in the morning he would call on Major and the Misses Rodney. He excused himself and set out in the returning fog to go back to the police station, and then home.

If Lady Cantlay had been startled to hear of Godolphin Jones's murder, Major Rodney was shattered. He sat in the chair like a man who has nearly been drowned. He gasped for breath, and his face was mottled with red.

"Oh, my God! How absolute appalling! Strangled, you say? Where did they find him?"

"In another man's grave," Pitt replied, unsure again whether to reach for the bell and call a servant. It was a reaction he had been totally unprepared for. The man was a soldier; he must have seen death, violent and bloody death, a thousand times. He had fought in the Crimea, and from what Pitt had heard of the tragic and desperate war, a man who had survived that ought to be able to look on hell itself and keep his stomach.

Rodney was beginning to compose himself. "How dreadful. How on earth did you know to look?"

"We didn't," Pitt said honestly. "We found him quite by chance."

"That's preposterous! You can't go around digging up graves to see what you will find in them—by chance!"

"No, of course not, sir." Pitt was awkward again. He had never known himself so clumsy. "We expected the grave to have been robbed, to be empty."

Major Rodney stared at him.

"We had the corpse whose grave it was!" Pitt tried to make him understand. "He was the man we first took to be Lord Augustus—on the cab near the theatre—"

"Oh." Major Rodney sat upright as though he were on horseback in a parade. "I see. Why didn't you say so to begin with? Well, I'm afraid there is nothing I can tell you. Thank you for informing me."

Pitt remained seated. "You knew Mr. Jones."

"Not socially, no. Not our sort of person. Artist, you know."

"He painted your picture, did he not?"

"Oh, yes—knew him professionally. Can't tell you anything about him. That's all there is to it. And I won't have you distressing my sisters with talk about murders and death. I'll tell them myself, as I see fit."

"Did you have a picture painted of them, also?"

"I did. What of it? Quite an ordinary thing to do. Lots of people have portraits."

"May I see them, please?"

"Whatever for? Ordinary enough. But I suppose so, if it'll make you go away and leave us alone. Poor man." He shook his head. "Pity. Dreadful way to die." And he stood up, small, slight, and ramrod stiff, and led Pitt into the withdrawing room.

Pitt stared at the very formal portrait on the far wall above the sideboard. Instantly he disliked it. It was grandiloquent, full of scarlets and glinting metal, a child in an old man's body playing at soldiers. Had it been intended as ironic it would have been clever, but again the colors were unsubtle and a little cloudy.

He went up to and found his eye drawn without consciousness to the left corner. There was a small caterpillar, totally irrelevant to the composition but cleverly masked in the background, a brown-bodied creature in a brown, mottled shadow.

"And I believe there is also one of your sisters?" He stepped back and turned to face the major.

"Can't think what you want to see it for," the major said with surprise. "Quite ordinary painting. Still, if you like—"

"Yes, please," Pitt went after him into the next room. It was on the facing wall, between two jardinieres, a larger work than the first. The pose was fussy, the scenery cluttered with far too many props, the colors a little better but with too much pink. He looked in the left corner and found the same caterpillar, exactly the same stylized hair and legs, but green-bodied, to hide against the grass.

"What did you pay for them, sir?" he asked.

"Sufficient, sir," the major said huffily. "I cannot see that it concerns your investigation."

Pitt tried to visualize the figures after the caterpillars in the little book, but there had been so many of them, more caterpillars than anything else, and he could not remember them all.

"I do need to know, Major. I would prefer to ask you personally than have to discover by some other means."

"Damn you, sir! It is not your business. Inquire as you like!"

Pitt would get nowhere by pressing the point, and he knew it. He would find the figures in the notebook in the column under £350, in line with the beetle, and total all those next to caterpillars. He would then try Major Rodney with that sum and observe his reaction.

The major snorted, satisfied with his victory. "Now, if that is all, Inspector?"

Pitt debated whether to insist on seeing the Misses Rodney now and decided there was little to learn from them. He could more profitably go and question the other person who had bought a Jones portrait, Lady St. Jermyn. He accepted the major's dismissal and, a quarter of an hour later was standing rather uncomfortably in front of Lord St. Jermyn.

"Lady St. Jermyn is not at home," he said coolly. "Neither of us can help you any further with the affair. It would be best left, and I counsel you to do so from now on."

"One cannot leave murder, my lord," Pitt said tartly. "Even did I wish to."

St. Jermyn's eyebrows rose slightly, not surprise so much as contempt. "What has made you suddenly believe that Augustus was murdered? I suspect a prurient desire to inquire into the lives of your betters."

Pitt ached to be equally rude; he could feel it like a beat in his head. "I assure you, sir, my interest in other people's personal lives is purely professional." He made his own voice as precise and as beautiful as St. Jermyn's, coolly caressing the words. "I have no liking either for tragedy or for squalor. I prefer private griefs to remain private, where public duty permits. And as far as I know, Lord Augustus died naturally—but Godolphin Jones was unmistakably strangled."

St. Jermyn stood absolute still; his face paled and his eyes widened very slightly. Pitt saw his hands clasp each other hard. There was a moment's silence before he spoke.

"Murdered?" he said carefully.

"Yes, sir." He wanted to let St. Jermyn say all he would, not lead him and make his answers easy by suggesting them. The silence was inviting.

St. Jermyn's eyes stayed on Pitt's face, watching him, almost as if he were trying to anticipate.

"When did you discover his body?" he asked.

"Yesterday evening," Pitt answered simply.

Again St. Jermyn waited, but Pitt did not help him. "Where?" he said at last.

"Buried, sir."

"Buried?" St. Jermyn's voice rose. "That's preposterous! What do you mean 'buried'? In someone's garden?"

"No, sir, properly buried, in a coffin in a grave in a churchyard."

"I don't know what you mean!" St. Jermyn was growing angry. "Who would bury a strangled man? No doctor would sign a certificate if the man was strangled, and no clergyman would bury him without one. You are talking nonsense." He was ready to dismiss it.

"I am relating the facts, sir," Pitt said levelly. "I have no explanation for them, either. Except that it was not his own grave; it was that of one Albert Wilson, deceased of a stroke and buried there in the regular way."

"Well, what happened to this—Wilson?" St. Jermyn demanded.

"That was the corpse that fell off the cab outside the theatre," Pitt replied, still watching St. Jermyn's face. He could see nothing in it but dark and utter confusion. Again for several moments he said nothing. Pitt waited.

St. Jermyn stared at him, eyes clouded and unreadable. Pitt tried to strip away the mask of authority and assurance and see the man beneath—he failed entirely.

"I presume you have no idea," St. Jermyn said at last, "who killed him?"

"Godolphin Jones? No, sir, not yet."

"Or why?"

For the first time Pitt overstepped the truth. "That's different. We do have a possible idea as to why."

St. Jermyn's face was still very pale, nostrils flared gently as he breathed in and out. "Oh? And what may that be?"

"It would be irresponsible of me to speak before I have proof." Pitt evaded it with a slight smile. "I might wrong someone, and suspicion once voiced is seldom forgotten, no matter how false it proves to be later."

St. Jermyn hesitated as if about to ask something further,

then thought better of it. "Yes—yes, of course," he agreed. "What are you going to do now?"

"Question the people who knew him best, both professionally and socially," Pitt replied, taking the opening offered. "I believe you were one of his patrons?"

St. Jermyn gave an answering smile, no more than a slight relaxation of the face. "What a curious word, Inspector. Hardly a patron. I commissioned one picture, of my wife."

"And were you satisfied with it?"

"It is acceptable. My wife liked it well enough, which was what mattered. Why do you ask?

"No particular reason. May I see it?"

"If you wish, although I doubt you will learn anything from it. It is very ordinary." He turned and walked out of the door into the hallway, leaving Pitt to follow. The picture was in an inconspicuous place on the stair wall, and, looking at the quality of it compared with the other family portraits, Pitt was not surprised. His eye scanned the face briefly, then went to the left-hand corner. The insect was there, this time a spider.

"Well?" St. Jermyn inquired with a touch of irony in his voice.

"Thank you, sir." Pitt came down the stairs again to stand level with him. "Do you mind telling me, sir, how much you paid for it?"

"Probably more than it's worth," St. Jermyn said casually. "But my wife likes it. Personally, I don't think it does her justice, do you? But then you wouldn't know; you haven't met her."

"How much, sir?" Pitt repeated.

"About four hundred and fifty pounds, as far as I can remember. Do you want the precise figure? It would take me some time to find it. Hardly a major transaction!"

The vast financial difference between them was not lost on Pitt.

"Thank you, that will be near enough." He dismissed it without comment.

St. Jermyn smiled fully for the first time. "Does that further your investigations, Inspector?"

"It may do, when compared with other information." Pitt walked on to the front door. "Thank you for your time, sir."

When he got home, cold and tired, Pitt was welcomed by the fragrance of steaming soup and dry laundry hanging from the ceiling. Jemima was already asleep, and the house was silent. He took his wet boots off and sat down, letting the calm wash over him, almost as capable of being felt with body as was the heat. For several minutes Charlotte said no more than a welcome, an acknowledgment of his presence.

When at last he was ready to talk, he put down the soup bowl she had given him and looked across at her.

"I'm making noises as if I knew what I was doing, but honestly, I can't see sense in any of it," he said with a gesture of helplessness.

"Whom have you questioned?" she asked, wiping her hands carefully and picking up an oven cloth before opening the door and reaching in for a pie. She pulled it out and put it quickly on the table. The crust was crisp and pale gold, a little darker in one corner, in fact, perilously close to burnt.

He looked at it with the beginning of a smile.

She saw him. "I'll eat that corner!" she said instantly.

He laughed. "Why does it do that? Scorch one corner!"

She gave him a withering look. "If I knew that, I would prevent it!" She turned out the vegetables smartly and watched the steam rise with appreciation. "Whom have you seen about this artist?"

"Everyone in the Park who has portraits by him—why?"

"I just wondered." She lifted the carving knife and held it in the air, suspended over the pie while she thought. "We had an artist paint a picture of Mama once, and another for Sarah. They were both full of compliments, told Sarah she was beautiful, made all sorts of outrageously flattering remarks; said she had a quality of delicacy about her like a Bourbon rose. She floated round insufferably with her head

158

in the air, looking sideways at herself in all the mirrors for weeks."

"She was good-looking," he replied. "Although a Bourbon rose is a little extravagant. But what is the point you are making?"

"Well, Godolphin Jones made his money by painting pictures of people, which in a way is the ultimate vanity, isn't it, having your face immortalized? Maybe he flattered them all like that? And if he did, I would imagine a fair few of them responded, wouldn't you?

Suddenly he perceived. "You mean an *affaire*, or several *affaires*? A jealous woman who imagined she was something unique in his life and discovered she was merely one of many, and that the sweet images were just part of his professional equipment? Or a jealous husband?"

"It's possible." She lowered her knife at last and cut into the pie. Thick gravy bubbled through, and Pitt totally forgot about the scorched piece.

"I'm hungry," he said hopefully.

She smiled up at him with satisfaction. "Good. Ask Aunt Vespasia. If it was anyone in the Park, I'll bet she knows, and if she doesn't, she will find out for you."

"I will," he promised. "Now, please get on with that and forget about Godolphin Jones."

But the first person he saw the following day was Somerset Carlisle. By now, of course, everyone in the Park knew of the discovery of the body, and he no longer had any element of surprise.

"I didn't know him very well," Carlisle said mildly. "Not much in common, as I dare say you know? And I certainly had no desire to have my portrait done."

"If you had," Pitt said slowly, watching Carlisle's face, "would you have gone to Godolphin Jones?"

Carlisle's expression dropped a little in surprise. "Why on earth does it matter? I'm a bit late now, anyway."

"Would you?"

Carlisle hesitated, considering. "No," he said at length. "No, I wouldn't."

Pitt had expected that. Charlotte had said Carlisle had spoken slightingly of Jones as an artist. He would have contradicted himself had he praised him now.

Pitt pursued it. "Overrated, would you say?"

Carlisle looked levelly at him; his eyes were dark gray and very clear. "As a painter, yes, Inspector, I would say so. As an admirer and companion, possibly not. He was quite a wit, very even-tempered, and had learned the not inconsiderable art of suffering fools graciously. It is difficult to command more than you are worth for long."

"Isn't art something of a fashion?" Pitt inquired.

Carlisle smiled, still meeting his eyes without a flicker.

"Certainly. But fashions are frequently manufactured. Price feeds upon itself, you know. Sell one thing expensively, and you can sell the next even more so."

Pitt took the point, but it did not answer the question as to why anyone should strangle Godolphin Jones.

"You mentioned other forms of worth," he said carefully. "Did you mean purely as a companion, or perhaps more—as a lover in an *affaire*—or even several?"

Carlisle's face remained impassive, amused. "It might be worth your while to investigate the possibility. Discreetly, of course, or you will rouse a lot of ill feeling that will rebound upon yourself."

"Naturally," Pitt agreed. "Thank you, sir."

Discretion began with Aunt Vespasia.

"I was expecting you yesterday," she said with slight surprise in her voice. "Where can you start? Is there anything you know about this wretched man? So far as I have heard, he had nothing to do with Augustus, and Alicia was one of the few beauties, or imagined beauties, around the Park that he did not paint. For goodness' sake, man, sit down; you give me a crick in my neck looking at you!"

Pitt obeyed. He still did not care to take the liberty of making himself comfortable before he was invited. "Was he a good artist?" he asked. He would value her opinion.

"No," she said baldly, "Why?"

"Charlotte said as much."

160

She looked at him a little sideways, her eyes narrowed. "Indeed. And what do you draw from that? You are trying to say something—what is it?"

"Why do you think he was able to charge so much, and get it?" he asked frankly.

"Ah." She leaned back a little, and a very small smile curved her mouth. "Portrait artists who paint society women have to be courtiers as well, in fact, possibly even courtiers first. The best of them can afford to paint as they please, but the others must paint to suit whoever holds the purse strings. If they have the skill, they flatter with the brush; if not, they must do it with the tongue. Some even do both."

"And Godolphin Jones?"

Her eyes flickered with amusement. "You have seen his work yourself—and you must know it was with his tongue."

"Do you suppose it went further than flattery?" He was not sure if she would be affronted by his assuming such a possibility and asking it so bluntly. But, on the other hand, there was no point in being evasive with her, and he was too weary of the case and confused to be subtle.

She was silent for so long he began to be anxious she was offended. Then at last she spoke, choosing her words.

"You are asking me if I know of anyone having an *affaire* with Godolphin Jones. I suppose if I do not tell you, you will have to pursue it yourself? I had rather tell you; I imagine that will be the least painful. Yes, Gwendoline Cantlay had an *affaire*. It was nothing serious, a relief from boredom of a pleasant but growingly uninterested husband; certainly not a grand passion. And she was extremely discreet about it."

"Do you know if Sir Desmond knew of it?"

She considered for a moment before replying.

"I should think he guessed but was tactful enough to look the other way," she said at length. "I find it very hard indeed to believe he would have killed the wretched little man over it. One does not react in such a way, unless one is completely unhinged."

161

Pitt had no understanding; he simply had to accept that she knew. He could not conceive of what his own behavior might have been had he discovered Charlotte in such a squalid involvement. It would shatter everything he cared about, desecrate and overturn all that was precious within him and held him islanded against daily wretchedness he saw. It was not beyond his imagination that he would strangle the man: the more so if it were merely part of his professional repertoire, and she were one of any number.

Vespasia was looking at him, perhaps reading something of what was going through his mind.

"You must not judge Desmond Cantlay by yourself," she said quietly. "But investigate the possibility, if you must. I suppose as late as this you cannot say when he was killed?"

"No; approximately three to four weeks ago, but that is hardly any use for establishing anyone's whereabouts to prove him innocent or guilty. I should imagine he was killed shortly after the last time his servants saw him, which was three weeks ago last Tuesday. But even that is not proven. We don't even know where he was killed yet."

"You seem to know remarkably little," she said grimly. "Don't go seeking your information by spreading suspicions. Maybe Desmond didn't know it. And doubtless, since it is a tool of his trade, Jones used it quite regularly."

Pitt frowned. "Probably. But would he dare with Lady St. Jermyn?" He pictured that dark head with its severe silver streak. There was a remarkable dignity about her. It would have been a brash artist indeed who had tried to soften her with over-flattery.

Vespasia's eyes widened very slightly, but her expression was beyond his reading.

"No," he said simply. "Nor with the Misses Rodney, I suspect!"

The idea of an *affaire* with the Misses Rodney was ridiculous, but few people are impervious to flattery, and perhaps Jones had been skilled enough when he wished.

"I'll have to find his other subjects," he agreed. "I have a list from the butler." He wanted to ask her more; in fact, he had a vague impression that she knew something that deliberately she was not telling him. A shield for Gwendoline Cantlay or for someone else? Surely not Alicia again? Or worse than that, Verity? There was no point in asking. It would only offend her.

He stood up. "Thank you, Lady Cumming-Gould. I appreciate your help."

She looked at him dubiously. "Don't be sarcastic with me, Thomas. I have been of uncommonly little help, and you know it. I have no idea who killed Godolphin Jones, but whoever it was, I have some sympathy with him. But I am really only marginally interested in the whole affair. It is a pity he could not have remained decently buried in the butler's grave. The parliamentary bill is a great deal more important than the death of one opinionated and indifferent little artist. Do you have any conception of what it could mean in the lives of thousands of children in this wretched city?"

"Yes, ma'am, I have," he said, equally soberly. "I have been in the workhouses and the sweatshops. I have arrested starving five-year-olds already schooled in thieving, and knowing of nothing else."

"I apologize, Thomas." She was unused to retreat, but this time she meant it.

He knew it. He smiled at her, brilliantly, honestly, and for an instant they were equals. Then it vanished. She rang the bell, and the butler showed Pitt to the door.

But there was something nagging at his mind, and, rather than take out the butler's list, he hailed a cab and traveled for more than two miles before alighting, paying the driver, and climbing a dingy staircase up to a small room that had a great south-facing window and an even greater skylight. A scruffy little man with enormous eyes looked up at him.

"Hello, Froggy," Pitt said cheerfully. "Can you spare me a few minutes?"

The man looked at him skeptically. "I ain't got nothing as I oughtn't to. You got no right to look!"

"I'm not looking, Froggy. I want your advice."

"And I ain't ratting on no one!"

"Your artistic advice," Pitt elaborated. "On the worth of a perfectly legitimate picture. Or, to be more precise, an artist."

"Who?"

"Godolophin Jones."

"No good. Don't touch it. But 'e's bleedin' hexpensive. Where d'you get that kind o' money? You bin takin' bribes, or suffink? D'you know what 'e sells for—four or five 'undred nicker a time, or near enough."

"Yes, I do know that, and I won't press you to tell me how you know. Why does he sell that highly, if he's no good?"

"Oh, now there you 'as one o' life's mysteries. I dunno."

"Maybe you're wrong, and he is good?"

"Now, there's no need to be rude, Mr. Pitt! I know my business. Couldn't sell one o' them Joneses, not if I was to give you a chicken with each one. People as buy from me wants suffink as they can keep for a while; then, when nobody's lookin' for it anymore, ship it out to some collector what ain't too choosy as to 'ow they come by fings. No collector wants a Jones. You ask why they pays so 'igh—maybe it's vanity? Don't understand the Quality, never 'ave—and you're wastin' your time if you thinks you can. They're a different sort of animal from you and me. No knowin' what they'll do, or why. Except I can tell you this—that Joneses never change 'ands; nobody sells 'em 'cos nobody buys 'em. Now, that's a rule, that is—if it's worth buying, somewhere, sometime, somebody's goin' to sell it!"

"Thank you, Froggy."

"That all?"

"Yes, thank you, that's all."

"Does it 'elp?"

"I've no idea. But I think I'm glad to know it all the same."

On his return to the police station before the end of the day, Pitt was greeted by the sergeant who had previously met him with news of one corpse after another. His heart sank as soon as he saw the wretched man's face flushed with excitement again.

164

"What is it?" he snapped.

"That plate, sir, the photographic plate from the dead artist's house."

"What about it?"

"You sent it to be developed, sir." He was practically fidgeting in his fever.

"Naturally——" Sudden hope seized Pitt. "What was on it? Tell me, man, don't stand there!"

"A picture, sir, of a naked woman, naked as a babe, but nothing like a babe, if you get my meaning, sir?"

"Where is it?" Pitt demanded furiously. "What have you done with it?"

"It's in your office, sir, in a brown envelope, sealed."

Pitt strode past him and slammed the door. With shaking fingers he picked up the envelope and tore it open. The photograph was as the constable had said, an elegant but highly erotic pose of a woman without a shred of clothing. The face was perfectly clear. He had never seen her before, either in life or in paint. She was a total stranger.

"Damn!" he said fiercely. "Damnation!"

Pitt spent the next day trying to discover the identity of the woman in the photograph. If she was a person of social standing at all, the picture alone was motive for murder. He gave the sergeant a copy and had him try all the police stations in the inner city to see if anyone recognized her, and he took another copy himself, this time with the body carefully blocked out, to see if anyone in society knew her. She did not have to be a lady; even a maid, seeking to make a little money on the side with such things, would lose not only her present employment but any hope of future employment with all its security, clothes, regular meals, companionship, and certain status of belonging. That, too, could be cause for murder.

Of course, he went back to Vespasia.

She hesitated a long time before replying, weighing her answer so carefully he was more than half prepared for a lie.

"She reminds me of someone," she said slowly, her head a little to one side, still considering it. "The hair is not right; I seem to feel it was done differently, if indeed I do know her. And perhaps it was a little darker.''

"Who is it?'' he demanded, impatience boiling inside him. She might actually have the last clue to murder on the back of her tongue, and she was havering like a nervous bride.

She shook her head. "I don't know—I just feel a certain familiarity.''

He let out his breath in a sigh of exasperation.

"There's no use trying to goad me, Thomas,'' she replied. "I am an old woman—''

"Rubbish!'' he snapped. "If you are going to plead infirmity of mind—I'll charge you with perjury!''

She smiled at him bleakly. "I do not know who it is, Thomas. Perhaps it is someone's daughter, or even someone's maid. Maybe I have normally seen that face under a lace cap? Hair makes a lot of difference, you know. But if I see her again, I shall send a messenger to you within the hour. You said you found this photograph in Godolphin Jones's house, in his camera? Why is it so important?'' She glanced at the picture still in her hand. "Is the rest of it indecent? Or is there some other person in it? Or perhaps both?''

"It is indecent,'' he replied.

"Indeed.'' She raised her eyebrows a little and handed it back to him. "Motive for murder then. I presumed so. Poor creature.''

"I must know who it is!''

"I appreciate your desire,'' she said calmly. "You have not need to reinforce it.''

"If everyone were to go around murdering witnesses to indiscretion—'' He was frustrated almost beyond the stretch of his temper. He was now nearly sure she was concealing something from him, if not knowledge, at least strong suspicion.

She cut across him. "I do not approve of murder, Thomas,'' she said staring up at him. "If I remember who it is, I shall say so.''

He had to be content with that. He knew perfectly well she

would say no more. He took his leave with as much grace as he could muster and went out into the thickening fog.

He spent most of the rest of the day inquiring, with the picture in his hand, but no one else was prepared to admit having known the woman, and by dusk he was cold, his legs and feet ached, there was a blister on his heel, and he was hungry and thoroughly miserable.

Then, as the fourth hansom cab passed him without stopping and left him islanded under the gas lamp in a sea of icy vapor, he had a sudden idea. He had temporarily forgotten all about the other corpses, presuming them incidental. They had all died naturally; only Godolphin Jones was murdered. But perhaps there was some bizarre connection? Horatio Snipe had been a procurer of women. Could his clientele have included Godolphin Jones—either for his own appetite or as subjects to photograph? Perhaps that was his particular fetish—lewd photography.

He ran out into the street, shouting at the next cab as it approached, and reluctantly it pulled to a halt.

"Resurrection Row!" he bellowed at the driver.

The man pulled a fearsome face but wheeled his horse round and started back, muttering angrily under his breath about darkness and graveyards, and what he hoped would happen to residents of such places if they hired cabs they could not pay for.

Pitt almost fell out at the other end, shoving coins at the alarmed driver, and strode down along the barely lit pavement to find number fourteen, where Horrie Snipe's widow lived.

He had to knock and shout loudly enough to make a nuisance and send windows opening along the street with cries of abuse before she came to the door.

"All right!" she said furiously. "All right!" She opened it and glared at him; then, as she recognized him, her expression changed. "What do you want?" she said incredulously. " 'Orrie's dead, and buried twice! You oughta know that! It was you w'ot came wiv 'im the second time. Don't say someone's dug 'im up again?"

"No, Mazie, everything's fine. Can I come in?"

167

"If you 'ave to. What do you want?"

He squeezed in past her. The room was small, but there was a fire burning strongly, and it was much cleaner than he would have expected. There was even rather a good pair of candlesticks on the mantel shelf, polished pewter, and lace antimacassars over the backs of the chairs.

"Well?" she demanded impatiently. "I ain't got nuffink in 'ere as isn't mine—if that's what you're thinking!"

"It wasn't what I was thinking." He pulled out the picture. "Do you know her, Maizie?"

She took it between her finger and thumb gingerly. "An' what if I do?"

"There's ten shillings in it for you," he said rashly. "If you give me her name and where I can find her."

"Bertha Mulligan," she said, without hesitation. "Lodges with Mrs. Cuff, down at number one thirty-seven, straight down on the left-'and side. But you won't find 'er at 'ome this time o' the evening. I shouldn't wonder. Beginning work about now."

"Doing what?"

She gave a snort of disgust at his stupidity for asking. "On the streets, o' course. Probably up in one of them cafés near the 'Aymarket. Good-lookin' girl, Bertha."

"I see. And does Mrs. Cuff have other lodgers?"

"If you mean does she run an 'ouse, then I says go and look for yourself. I don't talk about me neighbors, same as I don't expect no gossip about me, nor poor 'Orrie, when 'e was alive."

"I see. Thank you, Maizie."

"Where's my ten bob?"

He fished in his pocket and brought out string, a knife, sealing wax, three pieces of paper, a packet of toffees, two keys, and about a pound's worth of change. He counted out ten shillings for her, reluctantly; it had been a promise made in the heat of discovery. But her hand was out, and there was no going back on it. She snatched it, checking it minutely.

"Thank you." She closed her grip on it like a dying man's and put it into the reaches of her underskirts. "That's Bertha, all right. Why do you want to know?"

"Her picture was found in a dead man's house," he replied.

"Murdered?"

"Yes."

"Who was it, then?"

"Godolphin Jones, the artist." She might not have heard of him. Probably she could not read, and the murder would be of little interest in this quarter.

She did not seem in the least surprised.

"Stupid girl," she said imperturbably. "I told 'er not to go posin' for 'im; better to stick to what she knows. But not 'er, would try to better 'erself. Greedy, she was. I never like things on paper, meself; only leads to trouble."

He grabbed at her arm without thinking, and she pulled away sharply.

"You knew she posed for Godolphin Jones?" he demanded, holding onto her.

"Of course I did!" she snapped. "Do you take me for a fool? I know what goes on in that shop of 'is!"

"Shop! What shop?"

"That shop of 'is a number forty-seven, of course, where 'e takes all the photographs and sells them. Disgusting, I calls it. I can understand a man who wants a girl and can't get one for 'isself, like what 'Orrie used to provide for; but one what gets 'is fun out o' lookin' at pictures, now that's what I call un'ealthy!"

A flood of understanding washed over Pitt, and a whole world of possibilities opened.

"Thank you, Maizie." He clasped her hand with a warmth that positively alarmed her. "You are a jewel among women, a lily growing in a rubbish yard. May heaven reward you!" And he turned and charged out of the door into the thick darkness of Resurrection Row, crowing with delight.

9

ALICIA FIRST HEARD of the death of Godolphin
Jones from Dominic. He had spent a morning with Somerset Carlisle, going over the names of those they could count
on to support them when the bill came before the House in
a few days' time, and the news had come, whispered from
servant to servant around the Park. Carlisle's kitchen maid
had been keeping company with Jones's footman and had
been among the first to hear.

Dominic arrived at the Fitzroy-Hammond house before
luncheon, looking breathless and a little white. He was
shown straight into the room where Alicia was writing letters.

As soon as she saw him, she knew something else was
wrong. The joy she had expected to feel evaporated, and
she was aware only of anxiety.

"What is it?"

He did not take her hands as usual. "They found the body
of Godolphin Jones this morning. He was murdered." He
made no attempt to tell her gently or evade the unpleasantness. Perhaps association with Somerset Carlisle and the
workhouse in Seven Dials had made such qualities ridiculous, even an offense against reality. "He was strangled to
death about three or four weeks ago," he went on, "and

170

buried in someone else's grave—the man who fell off the cab and you first thought was Augustus. He turned out to be someone's butler.''

She was stunned, bemused by the rapidity of fact after fact, all new and jarringly ugly. She had never even thought of Godolphin Jones as having anything to do with the corpses. In fact, since Augustus was buried again, she had tried to dismiss the whole matter from her thoughts. Dominic was far more important, and over the last week her feelings about him had been becoming gradually less complete, tinged with an unhappiness, or perhaps an anxiety, that she had tried alternately to resolve or to put from her mind. Now she simply stared at him.

''Naturally, they'll be looking in the Park,'' he went on.

She was still confused, not understanding him.

''Why? Why should anyone in the Park kill him?''

''I don't know why anyone at all should kill him,'' he said a trifle tersely. ''But since you cannot strangle yourself, even by accident, obviously someone did.''

''But why here?'' she persisted.

''Because he lived here, and Augustus lived here, and Augustus's corpse turned up here.'' He sat down suddenly. ''I'm sorry. It's wretched. But I had to warn you because Pitt is bound to come. Did you know him—Godolphin Jones?'' He looked up at her.

''No, not really. I met him once or twice; he was socially acquainted. He seemed pleasant enough. He painted Gwendoline, and Hester, you know. And I believe all three of the Rodneys.''

''He didn't paint you?'' he asked, frowning a little.

''No, I didn't really care for his work. And Augustus never expressed any wish for a portrait.'' She turned away a little and moved closer to the fire. She was thinking of the murder, but it seemed very impersonal. No one she knew appeared to be involved; no one was threatened by an investigation. She remembered how terrified she had been when it had been Augustus—afraid other people would suspect her, then even worse, that they would suspect Dominic. To begin with, the idea had been something outside herself, outside both of them, and she had felt they stood together facing an undeserved suspicion from those whose ignorance or malice would eventually be proved wrong.

Then the old woman had sowed seeds in her mind of doubt that the circle was really so simple. Assuredly, there was the circle that enclosed both of them in a common motive and held them apart from others; but there was also another circle that enclosed her alone, and it was a double barrier. She was ashamed and frightened by it—but the thought had crept into her mind that Dominic might have killed Augustus. The old woman had said he did, and she had not brought the whole heart, the absolute conviction to denying it that she would have wished, indeed, expected. There was a streak in him, a childlike reaching for his wants, that had allowed her to believe it possible, even if only for an instant.

How well did she know him? She turned away from the fire to look at him now. He was still as handsome, with the elegant head and shoulders, the way the hair grew on his neck, strong, neatly curved to the nape. His face was the same, the lines of his smile, But how much more was there? What did he think, behind the face? Did she know those things, and did she love them, too?

When she looked at her own face in the glass, she saw even features, fine hair. When she moved closer, in the morning light, she saw all the tiny flaws, but she also knew how to disguise them. The whole was pleasing, even beautiful. Did Dominic see any more than that? Did he see the flaws and still love her, or would they disturb him, even repel him because it was not what he had looked for, believed in?

All he knew was the careful face she presented to him; her best. And perhaps she was at fault for that. She had taken so much trouble to hide all the other facets, the weaknesses and failings, because she wanted him to love her.

Had he wondered if she had killed Augustus? Was that why he had been cooler lately and so absorbed in this bill of

Carlisle's, not sharing it with her? She could have helped! She had every bit as many connections as he, in fact, more! If he had trusted her, felt that unity she believed was love, then he would have told her how he felt, what fear or pity Seven Dials had stirred in him. He would have tried to explain the confusion, in terms not of social wrong but of his own emotions.

He was looking at her now, waiting.

"I don't suppose it has anything to do with us," she said at last. "If Mr. Pitt comes here I shall see him, of course, but I cannot tell him anything of value." She smiled, the nervousness all gone. Her stomach was as calm as sleep. They both knew what had happened, and it was a kind of release, like silence after a crescendo of music, too long and too loud—now she was back to reality again. "Thank you for coming. It was kind of you to tell me. It is always easier to learn of bad news from a friend than a stranger."

He stood up very slowly. For a moment she thought he was going to argue, to try to pull back the threads; but he smiled, and for the first time they looked at each other without pretense or the delusionary quickening of the heart, the flutter, the urgent breath.

"Of course," he said quietly. "Perhaps it will be solved before it needs to trouble us. Now I must go and see Fleetwood. The bill comes up very soon now."

"I know several people I might approach," she said quickly.

"Do you?" His face was keen, Jones forgotten. "Would you ask them? Anything you want to know, call on Carlisle; he'll be terribly grateful."

"I have already written a few letters—"

"That's marvelous! You know, I think we really have a chance!"

After he had gone she felt a loneliness, but it was not a painful, anxious thing as it used to be, a longing to know when he would return, worrying about all she had said and done, whether she had been foolish, or too cold, or too forward, wondering what he felt, or thought of her. This was more like the emptiness of a summer morning when the whole sky is clear with the day before you, and you have no obligations and no idea what you intend to do.

The morning after he had spoken to Maizie Snipe, Pitt was back in Resurrection Row with a constable and a warrant to search the premises of number forty-seven.

It was what he had expected, a photographic studio complete with all the props necessary for rather glossy pornography: colored lights, animal skins, a few lengths of fabric of various vivid dyes, headdresses of feathers, strings of beads, and an enormous bed. The walls were covered with very skilled and very varied photographs, all of them highly erotic.

"Cor!" The constable breathed out tremulously, not sure what emotion he dare express. His eyes were as round as boiled sweets, and twice as glazed.

"Precisely," Pitt agreed. "A flourishing business, I should say. Before you disturb anything, look at everything very carefully and see if you can see any marks of blood, or evidence of violence. He may well have been killed here. I should think there are a couple of hundred motives hanging on these walls or stuffed in the drawers."

"Oh!" The constable stood motionless, appalled by the thought.

"Get on with it," Pitt urged. "We've a lot to do. When you've searched everything, start putting those photographs in order; see how many different faces we've got."

"Oh, Mr. Pitt, sir! We're never going to try and identify all them lot! It'll take years! And who's going to admit to it, anyway? Can you see any young girl saying 'Yes, that's me'? I ask you!"

"If it's her face in the picture, she can't very well argue, can she?" Pitt pointed to the far corner and jerked his head expressively. "Get on with it!"

"My wife'd have a fit if she knew I was doing this!"

"Then don't tell her," Pitt said sharply. "But I'll have one if you don't, and I'm much more of a force to be reckoned with than she is!"

The constable pulled a face and squinted at the photographs with one eye.

"Don't you believe it, sir," he said, but he obeyed and within a few minutes had discovered marks of blood on the floor and on an overturned stool. "This is where 'e was killed, I reckin," he said decisively, pleased with himself. "See it plain, if you know where to look. Reckin 'e was likely 'it with this." He touched the stool.

It was after the examination and the measuring that Pitt left the constable to begin the immense task of sorting the photographs to identify the girls. It was for Pitt to consider the other half of the trade—the clients. Naturally, Jones was more discreet than to write down names of those who might be sensitive, even violent, about their association, but Pitt thought he knew at least where he might begin: with the book of numbers and insects from Jones's desk in his house. He had seen four of those elegant little hieroglyphics on pictures in Gadstone Park. Now he would go and question their owners, Perhaps they held an explanation to at least one mystery: why anyone should pay so highly for the work of an artist that was at best of very moderate talent.

He began with Gwendoline Cantlay, and this time he came to the point after only the briefest of preliminaries.

"You paid a great deal of money for your portrait by Mr. Jones, Lady Cantlay."

She was cautious, already sensing something beyond trivial enquiry. "I paid the usual price, Mr. Pitt, as I think you will discover if you look a little further."

"The usual price for Mr. Jones, ma'am," he agreed. "But not usual for an artist of his rather indifferent quality."

Her eyebrows rose in disbelief. "Are you an art expert, Inspector?" she said heavily.

"No, but I have opportunity to counsel with experts, ma'am, and they seem to be agreed that Godolphin Jones was not worth anything like the prices he received here in the Park."

She opened her mouth and began a question, then stopped. "Indeed. Perhaps art is only a matter of taste, after all."

This was a scene he had played out so many times and always disliked. Secrets were almost always a matter of vulnerability, an attempt to hide or reject a hurt of some sort.

But he had no alternative. Plastering over truth was not his job, even though he would like it to have been.

"Are you sure, ma'am, that he was not selling something else with his painting—perhaps discretion?"

"I don't know what you mean." It was the standard response, and he could almost have said it for her. She was going to resist as long as possible, make him spell out his knowledge.

"Were you not at one time fonder of Mr. Jones than you would wish known, Lady Cantlay—especially, say, by your husband?"

Her face flushed scarlet, and it was several painful seconds before she could decide what to say to him, whether to continue to deny it, or if anger would help. In the end she recognized the certainty in his face and gave in.

"I was extremely foolish, carried away by the glamour of an artist, I suppose—and flattered—but it is all past, Inspector, some time ago. And yes, you are correct. I did commission the picture before my—relationship—and then paid rather more for it when it was completed, to insure his silence. I would not have accepted it for such an amount, otherwise." She hesitated, and he waited for her. "I—I would be obliged if you would not discuss it with my husband. He does not know of it."

"Are you quite sure?"

"Oh, yes, of course I am! He would be—" All the color drained from her skin. "Oh! Godolphin was murdered! You cannot think Desmond—I assure you, I give you my most absolute word—that he did not know! He could not have. It was all most discreet—only when I went to sit for my portrait—" She did not know what else to say to convince him, and she cast around for some form of proof.

It was against all his convictions to feel sorry for her, and yet he did. They had nothing in common, and her behavior had been self-indulgent and thoughtless, but he found that he did believe her and had no wish to prolong her fear.

"Thank you, Lady Cantlay. If he did not know of the matter, he would have had no cause to wish Mr. Jones any harm, so far as we know. I appreciate your candor. The subject need not be raised again." He stood up. "Good day."

She was too relieved to say anything but a faint, automatic "good day" in return.

Pitt called next on Major Rodney, and here his reception was totally different, wiping away every trace of the rather ebullient feeling with which he had left the Cantlays'. Self-satisfaction disappeared like water down a large sink.

"You are extremely insolent, sir!" the major said furiously. "And I have not the least notion of what you are imagining! This is Gadstone Park, not one of your back streets. I don't know what kind of behavior you are accustomed to, but we know how to conduct ourselves here! And if you persist in suggesting that my sisters have had some sort of liaison with this wretched artist, I shall sue you for slander, do you understand me, sir?"

Pitt tried with difficulty to keep his patience. The idea of Godolphin Jones in a romantic involvement with either of the two elderly jam-making ladies was ridiculous, and in taking refuge behind it, Major Rodney was obscuring the issue very effectively, whether on purpose or not. Pitt doubted him capable of the strategy, but the result was the same.

"I have not suggested anything of the kind, sir," he said as calmly as he was able, but the hard, frayed edges of his temper showed. "Indeed, the possibility had not occurred to me. Both because I would not have considered your sisters to be ladies of a temperament or an age to indulge in such things, nor did I know they had purchased the pictures themselves. I had believed it to be you who had commissioned Mr. Jones?"

The major was temporarily thrown off balance. His cause for outrage had vanished just as he was getting into his stride and all ready to demand that Pitt leave the house.

Pitt pressed home his advantage. "Are the ladies of private property?" he asked. They were both unmarried and could not be heiresses since they had a brother, so it was almost impossible, and he knew it.

The major was growing increasingly redder in the face. "Our financial affairs are not your concern, sir!" he snapped. "I dare say it would seem like wealth to you, but it is merely adequate for us. We do not care to be ostentatious, but we have means, certainly. And that is all I am prepared to say."

"But you did commission two large and expensive picture from Mr. Jones, costing nine hundred seventy-five pounds in total?" Pitt had added up the columns next to the caterpillars and had the satisfaction of seeing the major's face pale and his neck tighten with shock.

"I—I demand to know where you gained such information. Who told you?"

Pitt opened his eyes wider, as if the question were foolish.

"Mr. Jones kept records, sir, very precise records; dates and amounts of payments. I had only to add them up to find the total. It was hardly necessary to trouble anyone else."

The major's body went slack, and he sat like a well-trained child at table, eyes forward, hands still, but no substance inside him. For a long time he was silent, and Pitt hated the necessity for digging out of him whatever wretched secret it was that Jones had blackmailed him with. But there was no alternative. There was no time of the crime to use to eliminate people, no weapon but hands, the strength of which would almost certainly rule out a woman, certainly any society woman. Possibly a servant used to manual work, wringing heavy, wet laundry, might have had the power? At the moment he could think of no avenue except to learn all the truth he could.

The major was a small man, inarticulate, rigidly stiff within himself both bodily and emotionally, but he had been a soldier; he had seen death before and been taught how to kill, had learned to become familiar with the idea and to accept it as part of himself, to know that at times it could be his duty. Was his secret of sufficient importance to him that he would have strangled Godolphin Jones and then buried him in Albert Wilson's grave?

"Why did you pay so much for those two pictures, Major Rodney?" Pitt pressed again.

The major focused his eyes and looked at him with dislike.

"Because that was the man's price," he said coldly. "I am no expert in art. That was what everyone else paid him. If it was excessive, then I was misled. So were we all! The man was a charlatan, if what you say is true. But you will forgive me if I do not accept your opinion as final?" His voice was heavy with sarcasm, and from the weight of his tone, Pitt guessed it an unfamiliar sentiment.

Major Rodney stood up. "And now, sir, I have said all I have to say to you. I wish you good day."

There was no point in struggling, and Pitt knew it. He would have to find out the secret some other way and return when he had more ammunition. Perhaps it was only some foolishness, something Jones had discovered from another patron, possibly an indiscretion with a woman, and Rodney's sense of honor forbade him from saying so. Or maybe it was a genuine matter of shame to him, an incident of cowardice in the Crimea, or some other barrack-room weakness, a gambling debt welched on, or a drunken escapade.

For now he would have to leave it.

In the early afternoon he called on St. Jermyn and found that he was out, at the House of Lords. He was obliged to return in the evening, cold and tired and well past the best of his temper.

His lordship was also irritated at not being able to relax and forget the business of the day over a glass of something from the pick of his cellars before considering dinner. He was civil to Pitt with something of an effort.

"I have already told you everything I know about the man," he said tartly, moving over to the fire. "He was a fashionable artist. I commissioned a picture from him to please my wife. I expect I have met him socially on one or two occasions; after all, he lived here in the Park, but I meet hundreds of people. I recall he was a trifle odd-looking; rather too much hair." He gave Pitt a sour look, his eye going to Pitt's own scruffy head. "But then, one expects artists to be a little affected," he continued. "It was not enough to be offensive, just rather obvious. I'm sorry the fellow is dead, but I dare say he mixed with a few less salubrious people. Possibly he became over-familiar with one of his models. As well as society, artists frequently paint women of far lower classes who happen to have the coloring or the features they want. I imagine you know that as well as I do. I should look for a jealous lover or husband, if I were you."

"We haven't been able to trace any pictures of women other than society portraits," Pitt replied. "He doesn't seem to have been prolific at all; in fact, rather reserved. but anything he did do, he sold at greatly inflated prices."

"So you implied before," St. Jermyn said drily. "I don't have any comment on that. I would have thought portraits needed only to please the sitter. One seldom would wish to resell them. They usually get relegated to a back hallway or stair if one loses one's taste for them; otherwise, they remain wherever they were hung in the first place."

"You paid a considerable amount for the portrait of Lady St. Jermyn," Pitt tried again.

St. Jermyn's eyebrows rose. "You also remarked on that the last time you were here. She seemed to like the picture, which was all that concerned me. If I did pay too much, then I was duped. I'm really not very concerned about it. I don't see why you should be."

Pitt had already racked his brain to think of some reason, any at all, why Jones should have been able to put pressure on St. Jermyn to buy a picture he did not like, or at a price he thought unfair, but he had come up with nothing. To press Lady Cantlay in return for discretion would be easy, and recalling the stiff, nervous figure of the major, that was certainly believable, although he did not yet know the reason. A middle-aged, socially inarticulate man living with two maiden sisters—the probability was obvious—another indiscretion. Pride would force the major to pay for silence.

But St. Jermyn was a totally different man. There was no fear in him. He would cover his indiscretions, if there were any and he cared about them, which again was doubtful.

And there was no other crime that Pitt knew of. Lord Augustus had died normally, or if he had not it was unprovable, and of no interest he knew of to St. Jermyn either way. All the others—Arthur Wilson, Porteous, and Horrie Snipe—had also died naturally and again, as far as Pitt knew, had no connection with St. Jermyn.

"If it was a jealous lover or husband," Pitt said slowly, "why was he found in another man's grave?"

"To hide him, I presume!" St. Jermyn said impatiently "I would have thought that was obvious! A fresh-dug grave anywhere in London except in a graveyard would excite attention pretty quickly. You can't go digging up parks, and if you put it in your own garden it would be damning if it were found. In someone else's freshly turned grave, it would invite no remark at all."

"But why put the corpse of Albert Wilson on a cab box?"

"I really don't know, Inspector! It is your job to find that out, not mine! Possibly there was no reason at all. It sounds the bizarre kind of thing an artist might do. More likely the grave was already robbed, and he merely took an excellent opportunity when it was presented to him."

Pitt had already thought of that for himself, but he was still hoping for a new thread, some error of control, a slip of the tongue that would give him another line to follow.

"Did Lord Augustus Fitzroy-Hammond know Mr. Jones?" he asked as innocently as he could.

St. Jermyn looked at him coldly. "Not so far as I am aware. And if you are suggesting he might have had some sort of *affaire* with one of Jones's models, I think it highly unlikely."

Pitt had to admit to himself it would also be too much of a coincidence if Augustus had first killed Jones and taken advantage of the grave robber's activities to hide him, and then immediately afterwards died himself and become a victim of the same robber. He looked across at St. Jermyn and fancied he saw a perception of the unlikelihood in his face also, and a barely concealed and rapidly growing impatience.

181

Pitt tried to think of something else to ask, anything that might draw more information, but St. Jermyn was not a man who could be manipulated, and Pitt gave in, at least for the time being.

"Thank you, my lord," he said stiffly. "I appreciate your time."

"A matter of duty," St. Jermyn acknowledged drily. "The footman will see you out."

There was nothing to do but accept it with as much grace as possible, and he left the bright room and accompanied the liveried footman to the step and out into the thick, obliterating fog.

Dominic had seldom been so enveloped and excited by anything as he was by St. Jermyn's bill. Now that he had ceased to fight it in his mind and given himself over to it, he found more and more pleasure in Carlisle's company. He was literate, intelligent, and, above all, an enthusiast. He had the rare gift of being able to pursue even the most appalling facts about workhouse conditions without losing his optimism that something could be done to alleviate them, or his ability to find humor, however wry, in the midst of what would otherwise have been despair.

Dominic found it hard to emulate. He had sought out Lord Fleetwood with trepidation and some self-consciousness. The friendship had increased more easily than he had expected; his natural charm was something he always underrated. But he never managed to guide the conversation successfully into the reality of workhouse tragedy. Every time it was acknowledged in words, they rang hollow, like one reciting with perfect pronunciation a language he does not understand.

After two attempts Dominic became more conscious of the urgency and admitted frankly to Carlisle that he needed his help.

Accordingly, the day after, because of the influence Fleetwood might have, Carlisle joined Dominic and Fleetwood in the Park for a spanking drive at a speed that scattered the

182

few pedestrians and sent other drivers and riders into paroxysms of rage or envy, depending upon the strength and direction of their own ambitions.

Dominic had driven, and although it was with a recklessness he would not normally have dared, today he was past caring for anything so trivial as social outrage or a few thrown paraders landed hard upon their dignity on the damp ground.

"Marvelous!" Fleetwood said with delight, catching his breath. "My God, Dominic, you drive like Jehu! I swear I never though you had it in you. If you come and drive my team in the spring, I'll consider it a favor from you."

"Of course," Dominic agreed instantly, his mind on the workhouse, and a trade favor for favor. He would not even consider now how he could find the courage to drive in such a fashion in cold blood, and with weeks to contemplate it beforehand and to fully appreciate all the possible disasters. He thrust it away to some improbable future. "Delighted to!"

"Brilliant," Carlisle agreed, his tongue in his cheek, but Fleetwood did not see it. "You have a natural art, Dominic." He turned to Fleetwood, both their faces red with cold and the fierce wind of their passage. "But you have a very fine team, indeed, my lord. I've seen few better animals. Though I think perhaps the springing of your carriage could be improved a little."

Fleetwood grinned. He was a pleasant young man, not handsome, but of a countenance that spoke of abundant good nature.

"Bounce you around a bit, did it? Never mind, good for the digestion."

"Wasn't thinking of the digestion," Carlisle replied with a smile. "Or the bruises. Rather more of the balance of the thing. A well-balanced carriage is a lot easier on the horses, takes the corners better, and is less likely to overturn if you get some idiot run into you. And of course if you do get an excitable animal, less likely for the whole thing to get away with you."

"Damn, but you're right!" Fleetwood said cheerfully. "Sorry I misjudged you. Sold you short a bit. I'll have to get it seen to. Must have it right."

"I know a chap in the Devil's Acre who can spring a carriage to balance like a bird in flight," Carlisle offered with a casual air as if it were of no interest to him, merely a graceful gesture after an early morning's companionship.

"The Devil's Acre?" Fleetwood said incredulously. "Where the deuce is that?"

"Around Westminster." Carlisle threw it away. Dominic watched him with admiration. If he could have been so light, perhaps he could have interested Fleetwood. He had been too earnest, too full of urgency and the horror of it. No one but a ghoul wanted horror, least of all with breakfast!

"Around Westminster?" Fleetwood repeated. "You mean that awful slum area? Is that what they call it?"

"Appropriate, I would have thought." Carlisle's peaked eyebrows went up. "Filthy place."

"What took you there?" Fleetwood handed the horse over to the groom, and the three of them went together toward the public house where breakfast and a steaming drink awaited them.

"Oh, this and that." Carlisle dismissed it with a wave of his arm, as though it were gentleman's business that any other gentleman would understand and be too discreet to mention further.

"It's slums," Fleetwood said again when they were inside and well started on a rich and excellent meal. "How would anyone there know about balancing and springing a carriage? There isn't room to drive one, let alone race it."

Carlisle finished his mouthful and swallowed. "Used to be an ostler," he said easily. "Stole from his master, or anyway was accused of it, fell on hard times. Simple."

Fleetwood loved and understood horses. He felt a comradeship with those who tended them and were obliged to make a living. He had spent many a companionable hour swapping opinions and tales with his own grooms.

"Poor beggar," he said with feeling. "Maybe he'd be

glad of a job, a few shillings for seeing what he can do to improve that carriage of mine.''

"I should think so," Carlisle agreed. "Always try him, if you like. Moves around a bit, have to catch him soon."

"Good idea, if you'd do me the kindness. Appreciate it. Where do I find him?"

Carlisle smiled broadly. "In the Devil's Acre? You'd never find him alone this side of doomsday. I'll take you."

"I'd be obliged. Sounds an insalubrious spot."

"Oh, it is," Carlisle agreed. "It is, indeed. But skill is often to be found best where it grows the hardest. There is something in Mr. Darwin's idea of survival of the fittest, you know; as long as you count cleverest, strongest, and most cunning as the fittest and don't tangle it up with any moral ideas. Fittest needs to mean fittest to survive, not most virtuous, most patient, most charitable, or of most benefit to the rest of mankind."

Dominic kicked him abruptly under the table and saw his face tweak with pain. He was terrified he would spoil the whole issue by moralizing and lose Fleetwood even now.

"You're saying that the race does go to the swift and the battle to the strong, after all?" Fleetwood took himself another helping of kedgeree.

"No." Carlisle refrained from rubbing his ankle with difficulty, but he did not look at Dominic. "Only that places like the Devil's Acre breed peculiar skills, because without them the poor do not survive. The fortunate can be any kind of a fool and get by, but the unfortunate have to have a use to someone, or they assuredly perish."

Fleetwood screwed up his face. "That seems a little cynical, if I may say so. Still, I would like to see this fellow of yours; you've convinced me he knows what he's doing."

Carlisle smiled, his face suddenly alight with warmth. Fleetwood responded like a flower opening to the sun. He smiled back, and Dominic found himself included in the blithe good fellowship. He felt a little guilty because he knew what Fleetwood had in front of him, but he refused to think of it now. It was a good cause, a necessary one.

He smiled back with equal charm and an almost straight eye.

The Devil's Acre was horrific. In the pall of smoke and fog the great towers of the minster hung over them, their Gothic glory lost in wraiths of vapor. All the bracing air of the Park was stilled and dampened to a chill stagnancy that sat like dead water from the shadows of the towers in the sky, past the pillared and porticoed homes of the rich and business houses, down to the modest dwellings of traders and clerks. Below them was a separate world of its own, a world of creaking, rat-ridden tenements with teeming alleys, of walls that were forever wet and crumbling, of air that was soured by rimed mold. Idlers, beggars, and drunks littered the way.

Carlisle strode through it as though it were nothing to remark.

"Oh, God!" Fleetwood clutched his nose and darted a desperate glance at Dominic, but Carlisle was not waiting. If they were not to lose him they must follow closely— heaven forbid they should become lost in such a hellhole as this!

Carlisle appeared to know where he was going. He picked his way over sleeping drunks under a pile of newspapers, kicked an empty bottle out of the way, and climbed up a flight of rickety stairs. They swayed under his weight, and Fleetwood looked alarmed as Dominic hastened him onto them also.

"Do you think they'll hold?" he asked, knocking his hat askew on the beam above.

"God knows," Dominic replied, stepping past him and going up. A good deal of his mind sympathized with Fleetwood, recalling his own feelings in Seven Dials, which had been less fearful than this. But there was also a strong tide in him that enjoyed it, tasting what Carlisle knew, the passion to alter this world, to force the innocent, the unknowing to look at it, to see and taste all of it, and to care. The emotion inside him was fierce, almost volcanic. He went up the stairs two by two and dived after Carlisle into a fetid mass of rooms where families of tens and dozens sat in the sickly light, carving, polishing, sewing, weaving, or gluing together to make all manner of articles to be sold for a few pence. Children as small as three or four years old sat tied to their mothers by string so they did not wander from work. Every time one of them stopped his labor or fell asleep, the mother would clout him over the head to wake him up and remind him that idle hands made for empty stomachs.

The smell was fearful, a mixture of wet mold, smoke and coal fumes, sewage, and unwashed bodies.

At the far end of the particular tenement they emerged into a dank courtyard that must once have been a mews, and Carlisle stopped and knocked on a cutaway door.

Dominic looked at Fleetwood. His face was pale, and his eyes looked deep and frightened. Dominic guessed he would long ago have run away had he had even the faintest idea which way to go or how to get back to the world he knew. He must have seen things even his nightmares had not conjured up.

The door opened, and a lean, bent little man peered out. He seemed to be lop-shouldered, as if one side of him were longer than the other. It was a moment before he recognized Carlisle.

"Oh, it's you, is it? What do you want this time?"

"A little of your skill, Timothy," Carlisle said with a smile. "For a consideration, naturally."

"What kind of skill?" Timothy demanded, looking suspiciously over Carlisle's shoulder at Dominic and Fleetwood. "Not rozzers, are they?"

"Shame on you, Timothy!" Carlisle said with heavy disgust. "When did you ever know me to keep company with the police?"

"What skill?" Timothy repeated.

"Why, the balancing of fine carriages, of course," Carlisle said with a twist to his face. "His lordship here," he indicated Fleetwood, "has an excellent pair, and a fine chance of winning a few gentlemen's races, private wagers and the like, if he can get his carriage balanced to do justice to them."

187

Timothy's face lit up. "Ah! Course I can do suffink about that! Balancin' makes all the difference. Where's this 'ere carriage, then? You tell me, and I'll fix it for yer to run smooth as a weasel, I will. For a consideration, like?"

"Of course," Fleetwood agreed quickly. "Holcombe Park House. I'll write the address for you—"

"No good, guv—I don't read. Tell me—I remember anything. Reckon it dulls the memory, readin'? Don't do you no good, in the long run. Reckon them as writes down everythin' don't remember their own name, if they keeps it up long enough."

Carlisle never missed a chance. He took this one as a swift bird takes an insect on the wing, with barely a flicker.

"But there's work for men who can read and write, Timothy," he said, leaning on the door. "Regular work, in offices that close in the evening and send you home. Jobs that pay enough money to live on."

Timothy spat. "I'd die of hunger and old age afore I learn to read and write now!" he said in disgust. "Don't know what you want to say a thing like that for!"

Carlisle patted the man's shoulder. "For the future, Timothy," he said quietly. "And for those who don't know how to balance a racing gig."

"There's 'undreds o' thousands what can't read nor write!" Timothy looked at him sourly.

"I know that," Carlisle conceded. "And there are hundreds of thousands who are hungry—in fact, I believe it's roughly one in four in London—but is that any reason why you shouldn't have a good meal, if you can get it?"

Timothy's face screwed up, and he looked at Fleetwood.

Fleetwood rose to the occasion.

"A good meal, all you can eat before you do the job," he promised. "And a guinea afterwards. I'll make a wager—a fiver if I win the first race with it after that—"

"You're on!" Timothy said instantly. "I'll be there for dinner tonight, start work in the morning."

"Good. You can sleep in the stable."

Timothy lifted his scruffy hat in a sort of salute, perhaps a sealing of the bargain, and Carlisle turned to leave again.

Fleetwood repeated the address, with instructions on how to reach it, then ran after Carlisle before he was lost to sight and he found himself marooned in the nightmare place.

They passed through the worst of the rookery again and toppled out into the fine rain of a narrow street almost underneath the shadow of the church.

"Dear God!" Fleetwood wiped his face. "Makes me think of Dante and the gates of hell—what was it written over the cave?"

" 'Abandon hope, all ye who enter here,' " Carlisle said quietly.

"How in the name of humanity do they bear it?" Fleetwood turned up his collar and drove his hands into his pockets.

"It's better than the workhouse," Carlisle replied. "At least they reckon it is. Personally, it seems much the same to me."

Fleetwood stopped. "Better!" he said in broad disbelief. "What are you talking about, man? The workhouse provides food and shelter, safety! It's a charitable place."

All the anger was purged out of Carlisle's face; his voice was a gentle as milk. "Have you ever been to one?"

Fleetwood was surprised. "No," he said honestly. "Have you?"

"Oh, yes." Carlisle started walking again. "I've been working quite hard on this bill of St. Jermyn's. I dare say you've heard of it?"

"Yes," Fleetwood said slowly. "Yes, I have." He did not look at Dominic, and Dominic did not dare to look at him. "I suppose you'd like my help when it comes up in the House?" Fleetwood said casually.

Carlisle flashed him a dazzling smile.

"Yes—yes, please, I would."

Alicia had written to everyone she could think of, recalling a good few of Augustus's relatives who had married well and whom she would never have contacted for any other reason. She found most of them insufferably dull, but the cause overrode all her previous inhibitions.

189

When she had exhausted her imagination on the subject and everything was sealed and in the post, she decided to go for a walk in the Park, in spite of the miserable weather. She had a feeling of good spirits inside her that simply cried for exercise, for the stretching of the body and opening of the lungs. Had it not been so absolutely ridiculous she would have liked to run and skip like a child.

She was striding along in a fashion unbefitting a lady, her head in the air, enjoying the bleak beauty of the trees against the ragged clouds far above. In the Park it was almost still; heavy drops glistened and dripped from twigs. She had never considered February had any loveliness before, but now she took pleasure in the stark simplicity of it, the soft, subdued colors.

She had stopped to watch a bird in branches above her when she was aware of overhearing a conversation immediately the other side of the tree.

"Did you really?" The voice was so soft that she did not at first recognize it.

There appeared to be no answer.

"Come and tell me all about it then," the voice continued.

Again there was silence, except for a faint squeak.

"My, well, how about that! You are a clever girl."

Then she knew it; at least she was almost sure she did. It sounded too soft, too American to be anyone but Virgil Smith.

But whom on earth was he talking to?

"My, you are beautiful! Well, come on now, tell me all about it."

An appalling thought came to her; he must be making advances to some servant or streetwalker! How dreadful! And she had accidentally come upon him. How could she possibly get away without embarrassing them both quite unforgettably? She froze.

Still there was no reply from whomever he was speaking to.

"You pretty thing." He was still talking gently, softly. "You beautiful girl."

She could not stay any longer overhearing a conversation

that was obviously desperately private. She took a step to creep, in the lee of the tree trunk, till she was back on the path and could affect not to have noticed him.

Her foot cracked on a twig, and it broke loudly.

He stood up and came around, enormous in a greatcoat; square, like the tree itself.

Alicia shut her eyes, her face burning up with her distress for him. She was sure it must be scarlet. She would have given anything not to have been witness to his shameful conduct.

"Good morning, Lady Alicia," he said with the softness she had heard in it before.

"Good morning, Mr. Smith," she replied, swallowing hard. She must force herself to carry it off with some aplomb. He was an American and a social impossibility, but she should know how to conduct herself whatever the occasion.

She opened her eyes.

He was standing in front of her, holding a little calico cat that was stretching and curling under his arms. He saw her glazed look and glanced down at the animal, his fingers running gently over its fur. She could hear the little creature singing even from where she was.

The color rose up to his face also when he realized she had overheard him talking to it.

"Oh," he said a little awkwardly. "Don't mind me, ma'am. I often talk to animals, especially cats. I'm kind of fond of this one in particular."

She breathed out a sigh of immense relief. She found she was grinning foolishly, a sudden, bubbling happiness inside her. She stretched out her fingers to touch the cat.

Virgil Smith was smiling, too, a shining tenderness in his face.

For the first time she recognized it and knew what it was. Only for a moment did it surprise her; then it seemed like something familiar, amazing and beautiful, like the leaves bursting open in the milky sunshine of spring.

10

PITT CONSIDERED what might be reasonable, what he might expect to receive, and then requested three additional constables to help him with the enormous task of sorting and identifying the photographs in Godolphin Jones's shop.

He was granted one, along with the one he already had.

He dispatched them both back to Resurrection Row with instructions to find a name for every face, and then an occupation and a social background, but not to allow any part of the picture to be seen other than the head and to ask no questions and to give no information as to where or in what circumstances the photographs had been found. This last instruction had been repeated to him by his superiors with much anxiety and a great deal of hemming and hawing as to whether there might not be some other way of tackling the whole matter. One superintendent even suggested tentatively that perhaps it would be advisable to overlook the tragedy as insoluble and turn their attention to something else. There was, for example, a nasty case of burglary that was still outstanding, and it would be a most useful thing if they could recover the property.

Pitt pointed out that Jones had been a society artist and that anyone who had lived in an area like Gadstone Park could not be murdered and then merely forgotten, or other residents of such areas would feel distinctly uneasy as to their own future safety.

The point was conceded him, unhappily.

Then Pitt himself went back to the Park and Major Rodney. This time he would not be put off by the major's anger or protestations; he could no longer afford to be. If the murderer of Godolphin Jones had taken advantage of the grave robbings to hide his own crime, as St. Jermyn had suggested, then the death of Lord Augustus was irrelevant. There was no point in looking any further for sense or connection between Albert Wilson, Horrie Snipe, W. W. Porteous, and Lord Augustus, because there was none. As far as either motive or means was concerned, the murder of Godolphin Jones stood alone. The key to them surely lay in the pornography shop in Resurrection Row, or in the little book with its hieroglyphic insects, or both.

It was possible the murderer was one of any number of women whose faces were on those photographs, or perhaps someone else he had blackmailed as he had done Gwendoline Cantlay. But surely the number of *affaires* he had had must be severely limited by both time and opportunity. By all accounts he was not an abnormally charming man. He might have flattered liberally, but society beauties were used to that. On the whole, Pitt inclined to think his romantic opportunities slight. The blackmail must lie in other areas as well, which brought Pitt back once again to Resurrection Row and the photographs.

He was at Major Rodney's door. The butler answered and suffered him to enter with the look of weary acceptance of one who is resigned to something unpleasant but inevitable. Pitt had felt the same when toothache had finally driven him to the dentist.

The major received him with ill-concealed impatience.

"I have nothing else to add, Inspector Pitt," he said, waspishly. "If you cannot do better than to go over and over old ground, pestering people, then it would be better if you were to pass the case over to someone more competent. You are making a nuisance of yourself!"

Pitt would not be pressured to apologize. It stuck in his

throat. "Murder is an untidy and annoying business, sir," he replied.

He towered over the major, putting him at a disadvantage. The major waved to a chair and ordered Pitt to sit down. He sat on a straight-backed chair himself, ramrod-stiff, reversing the advantage so now he could look down on Pitt, sprawled in a deep sofa, his coat falling open and his scarf undone in the warmth of the room.

The major's confidence was somewhat restored.

"Well, what is it now?" he demanded. "I have told you that I had very little personal acquaintance with Mr. Jones, no more than civility required, and I have shown you the portraits. I really cannot think of anything else. I am not a man to make other people's business my concern. I do not listen to gossip, and I will not permit my sisters to repeat such as they cannot help overhearing, since it is in the nature of women to talk, mostly upon trivial matters."

Pitt would like to have argued—he could imagine what Charlotte would have said to such a condemnation of women—but the major would not have understood him, and he had no place to discuss such subjects. This was not a friendship and they were not equals; it was not for him to question the major's convictions.

"Indeed," he replied. "Gossip can be a great evil, and much of it is false. Although I have often gained valuable insight into the nature or personality of people by listening to it. What one man says of another may be false, but the fact that he says it at all tells me—"

"That the man is a gossipmonger and a liar to boot!" the major snapped. "I have nothing but contempt for you, or for an occupation which obliges you to indulge in such vices!" He stared at Pitt fiercely, seeming to burn him with indignation.

"Precisely," Pitt agreed. "What a man says may tell nothing of the object of his speech, but it tells a great deal about him."

"What?" The major was startled. It took him several moments to digest Pitt's meaning.

"When you open your mouth you may or may not betray

194

another, but you assuredly betray yourself,'' Pitt repeated. A new thought had come to him, about Major Rodney and his feelings towards women.

''Huh!'' the major snorted. ''Never went in for sophistry. Soldier—all my life. Man for doing things, not sitting around talking about it. Better for you if you'd been in the army, make a man of you.'' He looked at Pitt's clothes, the way he was sitting, and Pitt could almost see in his face the vision of the drill sergeant, the barber, and the parade ground, and the miraculous change that could be wrought in a man. He smiled, blissful that it would never be.

''Of course, there are many women with mischievous tongues,'' Pitt observed, feeding the major the thoughts he wanted. ''And idleness is a schoolmaster of evil.''

The major was again surprised. He had not expected such perception in a policeman, especially this one. ''Quite,'' he agreed. ''That is why I do all I can to see that my sisters are kept occupied. Good, homely tasks, and of course such study as they are capable of, in the care of homes and gardens, and so forth.''

''What about current affairs, or a little history?'' Pitt inquired, leading him gently.

''Current affairs? Don't be foolish, man. Women have neither the interest nor the capacity for such things. And it is unsuitable in them. I see you don't know women very well!''

''Not very,'' Pitt lied. ''I believe you were married, sir?''

The major blinked. He had not anticipated the question. ''I was. My wife died a long time ago.''

''Very unfortunate,'' Pitt commiserated. ''Were you married long?''

''A year.''

''Tragic.''

''All over now. Got over it years ago. Not like getting used to a thing. Hardly knew her, really. I was a soldier— away fighting for my Queen and country. Price of duty.''

''Quite so.'' Pitt did not have to affect pity; he was beginning to feel it like a welling, bitter spring inside him as his idea grew stronger. ''And women are not always the companions one hopes,'' he added.

The major's face sank into lines of quiet reflection, looking back on disillusions. The reality was unpleasing, but the recognition of it gave him a certain satisfaction in having overcome, even a sense of superiority over those who had yet to face it.

"They are different from men," he agreed. "Shallow creatures, for the most; nothing to talk about but fashion, the way they look, and other similar foolishness. Always laughing at nothing at all. A man cannot take much of that, unless he's as big a fool as they are."

The idea crystallized in Pitt's brain. Now was the time to put it to the test. "Extraordinary thing about these bodies," he said casually.

The major's head jerked up. "Bodies? What bodies?"

"Keep turning up." Pitt watched him. "First the man on the cab box, then Lord Augustus, then Porteous, then Horatio Snipe." He saw the major's eye flicker and his Adam's apple move. "Did you know Horrie Snipe, sir?"

"Never heard of him." The major swallowed.

"Are you sure, sir?"

"Do you question my word?"

"Shall we say, your memory, sir?" Pitt hated it, but he had to continue, and the more quickly it was done, the shorter the pain. "He was a procurer of women, and he worked in the Resurrection Row area. The same place Godolphin Jones kept his pornography shop. Perhaps that revives your recollection a bit?" He caught the major's eye and held it in a hard, candid gaze that allowed no retreat, no mercy of pretended ignorance.

The color wavered, then swept up the major's mottled skin. He was ugly and pathetic, hurting Pitt in a way perhaps he did not hurt himself. He could not see how fragile, how unused he looked, how much of him had never grown.

He could find no words. He could not admit it, and he dared no longer deny it.

"Was that what Godolphin Jones was blackmailing you with?" Pitt asked quietly. "He knew about Horrie Snipe's woman, and he sold you photographs?"

The major sniffed. Tears started running down his cheeks,

196

and he was furious with himself for showing weakness, hating Pitt for seeing it.

"I did—I did not kill him!" he said between gulps to control himself. "Before God, I did not kill him!"

Pitt did not doubt it for a moment. The major would never have killed him—he needed him for his private dreams, his pictures and fantasies where he could live out the mastery he could never achieve in life. Jones was doubly precious to him since Horrie Snipe had died just before him, cutting the major off from his brief, wild adventure into the realms of live women.

"No," Pitt said quietly. "I don't suppose you did." He stood up, looking down on the rigid little man, wanting to get out into the fog and drizzle, and escape from the despair inside. "I'm sorry it has been necessary to discuss this. It need not be mentioned again."

The major looked up, his eyes watering. "Your—report?"

"You are not a suspect, sir. That is all I shall say."

The major sniffed. He could not bring himself to thank Pitt.

Pitt let himself out and breathed in the bitter fog with a sense of release, almost of warmth within him.

But it was not a solution. Suddenly the little notebook seemed much less promising. Without searching the drawing rooms of London, he knew of no way of finding all the rest of the pictures that carried the hieroglyphic insects. And there was no proof that the owners were all victims of blackmail, or any other sort of pressure. Possibly they were simply customers for the photographs as well, and Godolphin Jones had chosen this disguised and highly profitable way of collecting his fee. To have his art paid for at such inflated prices was a double reward, because it enhanced his professional reputation in a way his skill never could. Pitt was obliged to admire his ingenuity, if nothing else about him.

But if they were customers for his pornographic pictures, they would be the last people to wish him dead! One did not cut off one's source of supply, especially of something that one desperately wished to be kept secret and that was presumably, in its own way, addictive.

There was, of course, another possibility: a rival in the market. That was a thought that had not occurred to him before. Jones's work was good; at least he had a better eye than most practitioners in the field that Pitt had come across, although admittedly his experience was slight. He had not worked in the vice areas by choice, but it fell to the lot of every policeman now and again. And all the photographs he had seen before had been pathetic and obvious in their banality: portrayals of nakedness, and very little more. These of Jones's had at least some pretensions to art, of a decadent sort. There was a little subtlety in them, a use of light and shade, even a certain wit.

Yes, very possibly some other merchant in the same trade had found himself squeezed out of the market and had rebelled in the only way he knew how; effective—and permanent.

Pitt spent the rest of that day and all the following one questioning his colleagues in all of the stations within three or four miles of either Gadstone Park or Resurrection Row to catch up on whatever was known about current dealers in pornographic pictures. When he finally reached home after seven o'clock and found Charlotte waiting for him a little anxiously, he was beyond giving her an explanation and inside himself blessed her for not asking one. Her silence was the most companionable thing he could think of. He sat all evening in front of the fire without speaking. She was wise enough to occupy herself with knitting, making no sound but the clicking of her needles. He did not wish to relive the squalor he had seen, the twisting of minds and emotions until all affections became mere appetites, and the titillation of those appetites for financial gain. So many sad little people clutching paper women, fornicating in and dominated by fantasies: all flesh and prurient, frightened mind, and no heart at all. And he had learned nothing of use, except that no one knew of a rival with either the need or the imagination to have killed Godolphin Jones and buried him in Albert Wilson's grave.

In the morning he set out again with nothing left but to return to the shop in Resurrection Row and the photographs. The two constables were there when he arrived. Both of them leaped up, red-faced, as he opened the door.

"Oh! It's you, Mr. Pitt," one of them said hastily. "Didn't know who it might be!"

"Does anyone else have a key?" Pitt asked with a twisted smile, holding up the one he had had cut.

"No, sir, not exceptin' us, o' course. But you never know. 'E might 'ave 'ad—" He trailed off; the idea of an accomplice was never likely, and the look on Pitt's face told him it was useless. "Yes, sir." He sat down again.

"We just about got 'em all sorted," his companion said proudly. "I reckon as there's about fifty-three different girls, all told. Lot of 'em 'e used a fair number o' times. I suppose there aren't that many women as can do this sort o' thing."

"And not for long," Pitt agreed, his amusement vanishing. "A few years on the streets, a few children, and you can't strip off in front of the camera any more. Unkind thing, the camera; doesn't tell any comfortable lies. Do you know any of the girls?"

The constable's back went rigid and his ears burned red. "Who, me, sir?"

"Professionally." Pitt coughed. "Your profession, not theirs!"

"Oh." The other constable ran his fingers round his collar. "Yes, sir, I 'ave seen one or two. Cautioned 'em, like. Told 'em to move on, or go 'ome and be'ave theirselves."

"Good." Pitt smiled discreetly. "Put them on one side, with names if you remember them. Then give me the best picture of each, and I'll start checking."

"The best one, sir?" The constable's eyes opened wide, his eyebrows almost to the roots of his hair.

"The clearest face!" Pitt snapped.

"Oh—yes, sir." They both started sorting rapidly and in a few moments handed Pitt about thirty photographs. "That's all we're sure of so far, sir. We should 'ave 'em all by lunchtime."

"Good. Then you can start round the brothels and rooming houses as well. I'll begin in Resurrection Row, going north. You can go south. Be back here by six o'clock, and we'll see what we have.''

"Yes, sir. What are we looking for, sir, really?"

"A jealous lover or husband, or more likely a woman who had a great deal to lose if people found out she posed for this sort of picture."

"Like a society woman?" The constable was dubious, picking up one of the photographs and squinting at it.

"I doubt it," Pitt agreed. "Possibly middle-class, after something a little daring to do, more likely respectable working-class hard up, or a servant with aspirations."

"Right, sir. We'll get this lot sorted and be on our way."

Pitt left them to it and went out into the Row to begin. The first rooming house got rid of three on his list. They were handsome, professional prostitutes who had been glad of the extra money and rather amused by the whole thing. He was about to leave when, on a sudden chance, he decided to show them the rest of the pictures.

"Oh, now, love." A big blond one shook her head at him. "You wouldn't expect me to go around naming other people, would you? What I do meself is one thing, but talkin' about other girls is something else."

"I'm going to find them, anyway," he pointed out.

She grinned. "Then good luck to you, love. You 'ave fun lookin'.''

He did not want to say anything about murder. He had not said anything about it to the landlady, either. It was a crime for hanging, and everyone knew it. The shadow of the gallows closed even the most garrulous moths. If they did not know, so much the better.

"I'm only looking for one girl," he said reasonably. "Just have to eliminate all the rest."

She narrowed bright blue painted eyes at him. "Why? What's she done? Somebody made a complaint?"

"No." He was perfectly honest, and he hoped it showed. "Not at all. As far as I know, all your customers are perfectly satisfied."

She gave him a wide smile. "You got a quid to spare then, love?"

"No." He smiled back good-naturedly. "I want to know how many of the rest of these are regular working girls who don't have any objection to anyone knowing what they do."

She was quick. "A touch o' the black, is it?"

"That's right." He was startled by her perception. He must not underrate her again. "Blackmail. Don't like blackmailers."

She screwed up her face. "Give us them again, then."

He passed one over hopefully, then another.

She looked at it, then reached for the next.

"Cor!" She let out her breath. "Bit much of 'er, ain't there? Don't 'ardly need a bustle, do she? Backside like the Battersea gasworks!"

"Who is she?" He tried to keep a straight face.

"Dunno. Gimme the next one. Ah, that's Gertie Tiller. She'd a done that for a laugh. Nobody'll black 'er for it. Tell 'em where to go, she would." She handed it back, and Pitt put it in his left pocket with the others he had dismissed. "And that's Elsie Biddock. Looks better without 'er clothes on than she does with 'em! That's Ena Jessel. Although that's never all 'er 'air. Must be a wig. She looks damn silly in all them feathers."

"Could you put the black on her?" Pitt inquired.

"Never! Proud of it, like as not. Never seen 'er, reckon she's an amateur. You could try 'er. Amateurs is scared rotten, some of 'em. Poor bleeders just tryin' to get a bit on the side to make ends meet, pay the rent an' feed theirselves."

Pitt put it back in his right pocket.

"And 'er, don't know 'er neither."

Another for the right pocket.

"She's a looney, daft as a brush, she is. Couldn't black 'er; she 'asn't the sense to be scared of anything! Goes with all sorts. And 'er, two for a pair, they are."

"Thank you." Two more disposed of.

She took the rest, one by one. "You're goin' to be busy, aren't you, love? Sorry. Know a few o' their faces but can't remember where, and don't know their names or anythin' about them. That all?''

"That's a great help. Thank you very much.''

"You're welcome. Could you put in a good word for me with the local rozzers?''

Pitt smiled. "Least said the better," he replied. "I dare say if you don't bother them, they'll be happy enough to pretend they don't see you either.''

"Live and let live," she agreed. "Ta, love. Find your own way out?''

"I'll manage." He gave her a little salute with his hand and went back out into the street.

The next three places enabled him to write off a dozen more. This list was going down rapidly. So far there was no one who would be likely to be greatly concerned by any part of the affair, least of all their own involvement in it.

By the end of the day, the three of them had identified and dismissed all but half a dozen of the faces.

The following day was harder, as Pitt had known it would be. They had identified the professionals; now they were looking for the women driven to the streets by poverty and fear, those who would be ashamed. It was among these he expected to find the tragedy that had stretched and swelled until the burden was unbearable and had ended in murder.

He had talked to the constables, probably far too long, investing too much of his own feelings of anger and pity in his words. If they did not feel it themselves already, then they were not capable of understanding what his words could only frame. He had been aware of it at the time he was speaking, and yet he had still gone on.

By half-past ten he had found two women who had worked all day in a sweatshop sewing shirts with children pinned to their chairs and walked the streets at night to pay the rent. The sweatshop master looked sideways at him, but he snapped viciously back that all he wanted was to find the witness to an accident, and if he were not prepared to help the police the best he could, Pitt would see to it personally that the shop was turned over at least twice a week to look for stolen goods.

The man asked tartly how, if she was only a witness to an accident, Pitt came to have her photograph.

Pitt could not think of an answer to that, so he glared at the man and told him that it was a secret of police procedure and that unless he wanted a much closer relationship with the police than he already had, he would mind his own business.

That produced the desired silence on the subject and a grudging admission that at least two of the women worked for him and Pitt could speak to them if he must, but to be quick about it because time wasted was money lost, and the women needed all they earned. Policemen might get paid to stand around and talk, but they did not.

The afternoon was much the same: finding one frightened woman after another, ashamed of what she was doing, afraid of being exposed, and yet unable to manage on what sweatshop masters paid and terrified of the workhouse. At all costs they wanted to keep their children out of the institutionalized, regimented despair of the workhouses. They feared losing their children to fostering out, perhaps never to see them again, or even to know if they had survived to adulthood. What was taking off one's clothes for an hour or two to titillate some anonymous man one would never see again, in exchange for enough money to live for a month?

By the time he came back to the police station at nine o'clock, rain soaking his trousers and boots and running down the back of his neck, he had found only two exceptions. One was an ambitious and rebellious little maid who had dreams of becoming rich and starting her own hat shop. The other was completely different, a very practiced woman of nearer thirty, handsome, cynical, and obviously doing very well at the better end of the professional market. She admitted quite freely to posing for the pictures and defied Pitt to make a crime of it. If certain gentlemen liked pictures, that was their *affaire*. They could well afford it, and if Pitt were foolish enough to pursue the matter and make a nuisance of himself, he would very likely find his fingers burned by some gentlemen of considerable means, not to mention social standing.

She had rooms at a comfortable address; she made no trouble, paid her rent, and if she had gentlemen callers, what of it? She would admit to no husband, lover, or protector, still less to anything resembling a pimp or a procurer, and the confidence with which she said it made it impossible for Pitt seriously to doubt her.

He walked into his own office weary and disappointed. The best hope seemed the ambitious little maid, and she admitted to the existence of no man who might have cared, except perhaps her employer. Certainly she would be anxious, even desperate not to lose her position and the roof over her head.

The constables were waiting for him.

"Well?" Pitt sat down heavily and took his boots off. His socks were wet enough to wring out. He must have trodden in a puddle, or several.

"Not much," one of them replied grimly. "Only what you'd expect, poor devils. Can't see any of them murderin' anyone, least of all the only bloke what paid 'em a decent bit o' money. Reckon 'e was like Christmas to them."

The other one sat up a little straighter. "Mostly the same, but I turned up a couple o' really experienced bits, addresses what I wouldn't mind even visitin', let alone livin' in. Reckon any feller what goes to them for 'is fun must 'ave money to burn."

Pitt stared at him, one wet sock in his hand, the dry ones in the drawer forgotten. "What addresses?" he demanded.

The constable recited them. One was the same as that of the women Pitt had found; the other was different, but in the same area. Three prostitutes in business for themselves, and a coincidence? Or at least one very discreet bawdy house?

Up to that point Pitt had had every intention of going straight home. In half his mind he was already there, feet dry, hot soup in his hand, Charlotte smiling at him.

The constables saw the change in his face and resigned

themselves. They were constables and he was an inspector; there was nothing else they could do. Brothels did their trade largely at night.

Charlotte had long ago disciplined herself to accept Pitt's late and erratic hours, but when he was not home by eleven o'clock she could no longer pretend to herself that she was not worried. All sorts of people had accidents, were struck down in the street; policemen especially invited attack by interfering in the affairs of those who made a business of violence. A murdered body could be dumped in the river, dropped down a sewer, or simply left in the rookeries where it might never be found. Who would know one pauper corpse from another?

She had almost convinced herself that something appalling had happened when at midnight she heard the door. She flew down the hallway and flung herself at him. He was thoroughly wet.

"Where have you been?" she demanded. "It's the middle of the night! Are you hurt? What happened to you?"

He heard the rising fear in her voice and swallowed back his instinctive answer. He put both arms around her and held her close, ignoring the fact that he was wetting her dress with the rain still sliding off him.

"Watching a very high-class brothel," he replied, smiling into her hair. "And you'd be surprised who I saw going in there."

She pushed him away but still gripped his shoulders. "Why do you care?" she demanded. "What case are you on now?"

"Still Godolphin Jones. Can we go into the kitchen? I'm frozen."

"Oh!" She looked at herself in disgust. "And you're soaking!" She turned and led the way smartly back to the kitchen and threw another piece of coal on the stove. One by one she took his wet outer clothes, then his boots and his new socks. Lastly, she made tea with the kettle that had been simmering all evening. Five times she had got up and put more water in it, waiting his return.

"What has Godolphin Jones got to do with brothels?" she asked when she sat down opposite him at last.

"I don't know, except that most of the women he photographed also work in brothels."

"You think one of them killed him?" Her face was full of doubt. "Wouldn't it be pretty hard for a woman to strangle a man, unless she drugged him or hit him first? And why should she, anyway? Didn't he pay them?"

"He was a blackmailer." He had not told her about Gwendoline Cantlay or Major Rodney. "Blackmailers often get killed."

"I'm not surprised. Do you think one of them might have received an offer of marriage, or something of that sort, and wanted her pictures destroyed?"

It was a motive that had not occurred to him. Prostitutes quite often did marry, in their heyday, before their looks were gone and they slowly drifted to lower and lower brothels, earning less and less, and disease began to catch up with them. It was a decided possibility.

"Why were you watching a brothel?" she continued. "What could that tell you?"

"First of all, I wasn't sure that it was a brothel—"

"But it was?"

"Yes, or, more correctly, a set of apartments used for that purpose; rather more luxurious than a regular brothel, less communal."

She screwed up her face but said nothing.

"I thought I might find a procurer, or a pimp. He could have an excellent motive for getting rid of Godolphin Jones. Maybe Jones was poaching on his women, paying them higher rates and not giving the pimp his cut."

She looked at him very steadily. The polished pans gleamed on the dresser behind her. One of them was a little askew, and she had missed the handle.

"I think that's where we'll find the murderer." He stretched and stood up, easing his feet now that they were free of their boots. "It'll have nothing to do with Gadstone Park at all. Or the grave robbers, for that matter, except that he made use of them. Come on up to bed. Tomorrow'll come too soon as it is.''

In the morning she dished the porridge solemnly, then sat down opposite him instead of getting her own or bothering with Jemima.

"Thomas?"

He poured milk on the porridge and began to eat; there was no time to waste. They had been a little late up anyway.

"What?"

"You said Godolphin Jones was a blackmailer?"

"So he was."

"Whom did he blackmail, and over what?"

"They didn't kill him."

"Who?"

The porridge was too hot, and he was obliged to wait. He wondered if she had done that on purpose.

"Gwendoline Cantlay, over an *affaire*, and Major Rodney because he was a customer. Why?"

"Could he blackmail a pimp or a procurer? I mean, what would they be afraid of?"

"I don't know. I should think greed, professional rivalry is far more likely." He tried the porridge again, a smaller spoonful.

"You said the houses where these women worked were better than ordinary brothels?"

"So they were. Pretty good addresses. What are you getting at, Charlotte?"

She opened her eyes very wide and clear. "Who owns them, Thomas?"

He stopped with the spoon halfway to his mouth.

"Owns them?" he said very slowly, the thought mushrooming in his mind as he stared at her.

"Sometimes the oddest people own property like that," she went on. "I remember Papa knew someone once who made his money from property leased out as a sweatshop. We never had anything to do with him after we found out."

Pitt poured milk on the rest of the porridge and ate it in

five mouthfuls; pulled on his boots, still damp; grabbed his coat, hat, and scarf; and left the house as if it were a sinking ship. Charlotte did not need an explanation. Her mind was with him, and she understood.

It took him three hours to discover who owned those properties, and six more like them.

Edward St. Jermyn.

Lord St. Jermyn made his money from the rent of brothels and a percentage from each prostitute—and Godolphin Jones knew!

Was that the reason St. Jermyn had bought the picture from him? And then refused to pay him again—and again? That was most certainly a motive for murder.

But could Pitt prove it?

They did not even know what day the murder had been committed. Proving St. Jermyn had been in Resurrection Row would mean little. Jones had been strangled—any fit man, and many women, could have done it. There was no weapon to trace.

Jones was a pornographer and a blackmailer; there could be dozens of people with motives. St. Jermyn would know all these things, and Pitt would never even get as far as a warrant.

What he needed was a closer link, something to tie the two men together more irredeemably than Major Rodney or Gwendoline Cantlay or any of the women in the pictures.

The largest house had a landlady, no doubt the madame who kept the money, took the rents and the percentages and passed them to St. Jermyn, or whoever was his agent.

Pitt was outside in the street now, walking briskly. He knew where he was going and what he intended to do. He hailed a cab and climbed in. He gave the driver the address and slammed the door.

Then he sat back in the seat and planned his attack.

The house was silent in the empty street. A rising wind blew sleet out of a gray sky. A maid came up the areaway steps and then disappeared again. It could have been one of any number of well-to-do residences just before the midday meal.

Pitt dismissed the cab and went up to the front door. He had no warrant, and he did not think he could get one merely on the strength of his beliefs. But he did believe, with something growing toward certainty, that St. Jermyn had killed Godolphin Jones, and the reason had been Jones's knowledge of the source of his income. It was certainly motive enough, especially if St. Jermyn was seeking to earn a high office for himself in government as a great reformer with his workhouse bill.

Pitt lifted his hand and knocked sharply on the door. He did not like what he was about to do; it was not his usual manner. But without it there was no proof, and he could not let St. Jermyn go, in spite of the bill. Although the thought was in his mind to put off collating the final evidence, if he should find it, until after the bill had been through the House. One murderer, even of St. Jermyn's order, was not worth all the children in all the workhouses in London.

The door was opened by a smart girl in black with a white lace cap and apron.

"Good morning, sir," she said with total composure, and it flashed through Pitt's mind that perhaps the place did business even at midday.

"Good morning," he replied with a bitter smile. "May I speak to your mistress, the landlady of these apartments?"

"None of them are to lease, sir," she warned, still standing in the doorway.

"I don't imagine so," he agreed. "Nevertheless, I wish to speak to her, if you please. It is a matter of business, with regard to the owner of the property. I think you had better permit me to come in. It is not something to be discussed on the front steps."

She was a girl of some experience. She knew what the house was used for and perceived the possibilities of what Pitt said. She made way for him immediately.

"Yes, sir. If you come this way, I will see if Mrs. Philp is at home."

"Thank you." Pitt followed her into a remarkably comfortable room, discreetly furnished, with a strong fire burning in the grate. He had only a few minutes to wait before Mrs. Philp appeared. She was buxom, growing a little fat now but handsomely dressed; even at this hour her face was rouged and mascaraed as if for a ball. He did not need to be told she was a successful prostitute a little over the hill, promoted now from worker to management. Her clothes were expensive, her jewelry flashy, but Pitt judged it to be real. She looked at him with hard, shrewd eyes.

"I don't know you," she said, coming in and shutting the door with a snick.

"You're lucky." He was still standing, back to the fire. "I don't often work vice, especially not this class."

"A rozzer," she said instantly. "You can't prove anything, and you'd be a fool to try. The sort of gentleman that comes here wouldn't thank you for it."

"I don't doubt it," he agreed. "I've no intention of trying to shut you down."

"I'm not paying you anything." She gave him a look of contempt. "You go tell anyone you like. See where it'll get you!"

"I'm not interested in telling anyone either."

"Then what do you want? You want something! A little custom on the cheap?"

"No, thank you. A little information."

"If you think I'm going to tell you who comes here, you're a bigger fool than I took you for. Blackmail, eh? I'll have you thrown out and beaten so bad your own mother wouldn't know you."

"Possibly. But I don't give a damn who comes here."

"Then what do you want? You haven't come here out of curiosity!"

"Godolphin Jones."

"Who?" But there was a hesitation, only the fraction of a second, a flicker of an eyelid.

"You heard me. Godolphin Jones. I'm sure you're very competent to handle anything to do with prostitution—you've had enough practice to outwit most of us—but how about murder? Do you feel like fighting me over that? That's what I'm good at, proving murder."

The painted rouge stood out on her cheeks. Without it she would still have been handsome.

"I don't know anything about no murder!"

"Godolphin Jones knew about this house and its business because he photographed a few of your girls."

"So what if he did?"

"Blackmail, Mrs. Philp."

"He couldn't blackmail me! What for? Whom would he tell? You? What can you do about it? You're not going to shut me down. Too many rich and powerful people come here, and you know it."

"Not blackmail you, Mrs. Philp. You are what you are and don't pretend to be anything else. But who owns this building, Mrs. Philp?"

Her face went white, but she said nothing.

"Whom do you pay rent to, Mrs. Philp?" he went on. "How much do you take from the girls? Fifty percent? More? And how much do you give him at the end of the week, or the month?"

She swallowed and stared at him. "I dunno! I dunno 'is name!"

"Liar! It's St. Jermyn, and you know it as well as I do. You wouldn't pay a landlord you didn't know; you're too fly by half to do that. You'll have an agreement all detailed out, even if it isn't written."

She swallowed again. "So?" she demanded. "What if it is? What about? You can't do nothing!"

"Blackmail, Mrs. Philp."

"You goin' to blackmail 'im? St. Jermyn? You're a fool, a crazy man!"

"Why? Because I'd wind up dead? Like Godolphin Jones?"

Her eyes widened, and for a moment he thought she might faint. There was a funny dry rattle in her throat, a gasping.

"Did you kill Jones, Mrs. Philp? You look strong enough. He was strangled, you know." He looked at her broad, well-padded shoulders and her fat arms.

"Mother of God—so I did not!"

"I wonder."

"I swear! I never went near the little sod, except to give him the money. Why would I kill him? I keep a house, it's my business, but I swear to God I never killed anyone!"

"What money, Mrs. Philp? Money from St. Jermyn to keep him quiet?"

A look of cunning came into her face, then vanished again in uncertainty. "No, I didn't say that. Far as I know, it was money for a whole lot o' pictures Jones was going to paint, all of St. Jermyn's children and himself. 'Alf a dozen or more. Jones wanted the money in advance, and this was the best place to get the ready cash. It was several weeks' earnings. St. Jermyn couldn't get all of that much out of 'is regular bank."

"No," Pitt agreed. "I'll bet he couldn't, nor would he want to. But you see, we never found it on Jones's body or in his shop in Resurrection Row or in his house, nor was it paid into his bank."

"What do you mean? He spent it?"

"I doubt it. How much was it?—and you'd better be right. One lie, and I'll arrest you as an accessory to murder. You know what that means—the rope."

"Five thousand pounds!" she said instantly. "Five thousand, I swear, and that's God's truth!"

"When? Exactly?"

"Twelfth of January, midday. 'E was here. Then 'e went straight to Resurrection Row."

"And was murdered by St. Jermyn, who took back the five thousand pounds. I think if I check with his bank, which will be easy to do now with your information, I shall find that five thousand pounds, or something near it, was deposited again, which will prove beyond any reasonable man's doubt that his lordship murdered Godolphin Jones, and why. Thank you, Mrs. Philp. And unless you want to dance at the end of a rope with him, you'll be prepared to come into court and tell the same story on oath."

"If I do, what will you charge me with?"

"Not murder, Mrs. Philp; and if you're lucky not even

keeping a bawdy house. Queen's evidence, and you might find us prepared to turn a blind eye."

"You promise?"

"No, I don't promise. I can't. But I can promise no charge of murder. As far as I know, there's nothing at all to prove you ever knew anything about it. I don't so far intend to look."

"I didn't! As God is my judge."

"I'll leave that to God, as you suggest. Good day, Mrs. Philp." And he turned and went out, allowing the maid to open the door for him into the street. The light snow had stopped, but there was a watery, blue-white sunshine.

The next thing he did was return to Gadstone Park, not to St. Jermyn's house but to Aunt Vespasia's. He needed only one final piece of evidence, a statement from St. Jermyn's bank, if the money was there, or alternatively a warrant to search his house, although it was highly unlikely he would keep that amount of cash in a household safe. It was more than most men earned in a decade, more than a good servant would earn in a lifetime.

Also, there would be a withdrawal of capital from the bank before the payment, or the sale of some property; either would be easily traceable. As Mrs. Philp had said, he could not have immediately laid his hands on that kind of cash; he certainly would not have sought a loan.

But before Pitt did anything so final, he wanted to know from Vespasia when, the precise day, the bill was coming up before Parliament. If there was any way at all he could put off his last, irreparable task, he would—at least that long.

She received him without her usual acid humor. "Good afternoon, Thomas," she said with a touch of weariness. "I presume this is business; you have not called for luncheon?"

"No, ma'am. I apologize for the inconvenient hour."

She brushed it aside with a slight gesture. "Well, what is it you wish to ask this time?"

"When does St. Jermyn's bill go before Parliament?"

She had been staring at the fire; now she turned to face him slowly, her old eyes bright and tired. "Why do you want to know?"

"I believe you already know the answer to that, ma'am," he said quietly. "I cannot let him get away with it, you know."

She gave a little shrug. "I suppose not. But can you not leave it at least until after the bill? It will be over by tomorrow evening."

"That is why I came here to ask you."

"Can you?"

"Yes, I can leave it that long."

"Thank you."

He did not bother to explain that he was doing it because he believed in it and cared just as much as she or Carlisle, and probably more than St. Jermyn himself. He thought she knew that.

He did not stay. She would not do anything, not communicate with St. Jermyn. She would just wait.

He went back to the police station, obtained the warrants for the house and the bank, and contrived to get them too late to execute them that day. He was home by five o'clock and sat by the fire, eating muffins and playing with Jemima.

In the morning he started late, moved slowly, and it was the end of the afternoon before he had assembled all his evidence to his entire satisfaction and made out an appropriate warrant for St. Jermyn's arrest.

He took only one constable and proceeded to the House of Lords at Westminster to wait in one of the anterooms until the voting was finished and their lordships left for the night.

He saw Vespasia first, dressed in dove gray and silver, head high. But he knew from the tightness in her, the rigid walk, the unblinking eyes that they had failed. He should have had more sense, more knowledge of reality than to hope; it was too early, too soon. Yet the disappointment rose up inside him like sickness, a tangible pain.

They would go on fighting, of course, and in time, five years, ten years, they would win. But he wanted it now, for the children it would be too late to save in ten years' time.

Behind Vespasia was Somerset Carlisle. As if drawn by the misery Pitt was feeling, he turned and caught Pitt's eye. Even in this moment of defeat there was a bitter irony in him, something like a smile. Did he, like Vespasia, know what Pitt had come for?

He moved through the crowd toward them, only dimly aware of the constable coming from the other side. St. Jermyn was behind them. He showed the least mark of hurt. He had fought a good battle, and it would be remembered. Perhaps that was all that had ever really mattered to him.

Vespasia was talking to someone, leaning a little. She looked older than Pitt had ever seen her before. Perhaps she knew she would not live to see the bill passed. Ten years for her was too long.

Pitt moved sideways to see whom she was talking to, who held her arm and supported her. He hoped it was not Lady St. Jermyn.

They were within yards now. He could see the constable moving to cut off any retreat.

He was almost in front of them.

Vespasia turned and saw him. It was Charlotte beside her!

Pitt stopped. They were facing each other, the constable and Pitt in front of St. Jermyn, Carlisle, and the two women.

For a wild moment Pitt wondered if Charlotte had known all along who had killed Godolphin Jones. Then he dismissed it. There was no way she could have. If she had guessed lately, then he would never know it.

"My lord," he said quietly, meeting St. Jermyn's eyes. He looked surprised; then, reading Pitt's face, the certainty in it, the relentless, unturnable knowledge, he showed a trace of fear at last.

There was only one thing incomplete in Pitt's mind. Looking at St. Jermyn—the recognition of defeat in him while the arrogance remained, the hatred, even now a contempt for Pitt, as if it were chance that had beaten him, ill

215

luck and not anyone else's skill—he could not see in him any trace of the bizarre imagination, the black grave-wit that had draped Horrie Snipe over his own tombstone, or had set old Augustus in his family pew, Porteous on the park bench, and the unfortunate Albert Wilson to drive a hansom. He must have known the grave of Wilson would eventually be found, with Godolphin Jones in it. He could not have hoped to escape forever. And his ambitions were long-term. This bill was only a step on the way to high office and all it meant; he did not care about it for itself.

To have changed those graves required a man of passion, a man who cared enough for the bill to exercise all his black humor to hold off the arrest just long enough—

His eyes move to Carlisle.

Of course.

St. Jermyn had killed Godolphin Jones—but Carlisle had known about it, perhaps even feared it and followed him, finding the body. It was he, after St. Jermyn had gone, who had buried him in Albert Wilson's grave and moved the bodies one by one, to keep Pitt confounded just long enough. That explained why St. Jermyn had been so confused when Jones had turned up in Wilson's grave and not Resurrection Row!

Carlisle was staring back at him, a small, bleak smile in his eyes.

Pitt returned the shadow of the smile and then looked back at St. Jermyn. He cleared his throat. He could never prove Carlisle's part, and he did not wish to.

"Edward St. Jermyn," he said formally. "In the name of the Queen, I arrest you for the willful murder of one Godolphin Jones, artist, of Resurrection Row."

216